Seaside Letters

OTHER NOVELS BY DENISE HUNTER

Surrender Bay

The Convenient Groom

Sweetwater Gap

Seaside Letters

DENISE HUNTER

THOMAS NELSON
Since 1798

NASHVILLE   DALLAS   MEXICO CITY   RIO DE JANEIRO   BEIJING

Published in Nashville, Tennessee, by Thomas Nelson. Thomas Nelson is a registered trademark of Thomas Nelson, Inc.

Thomas Nelson, Inc., titles may be purchased in bulk for educational, business, fund-raising, or sales promotional use. For information, please e-mail SpecialMarkets@ThomasNelson.com.

Publisher's Note: This novel is a work of fiction. Names, characters, places, and incidents are either products of the author's imagination or used fictitiously. All characters are fictional, and any similarity to people living or dead is purely coincidental.

Library of Congress Cataloging-in-Publication Data

Hunter, Denise, 1968–
    Seaside letters / Denise Hunter.
      p. cm.
    ISBN 978-1-59554-260-1 (pbk.)
    I. Title.
PS3608.U5925S44 2009
813'.6—dc22   2009027368

Printed in the United States of America

09 10 11 12 13 RRD 5 4 3 2 1

ED55 - 2011

Sweetpea: Betrayal flips a switch you didn't know existed. Suddenly you're on guard. No one is above suspicion, no one is as honest as they seem, and it's all because of this basic truth: You're too afraid to risk it all again.

Chapter One

Sabrina Kincaid heard the jingle of the café's glass door opening and glanced at the clock above the workstation: 7:12 on the dot.

She grabbed the fresh pot, turned toward the tables crowding the Cobblestone Café, then headed straight to his table—might as well get it over with—table seven, a two-topper near the front.

He would be seated against the beadboard wall, facing the kitchen, unfortunately. He would be wearing a blue "Cap'n Tucker's Water Taxi" cap, a light-colored T-shirt, and a crooked grin. She would offer him coffee, he would accept, then he would spread open *The Inquirer and Mirror* and take thirty minutes on all twelve articles while she waited on other customers, her bony knees knocking together like bamboo wind chimes.

"Evan," Gordon called from the kitchen. "Table twelve needs to be bussed."

Evan's blond ponytail flipped over his shoulder as he turned and wiped his hands on his stained brown apron. "Right, dude."

Sabrina stopped a foot from the scarred maple table, avoiding eye contact, looking only at the fat rim of the ivory mug as he slid it toward her.

How many words had they exchanged in the year he'd been coming to the café? One hundred? Two hundred? Couldn't be much more than that.

As always her expression was free of emotion, though a powerful hurricane brewed inside. It was a skill she'd learned early, perfected well, and if that had earned her the title of Ice Princess, so be it.

"Morning, Sabrina." Tucker's deep voice was raspy. And, as usual, he cleared his throat after the greeting.

Was she the first person he spoke to each morning? The thought made her hand tremble. A stream of hot coffee flowed over the cup's rim and onto Tucker's thumb. He jerked his hand back.

Idiot! Her first spill in months and it had to be Tucker. And with hot coffee.

"I'm sorry. Let me fetch a towel." She turned toward the kitchen, heat flooding her face.

He stopped her with his other hand. "I'm fine." He wiped his thumb on a napkin and held it out. "See?"

Sabrina made the mistake of meeting his eyes. Oh, yes. She saw, all right. Under the brim of his cap, his blue eyes contrasted with his summer-brown skin. One strand of dark hair curled like a backward *C*, nearly tangling with his eyelashes. He disliked his curly hair, but hated going to the barber so much that he procrastinated until it was an unruly mop. He wore contacts because he was nearsighted and because glasses would blur under the sprays of water as he guided his boat.

He was still looking at her.

She was still looking at him.

Look away. Say something. "Anything else?"

"A smile?" Tucker's own grin lifted the tiny scar near the corner of his mouth—a souvenir from the time his twin sister dared him to jump from his second-story bedroom window when he was nine.

But Sabrina wasn't supposed to know about that. She pulled at the tip of her ponytail with her empty hand.

"Give it up, McCabe." Behind her, Oliver Franklin's voice was a lifeline. "Top me off, Sabrina?"

She turned, grateful for the distraction, and filled his cup. The sand-colored coffee darkened to caramel as she poured, the rich smell of the brew drifting upward on wings of steam.

"Not feeling particularly *efficacious* this morning?" Oliver tilted his round head, his hairline receding another inch as he hiked his bushy gray brows. He gripped the mug with fat hands calloused from garden tools.

"I'm as efficient as always, just a bit clumsy today." Sabrina took his egg-streaked plate and stacked a smaller plate on top.

"Dagnabit, Sabrina," he said as she walked away. "Is there a word you don't know?"

She deposited the plates into Evan's tub, set the pot on the warmer, and loaded a tray with table five's food. Was Tucker watching her? She always felt like he was, which was ludicrous. Still, it made her stand a little straighter, smile a little more—at other customers. He was good for her tips.

You're just some server he toys with. Nothing else.

When she turned with the loaded tray, her eyes pulled toward him. *Don't look. Just walk.* Look at the sun streaming through the glass front. Look at the family at table four, the toddler, crouched in the wooden high chair, letting loose a wail that could be heard clear down at the wharf. Sabrina pulled a packet of crackers from her apron pocket and slipped it to the mom as she passed.

When she reached table five, she served the food, then tucked the tray under her arm. "Anything else?"

"Tabasco sauce?" the mother asked. "Oh, and he needs a refill of juice." She handed Sabrina her son's cup. The overhead lights sparkled off a huge diamond.

"Be right back." She had to pass Tucker's table on the way.

He turned as she passed, his sandaled foot sliding into her path as he shifted into the aisle. "Sabrina. I know you're busy, but I was wondering if we could chat a minute."

The request stopped her cold. Sabrina didn't chat with customers. Char chatted with customers, even the rich ones. Evan chatted with customers too. But not Sabrina, and certainly not with Tucker. It broke her unspoken line between customer and server, and that line was the only thing separating her from disaster. "I—I have too many tables."

"Miss, some decaf, please?" An elderly tourist, seated at the table behind Oliver's, corroborated her excuse.

"Of course." Sabrina went to fill the cup with juice, grabbed a bottle of Tabasco and the decaf pot. What could Tucker want? As far as he knew, she was only a server at the café.

Maybe he knows.

But he couldn't. She'd been so careful.

Yeah, so careful she'd lost her heart to the man.

I have not lost my heart. He's just a friend. A dear friend who would be lost forever with one little slip of the tongue. The relationship was hanging by a thread and she knew it.

Sabrina dropped off the two items for the family, then poured the decaf. She'd no sooner turned the carafe upright when Tucker stopped her again. His cup was empty. "I'll be right back with the regular," she said, even though she knew it wasn't coffee he wanted. It was a feeble stall that would buy her thirty seconds.

She stopped on the way to the coffee station and took the orders of a middle-aged couple, buying herself a few more minutes. Maybe if she took too long, Tucker would leave.

Sabrina put the order on the wheel and reviewed the lunch special with Gordon. She filled glasses with orange juice and ice water, set them on a tray, and delivered them to the table. In her peripheral vision, she saw Tucker waiting, his arms folded across the newspaper, rooted like a hundred-year-old oak tree. He wasn't going anywhere.

Reluctantly, she retrieved the coffeepot and returned to his table, filling his cup carefully.

"How about after work?" he asked, picking up the conversation as if it were only seconds later.

What did he want? Maybe he wanted to ask her out. The thought filled her, expanding her lungs like an inflated balloon. Then she felt the prick of jealousy. *Pop.*

She nearly rolled her eyes at the irony. "I have to be somewhere."

Behind her, Oliver chuckled, and Tucker shot him a look. He gave the brim of his hat a sharp tug.

Sabrina walked away. Her second job had flexible hours, but he didn't know that. Besides, Renny was expecting her. She had to find the perfect poison, and that would take a while.

The bell at the kitchen window dinged.

She was at the coffee station before she realized Tucker had followed her. His large frame made her feel small and cornered. He'd never gone farther than his table, and the fact that he did so today confirmed her suspicion that he wanted something more than idle conversation. And he wasn't giving up.

The rubber heels of her shoes brushed the wall behind her, and she straightened, meeting his gaze.

"Just a few minutes, all I'm asking."

His nearness sucked the moisture from her mouth and the thoughts from her head. She smoothed her thick hair toward her low ponytail. *Say something. Anything.*

"All right," she blurted. *Anything but that.*

His mouth relaxed, and the relief in his blue eyes made something twist in the pit of her stomach. "Thank you. I won't take much of your time. I'll meet you out front if it's all right with you? There's a bench down the way . . ."

She nodded, all at once relieved and disappointed they were meeting someplace so public. *What is wrong with you?*

His lips quivered at the corners, and the faint lines around his eyes relaxed. He touched his fingers to the brim of his hat and retreated.

"What was that all about?" Char was a veteran waitress at the diner. Though not as efficient as Sabrina, her affability scored points with the regulars. "He finally making his move?" Her blonde hair had kinked into poodle curls, forecasting the day's weather.

Sabrina turned and put two slices of bread in the toaster. "Don't be ridiculous."

The kitchen bell dinged twice.

"Char, you want to stop your gabbing and come get this food before it turns to rubber?" Gordon called through the window, wiping the back of his hand across his fat jowls.

"Don't say I didn't tell you so." Char winked a wide green eye, the mascara-thickened lashes fluttering.

Sabrina watched her walk away, wondering if Char was right, hoping she was, then hoping she wasn't. She gave her head a sharp shake. She had five hours and four minutes to get her act together, and suddenly that didn't seem like nearly enough time.

***

Sabrina threw her apron in the laundry bin and pulled her bag from the cubby in the break room. At least, Gordon *called* it a break room. It was more of a large closet with a table, two chairs, and enough wattage to light up Main Street at midnight.

The five hours since Tucker left had dragged by. She told herself she was dreading the meeting, but if that were the case, time would've raced, wouldn't it?

She slid the purse onto her shoulder and met her own gaze in the black-speckled mirror Char had perched on a shelf. Bending her knees so she could see her face, Sabrina pulled the rubber band, loosening the ponytail, and freeing her brown hair. She raked her fingers through it, wishing for smooth, glossy strands like her cousins', but her fingers worked fruitlessly.

Giving up on her hair, she rubbed at a fleck of mystery food that clung to her temple. Maybe she should splash water on her face. She stood back and surveyed her reflection. Her brown eyes gazed back, her best feature, framed with dark lashes thick enough to make Char jealous.

What could Tucker want with her? Her respiration quickened at the thought of him. What if he knew? What if she'd slipped and said something that would ruin everything?

Char's words tweaked at the corners of her mind. *"He's finally making his move . . ."*

Oh, for Pete's sake. He is not making his move. Sabrina grabbed the rubber band from her pocket and gathered her hair. *He owns a company. Maybe he's hosting some event and wants you to serve.*

"Better not keep him waiting." Char's voice sounded from the doorway.

Her eyes tilted coyly, and Sabrina felt heat flooding her face at being caught primping in the mirror like some pathetic adolescent. How many times had she found Jaylee and Arielle artfully applying makeup in front of their mirrors? Of course, it had paid off for her cousins.

"Oh, no, you don't." Char reached behind Sabrina and freed her hair.

"What are you doing?"

"Wear it down. Why do you always wear this infernal ponytail?"

Sabrina shifted as Char fluffed her hair. "We work in the restaurant industry."

"If I had hair like yours . . ." Char leaned back. "There. Much better. No street clothes, huh? Well, I guess your uniform will have to do. At least you have nice legs. Now, go, before he thinks you chickened out."

She squeezed past Char.

"Good luck, honey."

Luck. She'd need it if she hoped to hold it together. She exited the café, blinking against May's bright sunlight. Her feet navigated the bumpy brick sidewalk, and she fell in step behind a cluster of tourists. If only she could squeeze into the middle and sneak past Tucker.

The bench was only three stores from the diner and, over the bobbing heads, she saw Tucker sitting there, elbows propped on his knees, staring across the street. There was no backing out now.

When she approached the bench, he stood. The group of tourists deserted her, leaving them alone on the sidewalk. In the distance, the ferry horn sounded, announcing its arrival at the wharf.

"Hi. Thanks for meeting me." He gestured toward the bench.

She lowered herself onto the wooden seat and set her bag in her lap. "You're welcome." *Act normal. This is nothing out of the ordinary. You are a server and he is your customer. Nothing more.*

"I know you have another job to get to, so I'll make this quick."

Quick would be good. Merciful. She gripped the leather handles of her purse and pulled it into her stomach.

"I was hoping to hire you for a project."

A curious mixture of relief and disappointment flooded Sabrina. She told herself it was relief that tightened her stomach. *Now it's just a matter of listening to his proposal and saying no. I can say no, then go home.* She envisioned the cozy loft above Renny's garage as if she could beam herself there. She pictured her favorite quilt spread across the bed, the built-in shelves brimming with novels, the antique desk in the corner where her computer awaited her.

Focus, Sabrina.

"Go on." Sabrina crossed her legs. A pedestrian passed with a golden retriever on a pink leash, and she shifted to make room. The movement left her facing Tucker. He had one elbow propped on the back of the bench, his hand curling dangerously close to her shoulder.

"Well, the idea came to me when Renny Hannigan contacted me about a trip to Tuckernuck Island. We started talking about her stories, and she told me you're the mastermind behind the mysteries she writes—"

Sabrina shook her head. "I just do a little research for her."

"You're being modest. Renny told me about the twists you come up with. She raved that the stories are unsolvable because you find fresh angles and innovative ways to confuse the reader."

If Sabrina were that good, Renny's stories would be published by now. It wasn't lack of writing skill that kept her from publication. But what did her work for Renny have to do with Tucker?

"The things Renny said about you, combined with what I already know, made me think you were the perfect person for this project."

"I already have two jobs. Between the diner and my research for Renny . . ." Her words petered out as he held up his hand.

"I know you're busy right now, but Renny said in another couple weeks you'd be finished with the book she's writing now, and that she'd need several weeks of editing time before she'd need your help again with her next story."

Renny. Sabrina clenched her teeth together. Why'd the woman have to go and tell Tucker that? Maybe she should close the door on this conversation before it went any further.

"I don't think—I was looking forward to the time off when I finished the research. I think it would be best if—"

"Just hear me out, okay? If you don't want to do it, that's fine."

His hand spread across his thigh. He had big hands with long fingers that tapered down to squared-off fingertips. He liked working with them. He carved wooden animals in his spare time and gave them as gifts to his family. He'd once wanted to give her a seagull he'd carved, but she'd refused the gift.

"Sabrina?"

She cleared her throat and watched a family of four squeeze into a taxi across the street, the brother and sister fighting over the middle seat. "I'm listening." *Please just say what you have to say and let me go home where my heart rate can return to normal.*

"Well, as I was saying, I have this project I need help with."

His voice was so deep it seemed to rumble through her body. *Practice saying no. It's not my cup of tea. I don't have time, but thank you for the offer.*

"It's kind of embarrassing, but here goes."

Now he had her attention.

"There's this girl—this woman, I mean."

Sabrina thought her heart was already in her toes, but it didn't quite hit the tips until then. She reached for the end of her ponytail but found her hair loose.

"I have feelings for her and—" He pulled off his cap and raked his hands through his curls. "Well, the sad fact is, I don't know where she is."

Sabrina looked at him. She couldn't help it. "What?" A missing person? He wanted help finding his missing girlfriend? But he didn't have a girlfriend, did he? A seed of pure jealousy, something she'd thought she'd banished from her life long ago, sprang up, twisting, leaving that familiar ache in its path.

"I'm bungling this, aren't I? Let me start at the beginning and maybe I can explain this better. There's this woman I've been exchanging letters with. Email. We've been communicating online for about a year."

Oh.

"We've gotten pretty friendly. Actually, she's an amazing woman."

He looked off into the distance, and Sabrina was relieved to have his eyes anywhere but on her. *This is not happening.*

"I want to meet her in person. I know it sounds clichéd and corny, but I have feelings for her."

He looked at her, and she swore he could see right into her. She clutched the leather purse straps until her short nails dug into the flesh of her palm.

"Yeah, I know. You're wondering how I could fall for someone I've never met, but this is different. It's not like we set out to date online; it just happened. And you're probably wondering why we don't just meet up and live happily ever after."

Sabrina tried to speak, but her voice had jumped off two exits ago.

"I'd like nothing more, but the problem is, she won't meet in person. I don't know why, but it doesn't matter. I need to find her."

"Find her?"

His eyes bore into hers. "I need your help."

"I can't."

"You're the perfect person for the job. I need someone who can string together clues. I have hundreds of letters filled with information, but she's been careful not to write anything overt about her location. I need someone smart and intuitive. Someone like you."

"I'm not the right person."

"Renny thinks you'd be perfect."

Renny. She'd wring the woman's neck! Sabrina needed another tactic. Anything. "This woman—obviously she doesn't want to be found. Maybe you should leave things alone and continue the relationship as it is."

"I want to be with her."

"Maybe—" Could she be so cruel? She pressed her spine to the bench. Desperate needs called for desperate measures. "Maybe she doesn't want to be with you. Maybe she's—I don't know—married or something."

"She's not married."

"How can you know?"

"She's not. I *know*."

Sabrina wet her lips. Brushed at a mustard spot on her uniform. "There has to be some reason she won't meet you."

He lowered his voice. "I'm sure there is. I think she's afraid of taking the next step or something, but I don't think she'll tell me until I find her."

She gulped. *What do I say? How do I get out of this?* If she said no, he'd find someone else to help him, and then what?

That would be ten times worse. If someone else helped him—if someone else sifted through the letters and figured out the truth—then he'd discover that the person he's trying to find is . . . *her*.

Harbormaster: No matter where you are or how long it takes until we can be together, I'll keep searching for you.

Chapter Two

Tucker pulled his eyes from Sabrina's, and it wasn't easy. He'd never seen her hair all flowy around her shoulders. He made himself watch a tour van pass slowly, stop for a bicyclist, then continue toward the First Congregational Church.

He pulled his arm from the splintered bench back and clasped his hands between his knees.

"If she doesn't want to be found," Sabrina's voice quivered, "maybe she has a good reason. Maybe you'll only be hurt or disappointed if you find her."

He wanted to look at her; he wanted to grasp her shoulders between his hands and tell her that could never be true. *Tone it down, buddy. You're going to scare her away.*

He sucked in a deep breath, letting the salty air permeate his lungs before he released it on a steady exhale. He wished he could jump inside her head and know what she was thinking. Was she thinking about telling him the truth right now? Was she wishing she'd never started the email relationship to begin with? She clutched her bag to her body like a shield, and he could almost feel the waves of fear rolling off her.

He had to back her into a corner, but the thought of it was killing him. Maybe he should forget it. Maybe he should drop the whole thing. The whole relationship felt so precarious. As if one little breeze would send it crashing to the ground.

Then he remembered his daily trip to the café, sitting at his table pretending to read the paper, pretending they were strangers. How long could he continue with the charade? And the hours sitting at the computer, reading her letters, wishing for more . . .

No. He'd made his decision, and he was going through with it.

He leaned back against the bench. "I'm going to find her, regardless of any disappointment or hurt it might bring. I can't go on like this. I think you're the best person for the job, but if you're not interested—I'll find someone else."

There. He'd done it. He could feel the realization sinking into Sabrina. The realization that if she didn't help him, someone else would. It was a cheap trick, but for his plan to work, she had to say yes.

Maybe she'd just admit who she was right now. _Come on, Sabrina, say it._

"You seem determined." Her words wobbled pitifully.

I am such a jerk.

But it was for her own good. She was so beautiful, inside and out. He'd never known anyone so unaware of it. It was as if she still saw herself as the girl with acne and a gapped smile. Time and braces had fixed the external, but the inside was permanently damaged. She wore invisible armor that let no one through. Only in her letters was she transparent. Only when she was hiding behind a computer. If only he could get that to translate over to real life. And he would. If only he could accomplish Step One.

"I'm going to find her. It's not a matter of if, only when."

"Have you looked through the emails yourself? Surely if she'd left clues, you would've seen them."

"I'm not much of a between-the-lines person. I'm not even a computer person, except for this one email relationship. I use the thing for my business, but that's it."

"What's her name?"

As if you don't know. "She goes by Sweetpea."

"You don't know her name?"

He nearly said he had her photo, but it wasn't hers, was it? Instead, he met her almond-shaped eyes and spent a couple seconds just floating there in the sea of chocolate. "I know I care about her. I know she's special. And I know I'm going to find her." *You want to be found, don't you, Sabrina? Deep down? What are you afraid of?*

She looked so rigid, her chin set, her mouth drawn into a flat line. But behind that tough mask, there was tender flesh, a warm heart, a vulnerable soul. If only she would agree, he could set his plan in motion. Maybe if she spent time with him, he could gain her trust.

But she trusts Harbormaster, and she still doesn't want to meet him, doesn't want the relationship to progress. He'd been through this a million times.

He set his cap back on his head, feeling suddenly weary. Had he thought it was going to be easy? "You can mull it over if you like.

I want to find someone by the end of the week, though, so if you could let me know if I need to look elsewhere—"

"No, I'll do it." Her chin tilted up stubbornly. She knew she'd been trapped.

His stomach did a funny flop at the thought of having her in his home, where he'd spent hours writing her, reading her letters, thinking about her. It was just a matter of time now. Surely, once they had time alone together, he could penetrate that wall she kept around her heart. Surely he could get her to admit who she was when he had all the right tools in place.

"I can start in two weeks, when I finish Renny's manuscript."

There was one more matter to discuss, but he felt a smile breaking out on his face and couldn't stop it. "That'll be fine. Your hours would be flexible, but evenings are best for me, if that works for you."

She rubbed her neck, and her charm bracelet slid down her wrist, making a soft jingling sound. "Evenings . . ." Confusion etched lines across her forehead. "Aren't you going to print off the emails for me?"

He was glad he'd thought this through. "I wouldn't feel right about that. I feel bad enough letting someone else read her personal thoughts, much less have printed copies floating around."

"I'd be exceedingly vigilant—"

"I know you would. I just don't feel right about it. I hope you understand."

She didn't understand at all, but that didn't matter so long as she agreed. He could see her wavering. He drove the last nail home. "If you'd rather I find someone else . . ."

"No. That won't be a problem." She scooted to the edge of the bench and stood, hanging her bag on her shoulder.

He stood with her. "Great, then. Two weeks." He extended a hand, and she returned his firm handshake before walking away. "But I'll see you at the café before that," he called to her stiffened back.

He watched her go, her long legs swallowing the distance. Operation Sweetpea was under way, and the future suddenly looked brighter than the sunlight glinting off Nantucket Harbor at noon.

Sweetpea: If I thought planning a wedding was time consuming, it was only because I'd never had to cancel one in six days.

Chapter Three

Sabrina stopped pedaling and coasted, taking a breather. She wished she'd stayed in bed for the day. How had she let herself be persuaded to spend hours alone with Tucker? Didn't she know how difficult the task would be? How could she maintain her composure, keep her focus with him nearby? She must be plumb crazy.

It wasn't as if I had a choice. He was prepared to hire someone else if she said no. She couldn't allow that, could she?

At least now she could control the outcome. She could read the emails, pretend to give her best effort, then tell him it was an impossible task. She could even manufacture red herrings to sidetrack him, just like in Renny's books.

But you'll be alone with him for hours . . .

Despite the warm air, the thought sent a shiver down her arms. The relationship had seemed so simple in the beginning, just a friend she traded quips with. She liked the way he valued her opinions and the way he was only a mouse click away. He listened without judging, a rarity in her experience. Her feelings had evolved slowly, and by the time she knew they'd gone too far, she was helpless to stop them.

She signaled left and made the turn onto Renny's lane. And now she would somehow have to hide them. It was difficult enough facing him at the café, pretending he was a stranger. How would she conceal her feelings when they were alone in close quarters? And she must conceal them. Tucker might think he wanted Sweetpea, but that was only because he didn't know who she was.

Sabrina followed the gravel lane toward Renny's two-story oceanfront home. The shaker shingles, previously a pale blue, had faded to gray under the relentless erosion of wind and sand. Lining the front walk, Renny's flower garden was a riot of pink, yellow, and white. A prolific vine of some kind clung to the front entryway, climbing the white columns and creeping onto the small roof that shaded the patio. Many of the islanders hired men like Oliver for landscaping, but Renny managed her own garden and had affectionately named it *Gan Eden*, Hebrew for Garden of Eden. The Hebrew language was another of Renny's interests.

Sabrina parked her bike in front of the garage that housed her loft apartment. She sifted through the mailbox for her mail, then climbed the wooden stairs along the west side of the house that led to her private entry.

A tall oak rose above the roofline, and her eyes searched the length of the closest limb until they came to a nest a robin had built that spring. Cradled in the nook of two intersecting branches, the nest was tilted to the side precariously. Each day Sabrina expected to find the nest gone, blown to the ground by a harbor breeze, but it still hung there.

Cool air and the remnants of Pine-Sol greeted her as she entered and set the mail on the desk, moving quickly, eager to see if Tucker had written before he left that morning.

Would he admit he was trying to locate her, or would he keep it a secret? She sat at the desk and opened her email. They had a predictable pattern. He wrote in the morning after she left for work, and in the afternoon she'd reply. Then when he returned in the evening, messages flew back and forth, mostly short quips about nothing in particular.

Her inbox appeared, and Sabrina scanned the few emails, her heart bailing when she saw nothing from Harbormaster. She browsed the four emails. Two were junk mail, one was a shipping notice from Amazon, and the other was from her cousin Jaylee. The sight of Jaylee's name jolted her from complacency. Of their own volition, her eyes scanned the subject:

IMPORTANT PLEASE READ.

Sabrina highlighted the email and gave the Delete button a hard tap. The message vanished in a split second. Instead of satisfaction, the action left her with a vague sense of unease. What could Jaylee want? Hadn't her cousin taken more than enough? For a moment she was tempted to retrieve the message, then decided it wasn't worth the feelings it would arouse.

But the emotions appeared at the door of her heart anyway,

like unwelcome guests. Jealousy, Bitterness, and their close friend, Aching Pain.

No. She would not entertain the feelings today. *I choose not to.* Willfully, she pushed the thoughts to the back of her mind for another day and closed the email program.

Normally, she looked forward to this time of day. Returning to her little loft with its efficient layout and familiar furnishings, anticipating a message from Tucker. Here she could be alone to read and think and escape. Today, though, offered her none of the above. Her mind whirled like a window fan. She needed to finish Renny's research, but instead she started a kettle of tea and wandered past the kitchen table to the window overlooking the ocean.

Clouds had gathered, obscuring the sun, muting the daylight. On the water, a blue, triangular sail dotted the horizon. She wondered about the people inhabiting the boat. Were they a vacationing family? A wealthy retired couple killing time? A married man seeking peace and solitude from a nagging wife and a gaggle of boisterous kids?

Other than the ferry that had brought her to Nantucket, Sabrina had never stepped foot on a boat. It seemed peculiar when she was surrounded by water.

She let the curtain fall into place, then went to change into shorts and a crew neck T-shirt. The weather was mild today. Maybe later she'd go for a jog.

When the kettle whistled, she made a cup of tea before settling into her computer chair. Renny needed a poison for her story— something that would leave no trace in a blood test—and she needed it by tomorrow.

Sabrina made it as far as opening her internet program before her restless mind took her hostage.

Spying the stack of mail, she sorted through it, tossing the junk into the can by the desk and slipping the bills into the cubby above her. When she saw the last envelope, she stopped.

Her name and address were slanted across the front of the delicate pink parchment envelope. She would recognize the neat script anywhere, even if not for the return address in the upper left-hand corner. Dread coated her tongue, sticking it to the roof of her mouth.

She wished she could delete the envelope as easily as she'd deleted the email, because the temptation to open it was overwhelming. Three-dimensional letters were apparently more difficult to resist.

Succumbing to curiosity, she turned the envelope and slid her index finger under the flap. The pink scalloped card slid out easily. Sabrina read the printed script: *Mr. and Mrs. Everett Daniels and Mr. and Mrs. Lloyd Tanner invite you to share in the joy of the marriage uniting their children, Jaylee Daniels and Jared Tanner, on Saturday, the twenty-second of August, at five thirty in the evening.*

Sabrina's eyes returned to Jared's name and rested there. The card trembled in her hand. How had it come this far without her knowing? Where was the warning, the announcement of the engagement, for heaven's sake?

Then she remembered the emails from Aunt Bev she'd deleted. She remembered the voice mails from Jaylee and Arielle she'd never returned.

She hadn't regretted the distance she'd put between herself and the relatives who'd raised her after her dad ... died. They'd hurt her. It was natural that she'd want space between them, natural that she'd avoid them.

Still, this was a harsh way to find out. It was cruel to pop a wedding invitation into her mailbox with no warning. They should've tried harder. She looked at the date again. Less than three months away.

This shouldn't be happening. How could life be so inequitable? *What does it matter now? I don't love him anymore.*

But she had. She'd loved him so much.

But that was over a year ago. She'd moved on. She'd learned from the experience. She was no longer a naive young woman waiting to have her heart trampled. She was savvier now. A well-protected fortress.

She walked to the trash basket and dropped the invitation. At the motion, her bracelet slid down her wrist, drawing her eye to it. She pulled her hand closer and found the dangling heart pendant. Her thumb ran over the familiar surface.

The old emotions welled up, stuffing her lungs with something thick and stifling. She wrapped her hand around her wrist, bracelet and all, as if she could contain the thoughts as easily.

She longed to throw on her tennis shoes now and run until she was out of steam. Run until she was too tired to think, too tired to feel. But she'd promised Renny an answer on the poison, and it might take all evening. So instead, she sank down into her chair. But still her thoughts rebelled.

Somewhere out there, Jaylee and Jared were choosing place settings and planning a honeymoon. Her aunt and uncle would spare no expense. Where was the event? Sabrina couldn't remember. Did she even want to?

She did. She wanted to know the truth, every last painful drop of it, because it wasn't the truth that hurt so badly, but the secrets that preceded it.

Harbormaster: My sister needs a miracle. But I'm not worried. I trust God to work it out. How about you, Sweetpea . . . do you trust God?

Sweetpea: God and me are kind of on the outs right now.

Chapter Four

Sabrina pedaled down Tucker's lane, parallel to the harbor. The cottages along Nantucket's wharf resembled enlarged birdhouses perched on pilings at the water's edge. Their front yards were the ocean, dotted with small, bobbing boats. In the winter these homes, mostly vacant, suffered relentless wind and bitter cold sprays of salt-laden water, but in the summer they drew hefty rental fees from tourists.

The day before, Tucker had jotted his address on a thin café napkin and asked her to arrive around six. His eyes had a boyish light behind them. Hope, she realized, feeling the pierce of guilt.

It was cruel to ignite a fire of hope when she planned to smother every last ember. She had stuffed her hands in her khaki pockets and squeezed the napkin into a tight ball.

She'd weighed her options a hundred times since he'd approached her two weeks earlier. There was no alternative. She would suck it up, and complete the task as quickly as possible.

She would read the emails as though detached from the people writing them. She would list harmless details, making sure they in no way offered any hope of pinpointing Sweetpea's location. That was her plan, and she was sticking to it. Once it was over, she and Harbormaster would continue their relationship as it was before. The relationship was too important to risk losing.

She arrived at Tucker's cottage and parked her bike. It was one of the smaller homes on the water, not much more than a dollhouse, but even these ran over a million. Tucker's house would fit into her loft twice over, but you couldn't argue with the charm of a harbor house. Weathered shaker shingles clothed the building, and its two front windows, like square eyes, flanked the Craftsman-style door at the top of a stoop. A potted plant was the home's only exterior adornment, and it looked as if it had been forgotten long ago.

Sabrina knocked, then tucked a loose strand of hair behind her ear. Her heart, beating up into her throat, seemed to have escaped her rib cage, and she wished she could tuck it in place so easily. Darkness hovered behind the windows. Maybe he wasn't home.

Don't get your hopes up. Of course he's home. He asked you to be here at six. Sabrina checked her watch. One minute before the hour. Well, she could hope, couldn't she? Maybe he'd let her work in peace. Maybe once she was acclimated to his computer, she could come directly after work. He'd be gone, and she could work alone. Maybe this wouldn't be so difficult after all.

The door opened, and Tucker's frame filled the doorway. He

wore a black T-shirt and faded jeans from which his bare feet poked. Sabrina forced her eyes to his face as he opened the door wider.

"Right on time." His cap was missing, and his loose curls were damp, as if he'd recently showered.

Sabrina's tongue felt stapled to the roof of her mouth. She smiled benignly as she squeezed past, catching a faint whiff of his woodsy cologne. The familiar scent drew her.

She held her breath until she was a safe distance away, then forced her eyes around the living room's dim interior. A lone lamp lit the space, its inverted cone of light splaying upward, highlighting a sparse, clay-colored wall. A sofa, two chairs, and a TV hogged the space. A line of carved marine animals perched on the low mantel.

"The office is back that way." He pointed to a short hall beyond the living room. "Can I get you something to drink? I have soda, juice, coffee . . ."

"No, thank you."

She followed him down the hall, her sandals clicking on the wood floor behind his padding feet. She wondered if she should've removed her shoes, but they were clean and, judging by the dust ball in the corner, Tucker wasn't exactly fastidious.

"Here we are. This is my office, slash computer room, slash junk room."

Everything in the room faded in the wake of the harbor view. Evening light flooded the space through a large bay window, tinting the room golden pink.

"Nice view." Strange that he'd never mentioned it in his letters. If she had such a view, she was certain she'd find it distracting. Then again, when she wrote Tucker, she was focused on him alone.

"I had the bay window installed after I bought the place. It's supposed to be a spare bedroom, but it makes a nice office."

Her eyes left the harbor to travel the small space. An oak desk anchored a large rug and faced a pale blue wall. In one corner, a louvered door covered what she assumed was a closet, and stacks of boxes lined the wall opposite the desk.

Tucker had pulled another chair to the desk and gestured toward it. Sabrina set down her bag and sank into the seat as Tucker settled behind the computer, inches away.

She focused on the screen, a fifteen-inch Dell. Several icons covered a photo of Nantucket's harbor. She'd just identified Tucker in the picture before he opened his email program.

"We've been writing about a year, so there are lots of messages to wade through. Most are just quick back-and-forth stuff, but some are longer. I've reread them, trying to figure things out, but like I said, that's not my thing."

Sabrina watched him navigate the screen, going to the oldest letters. Something strange filled her at the sight of her email address in his inbox. As he scrolled, she saw there were few messages from anyone else.

"Her email address is right here." He pointed to the screen. "Sweetpea."

At least her screen name revealed nothing. She folded her hands in her lap.

"Are you always this quiet?"

She should be asking questions, not acting as if she already knew the answers. Which she did. "I'm just observing."

"They say it's the quiet ones you have to watch out for."

"Who's 'they'?"

His eyes flickered away from the screen long enough to give her a grin. "I don't know, but they must know what they're talking about, because everyone quotes them."

The line was so like the tone of his emails, she nearly smiled, but caught it in time.

Questions. She needed to ask questions. "What kind of factual data do you have on your friend? Perhaps you can make a list of everything you know about her."

"Sure. Here, switch chairs and you can start reading."

His arm brushed hers as they passed, and the hairs on her forearm stood on end, drawn toward him as if he were a magnet. She settled into the leather chair and opened the first message.

He'd initially addressed her on Nantucket Chat, a community for those interested in Nantucket. The group was talking about the controversial offshore wind turbine program, a community hot-button issue, and after several days, Tucker emailed her privately.

"I wonder if she grows peas," he said now, jokingly.

"Sweet peas are flowers, not a vegetable."

"Oh. See, that's why I need your help."

She rolled her eyes. "You don't know her occupation, then?"

He pulled a pen and paper from a drawer in the desk and hunched over the corner, way too close. His knee was a fraction of an inch from hers. What if she shifted? What would it hurt to touch him? He'd assume it was an accident if he noticed at all. She wanted to touch him so badly her palms began sweating. If only she could erase the past. If only this could be a normal relationship.

Get a grip, Sabrina. Focus. Read the letter.

"I wish I did. Like I said, she's been careful. On the chat site where I met her, her screen name was SweetpeaKS. Maybe those are her initials or something."

His words were a sharp smack across the face, waking her from her careless daze. He couldn't know, could he? Of course he couldn't. She'd sent Arielle's picture, not her own. She didn't think he'd remember that screen name. It had been over a year ago.

Say something quick. Before he realizes those are your initials backward. "Maybe the KS is for Kansas."

The tip of his pen paused over the paper, and his head tilted sideways as he studied her. "Could be."

Relax. He doesn't know anything. Sabrina got caught in his eyes, sinking in the blue pools. How could a cool color feel so warm? Silver flecks splintered out from the center like shiny threads.

"It could stand for anything, I guess," he said softly.

She pulled her attention to the screen where it belonged. *For heaven's sake, you have got to focus.*

Pretend you're at the café. Why was it easier there? Because she was on her feet and busy? Because when things grew difficult, she could retreat? Because they weren't alone?

Tucker returned to his list, shifting until his knee grazed her thigh.

Because there was no actual touching involved? His body heat permeated the material of her khakis, warming her skin. She should move. She should shift, or cross her legs, or casually lean away. But the contact with him felt so good. So temptingly wonderful.

She didn't want to move away. What could it hurt anyway?

Sabrina crossed her legs and leaned forward, breaking contact for her own sanity. Now she could focus. She opened the next letter and scanned it. They were still discussing the wind farm. Nothing extraneous here.

She waded through several more letters, noting that two or three days separated their messages at this point.

"Just keep going," Tucker said. "I know there's little information in the early emails, but it gets better." He bowed his head over his list again. "Much better," he mumbled, or at least she thought he did.

She read three more, her thoughts going back all those months. She'd never reread the early letters. It had begun harmlessly, a casual exchange of information and ideas. It was in this email, three weeks into their correspondence, that he'd gotten personal:

You know a lot about the wind farm project. Are you from Nantucket? Or are you a summer person? I live near the harbor.

She remembered freezing at the question, recognizing it as a potential turning point. If she told him yes, would she open a can of worms? He seemed kind, but she wasn't ready for a relationship or even a friendship. Her bad track record had sworn her off men months ago.

But it wasn't really a relationship. She didn't know him, he didn't know her. It was just words on a screen. What could it hurt? And yet, now that she knew for sure he was here on Nantucket . . . the proximity was frightening. If he knew she lived here, would he want to meet? That question sealed the deal.

No to both, she'd answered, and technically she wasn't, though she lived here now.

"What do you think?" Tucker interrupted her thoughts.

Sabrina wasn't sure what he meant. "She seems nice."

His eyes teased her. "I'm not asking for a character reference. Have you found anything interesting yet?"

Her face warmed. "Oh." She curled her fingers on the keyboard. "No, I'm just getting to the good stuff."

"Maybe this will help." He handed her the list. "That's all I can think of right offhand. I'm going to get a soda. Can I get you one?"

"No, thank you."

When he left the room, she scanned the list.

Loves to read mysteries

Works until two or three in the afternoon—the service industry, I think??

Lives alone

Allergic to cats and peanuts

Reads poetry—partial to Longfellow

Likes to clean

Favorite foods: pasta, dark chocolate, cupcakes, drinks iced tea

Hates corn

Never married—no kids

Has an extended family—two cousins, aunt and uncle, where??

The list continued, covering both sides of the paper. She felt increasingly exposed with each item. He knew a lot about her. And the list didn't even include the personal experiences she'd shared, only the bland facts. Although no one detail was particularly telling, the summation was like a fingerprint, surely unique to her alone.

The revelation frightened her. What if she said or did something to reveal herself? She'd have to be extremely vigilant.

She scanned the list again and noted an oddity. For all the factual information on the list, there was not one description of her appearance.

Harbormaster: My mom encouraged me to follow in her footsteps and become an attorney. I wasted three years of higher learning pursuing that goal until I finally realized I wasn't trying to become a lawyer at all. I was trying to gain my mother's approval.

Chapter Five

Tucker pulled open the refrigerator door and considered the drink options. Pepsi, milk, orange juice, and an old can of root beer that was probably flat. He'd already finished two sodas today, but milk or juice didn't appeal. He wasn't even thirsty.

He ran his hand through his hair. The real problem was Sabrina was in his house, in his office, fifteen paces away, and nothing was different. She was no more than a stranger, yet she was so much more.

He shut the fridge door. She was this close. *This close.* His leg had been pressed to hers, and okay, he'd manufactured the event, but still. He knew it hadn't meant anything. From her perspective the contact was accidental, probably even unnoticed. But for an instant he'd let himself believe it was significant. He imagined that she initiated the contact. He wouldn't delve into all the reasons why that was so pathetic. But it didn't matter anyway.

She'd pulled away, and that pretty much busted his imaginary bubble.

This was hard. Harder than he'd expected. He'd decided not to put Operation Sweetpea into full swing just yet. Let her settle in first, get comfortable. Allow her to know him a little. He hadn't realized that having her here would be so torturous.

What was holding her back? He knew she'd been hurt by her ex-fiancé. Hurt badly enough to cause rifts in her family and a chasm between her and God. Was she afraid of relationships? Or was it something more? Something she hadn't mentioned at all?

He remembered the first time he'd seen her. He stopped at the café on a Monday morning and took a seat near Oliver. A new server entered the dining room, a full tray balanced on one hand. She unloaded the tray with quick, efficient movements. She was tall, and her long limbs were fluid, graceful. She moved like a dancer.

Char appeared, filling his coffee mug. "Good morning, Tucker. How are you this morning, hon?"

"Fine, thanks."

Char moved on, and Tucker found himself watching the new server. There was something about her. He tried to figure out what. She had dark hair, pulled tightly into a ponytail and secured with a white band. She reached for it now and then, playing with the frayed end. Delicate eyebrows arched over a pair of almond-shaped brown eyes. She was a natural beauty. Her face, unadorned by makeup, would be perfect for a Dove soap ad. She was completely unaffected, as if she didn't know there were a couple male customers checking her out.

"Fancy the new gal, do you?"

Oliver's voice interrupted his thoughts. Tucker tore his eyes from the retreating server and sipped his coffee. "Where's she from?"

Oliver shrugged. "Don't know. Why don't you ask her?"

Tucker watched the new employee prepare a fresh pot of coffee like someone who'd done it a hundred times. He imagined himself starting a conversation with her, then realized what was different about the woman. For all her grace, her shoulders were too rigid, her back too straight. Her eyes engaged no one. She was all business.

He wasn't afraid of a challenge. "Might do that," Tucker replied.

"She don't look real friendly." Oliver smoothed his sparse hair.

A few minutes later, the new server stopped and refilled his coffee.

"You must be new around here." Tucker gave a smile that usually warmed up a woman pretty well.

"I am." The server turned her back, filling Oliver's cup.

"Where are you from?" Tucker asked.

She set the pot down and pulled out her tablet. "The mainland. Char's on break. Can I get you anything?"

She was a tough cookie; it didn't take a genius to see that. The all-business-don't-get-too-close sort. He cleared his throat. "I usually just have coffee."

She nodded once and went to take a family's order.

Oliver snickered. "That went real well."

The same scene had replayed itself many times over, some more humiliating than others. But eventually, he'd figured a way around her defenses. Even if it hadn't been ideal.

Now, he heard the faint tapping of Sabrina's fingers on the keyboard, and drew a breath. They'd come so far since then. He knew her so well, and loved what he knew. Loved how she toyed with her hair when she felt insecure, loved how openly she communicated with him, loved how honest she was about herself. He even loved her wry sense of humor. If only he could get that to translate outside of cyberspace.

Why was he in the kitchen, obsessing over the problem, when she was in the next room? He needed to loosen her up, get her accustomed to him so she'd let down her guard. He needed to focus on his plan, which began with that list he'd just made her.

When he reentered the office, Sabrina didn't look up from the screen. She'd jotted her own notes on his list. The screen displayed a letter she'd written a few weeks into their relationship. She was moving too quickly. If she continued at this pace, she'd be done in two weeks.

"Find anything?" He settled in the chair beside her.

"Nothing conclusive. Just jotting a few notes."

A strand of hair had slipped loose from her ponytail and fell over the curve of her cheek while she leaned forward, intent on her notes. It was easy to forget how delicate her features were. Her hands-off approach made most people avoid her, and that's probably how she liked it. But she had so much to offer under that hardened shell.

Her words from a message replayed in his mind. She'd written it after telling him about her ex-fiancé.

I guess you never know another person entirely. The parts you do know are formed by that person's words and actions. The parts you don't know you fill in with wishful thinking, which you eventually convince yourself is fact. When you're not looking, this nugget of illusion will come back to smash you over the head.

They were the sad words of a disillusioned soul. He'd turned them over and over in his head that night.

Now, Tucker watched her press her lips together, returning her attention to the screen. His eyes roamed her face—her long, dark lashes, her perfectly shaped nose, her stubborn chin—and determination twisted strong and hard in his gut. *No matter how hard this is on me, Sabrina Kincaid, I'm going to prove to you that love doesn't have to hurt.*

The picture. Ask about the picture. Sabrina pinched the bridge of her nose. It was the obvious question: Do you have a picture of her?

So simple, yet she'd avoided asking. Could she bear hearing Tucker fawn over Arielle's beauty?

Tucker appeared for the third time. For heaven's sake, was he going to stare over her shoulder every minute? She closed the email she'd been staring at blindly and opened the next one.

"How's it going?" He sat beside her.

Just peachy. "Are you going to ask that every five minutes?"

"Will it make you work harder?"

"It will make me irritable."

"Is that why your eyes are shooting sparks?"

She leveled a stare at him.

"All right, all right, I'll be quiet." Chastened, he leaned back in his chair, going nowhere.

Sabrina sighed and returned her attention to the screen. She couldn't focus with him staring a hole through her head. Heat gathered at the base of her skull and climbed to her ears. Was it hot in here?

She should ask about the picture. Just get it over with. It can't be worse than this.

She wetted her lips. "You haven't said anything about what she looks like. Surely you've exchanged photos." She pretended to read the next email, then realized Tucker was taking too much time in answering.

When she looked at him, he wore a strange expression, but when he blinked it was gone. He leaned over and took the mouse, brushing her hand.

Sabrina jerked back, then covered her overreaction by tucking a strand of hair behind her ear.

"I'll have to find the email that had the photo attached." He leaned toward the screen, his shoulder touching hers. "I think it's the only one with an attachment, so it shouldn't be hard."

She was only aware of the three square inches where their shoulders touched. If she turned toward him, it would take no more than a tip of her head to plant a kiss on his jawline. Her breaths became shallow, and she made a concerted effort to regulate them. *Breathe. In. Out.*

Oh, this was ridiculous. What was taking him so long?

She reached for the mouse. "I'll find it."

"Here it is." He clicked on an email, finally settling back in his seat.

Arielle smiled in the photo taken on Florida's gulf coast. She'd been walking toward the ocean, and it looked as if someone had called her name. The photo was from the waist up, shot from behind, taken as she'd turned to face the camera. Her long, blonde hair was spinning. Her blue eyes were sparkling brighter than the ocean in the background. But it was her trademark wide smile, the one that had won her numerous beauty pageants, that stole the show.

Sabrina wasn't jealous of Arielle. She loved her and was proud of her achievements. But knowing Tucker was gawking at her beautiful cousin twisted her insides painfully. She wanted to close the photo, but that would seem strange when she'd just asked to see it.

Instead she cleared her throat and pried the words off her tongue. "She's beautiful."

Her heart beat unnaturally fast waiting for his concurrence. She steeled herself against the inevitable sting.

"She's a beautiful person."

It was an odd response. Not what your typical man would say, but then Tucker wasn't your typical man. He was still staring at the screen. At least, she thought he was. She wasn't about to check.

Say something. "It's not a close-up. And her face is kind of shadowed. Is this the only one you have?"

"Yeah."

It was odd that he hadn't printed the photo. She'd expected an eight-by-ten glossy framed, matted, and placed on his nightstand or desk. Maybe even a wallet photo so he could show her off to his buddies.

"I'm not sure how much it'll help," she said. "Unless we can narrow the search down to a small town where everyone knows everyone."

"She's on the beach obviously." He gestured to the screen.

"You don't have any idea where she lives?"

"She was on Nantucket Chat when we met. I know she's been here at some point."

Better if he thought she lived elsewhere. Somewhere far, far away.

"We'd recognize her if she lived here."

Sabrina could feel his gaze on her. "You'd think."

"There's only ten thousand residents."

"But there are four or five times that in the summer. And this photo was taken at a beach."

Shoot. "True." She searched the photo for something that might sidetrack him. "There's a shadow falling on the sand beside her."

"A big tree, I think."

"That rules out Nantucket." Not that big trees didn't grow on the island, but none that big near the shoreline.

"Yeah, I guess you're right." He seemed reluctant to agree.

Sabrina searched the photo for more clues. "The waves look pretty small."

"That rules out the east and west coasts."

"Well, that narrows it down to a mere five states," she said.

"Better than fifty."

"Unless it's a vacation photo."

"Boy, sunshine, you're just full of positive thoughts."

"Just trying to be realistic." She closed the photo. "I should probably start reading these letters." She opened the next one and read the first sentence five times before she could focus enough to comprehend it. Was he going to sit there watching her read? It would take her months at this rate.

He picked up a pencil and tapped it on the desk, the sharpened end ticking against the wood surface.

She read the second sentence again. *Focus, Sabrina. For heaven's sake, you could have read the whole email twice by now.*

The tapping continued, pulling her attention from her task.

Finally she turned to him, sighing hard.

His brows disappeared under a dark, wavy tendril. "Oh, sorry. Am I distracting you?"

You think? If only she could read the emails in her apartment. She could get this done much quicker. "Are you sure you can't print them off? Or you could forward them to me. I wouldn't be in your way every night, and I promise I'd be careful with them."

He stood, shaking his head. "I wouldn't feel right about it. I feel bad enough just letting you read them."

If only he knew.

Sweetpea: My nickname in elementary school was Money Mouth. That's what happens when the class bully finds out a quarter will fit into the gap between your teeth. Braces only fix the exterior. Inside, I'm still the wallflower watching her cousins dance.

Chapter Six

Three days later, Sabrina gathered the thick stack of manuscript pages and checked the digital clock. It was one o'clock, late by her own standards, but Renny would be up working. The woman swore creativity flowed after midnight, and maybe it did, because the story Sabrina just finished reading was stellar.

She slid into sandals and walked down the stairs. A cool breeze ruffled the leaves above her and raised gooseflesh on her arms. When she reached Renny's kitchen door, she knocked.

"Sabrina, good heavens, what are you doing up?" Renny's gray hair protruded in all directions, an indication the woman had been using her scalp massager again. *"It stimulates the creative neurons,"* Renny had told her when Sabrina caught her at the computer, rubbing her head with the thing. It looked like a silver squid had latched on and wasn't letting loose.

"I couldn't go to sleep, and it's all your fault." Sabrina held up the manuscript.

Renny opened the door wider, letting Sabrina pass. "You liked it?"

"I couldn't put it down. Honestly, I started reading it today and couldn't go to bed until I finished. The writing is crisp, the characters are compelling, and the plot was woven together so tightly . . . Renny, if this one doesn't sell, those publishers are just incompetent. Your agent will be so pleased."

"Oh, thank God. I'm so relieved you liked it. The plot you helped me with is fresh and unique, I know that." A light behind Renny's eyes dimmed. "But the writing—it's not as good as I wanted it to be."

Sometimes Sabrina wanted to shake her. "The writing is superb."

Renny sank into an oak chair and stared through the window into the dark night. She didn't believe Sabrina. Anyone could see that. She wore her black and gray Hawaiian shirt, a sure sign her mood was down.

Renny twisted her diamond-studded wedding set around her wrinkled finger.

"You said that about the last one too."

"Because it's true."

Renny picked up the scalp massager and tapped its legs on the table. "I think the characters need more fleshing out. Especially Drew. That male point of view gets me every time."

"Every character was beautifully drawn."

"I don't know. It lacks . . . *chai*!"

"Chai? Like the tea?"

"Life! It lacks life."

Renny's late husband had done a job on her confidence. He'd been gone for three years, long before Sabrina had arrived, but she didn't have to know the man to see the effects he'd had on Renny.

"It lacks nothing. I have a good feeling about this one," Sabrina said.

"Well." Renny's gaze flickered to the hutch along the wall, then out the window. "Well, it's all in God's hands anyway, right?"

Sabrina needed to turn in if she was going to be lucid for work in the morning. Yet one look at Renny's drawn cheeks and ruffled hair and she sank into the heavy chair opposite the woman.

"How's your next story coming?"

She let out a Darth Vader sigh. "It's not. I have nothing at all, and I've been praying about it all week."

"Maybe we can brainstorm tomorrow."

"You're working for the McCabe boy after the café. Honey, you don't have time for that."

"I'll make time, Renny. Besides, it's fun."

"Well, you're a genius at it, there's no doubt. Maybe I should just sign your name to these stories and be done with it." She gave a weak laugh.

"I couldn't write my way out of a paper bag. Has your agent heard from any publishers on *Danger in the Night?*" The quality of Renny's writing had taken a huge leap in her last story about a Nantucket family's murder.

Renny set down the massager and yawned. "No, no word. Heavens, I don't think the ideas are going to flow tonight. Tell me how things are going for you. Work? Have you heard from your family?"

"Work's fine." She thought of the wedding invitation, a part of her shriveling at the thought.

"And your family?"

"I got a wedding invitation in the mail. Jared and Jaylee's."

Renny sucked in a breath. "No!" Her brows creased into a V between her shiny eyes. Righteous indignation.

"Afraid so."

She laid her hand over Sabrina's. "Oh, *amita,* I'm so sorry. God will give you peace on this. I know it."

Sometimes Renny's faith felt like enough for both of them. This was not one of those times. Still, it did comfort her when Renny called her "friend" that way. "Thanks, Renny."

"Will you go? I could go with you."

"No, I—I'm not going. But thanks for the offer."

"Well, if you change your mind, you have only to let me know and I'll be packing my suitcase."

After Sabrina left, her thoughts went back to Renny's manuscript. She wondered if it would take a sale for Renny to believe in her work. If so, there was no need to worry, because Sabrina knew great writing, and Renny's recent stories were nothing short of that.

Tucker sipped the coffee Sabrina had poured, then spread out *The Inquirer and Mirror* and pretended to read. She was posting an order for two men in suits and neckties. They chatted quietly over a thin stack of papers, sipping their coffee between notations. It seemed a little early for business, but hey, better them than him. He relished the idea of a day spent on the open sea instead of chained to some desk.

Glancing around the café, he caught two high school boys ogling Sabrina all the way to the kitchen. One of them met his eyes, and Tucker stared until the kid looked away. *Aren't you a little young for her, pal?* They couldn't be more than eighteen and Sabrina was twenty-four. No, he reminded himself, she was twenty-five today. He'd thought she'd request the night off, but she hadn't.

He remembered his own twenty-fifth birthday. He'd gone home to New York for Thanksgiving break, and his family had thrown a surprise dinner party for him and his twin sister at Le Bernardin, complete with friends from high school and college.

He wanted to do something special for Sabrina, but an email greeting would have to suffice. Maybe he could make tonight special.

If only she would open up to him, even as a friend. She was so guarded. When she'd first come to the island, he'd tried for months to get to know her.

He'd begun to wonder if Oliver's sole reason for coming to the café wasn't to watch the show.

"Don't you have anything better to do than eavesdrop on my conversations?" he'd asked more than once.

"Last I checked, it took two to have a conversation."

Being publicly rejected on a regular basis wasn't much fun. Still, there was something about Sabrina. He sensed a vulnerability in her that drew him. Watching her reminded him of a quote he'd once heard: *"The people with the highest walls have the softest hearts."* Watching Sabrina, he suspected it was true. He wanted to know for sure. He wanted to know her, if only she'd let him in.

He'd never been so interested in someone who, apparently, didn't return the favor. Was it her thinly disguised vulnerability that drew him, or something else? He reflected on that often and came to the conclusion that it was those unguarded moments that captured him. She presented a disinterested front, but there were moments when she didn't think anyone was looking that he caught an unvarnished glimpse of the real Sabrina.

One evening after she'd first started working at the café, he'd seen her resting on a bench at Jetties Beach. The sun was low in the sky, and the beach crowd was gone for the day. It was just Sabrina, watching the sunset. She had a little smile on her face and was so caught up in the view she didn't notice him, only twenty feet away. He wanted to stroll over and say hi. But she looked so peaceful, and though he hadn't known her long, he knew the instant she saw him, her guard would go up. He didn't want to spoil her relaxing evening.

So he continued to try and spark conversations at the café. Just when he was about to give up, he'd catch a glimpse of her chatting with Char or coming off break and see her unmasked. He was determined to find out who she really was, why she kept such a distance between herself and others.

The first time he'd asked her out, he'd been more nervous than ever before. Of course, he didn't normally ask out a woman who'd given him no encouragement. He dismissed his failed attempts at conversation. She was busy during breakfast, and he got to thinking that if he came at a slower time, she might be more receptive.

So on a chilly fall day during slow season, he showed up after the lunch hour and took a seat at his regular table. He saw the surprise on Sabrina's face before she could mask it.

He opened the menu and surveyed the lunch selection. The thought of food made his stomach turn.

"Coffee?" she asked.

He flipped his mug over and gave her what he hoped was a charming smile. "Sure." He thought she might comment about his unscheduled appearance, but she didn't.

Instead she pulled out her order pad and poised a pen over it. "What can I get you?"

Now, there was a loaded question. He considered whether to order or just say what he'd come for. His heart drummed wildly in the pause.

Her brows lifted ever so slightly.

He closed his menu. "Actually, to be honest, I didn't come here to eat."

She hardly missed a beat. "Just coffee then?"

"No," he said quickly before she could skedaddle away. "No, I—" He sat up straight in his chair as if the boost would raise his confidence. "I wanted to ask if you'd like to go out for coffee sometime. Or dinner. My friend works at DeMarco and could probably even get us in—"

"I can't," she said. "I'm sorry." She scooted off toward the coffee station while he gathered what was left of his pride. Not even a reason, just *"I'm sorry."* Was she dating someone? Wouldn't she have said so if she were? He never saw her with anyone else, and neither had anyone else, because he'd asked around. No, he didn't think she was taken. And that only made the rejection worse.

But he'd survived it and had even gotten up the courage to ask again. With the same results.

It was only when he'd overheard a conversation between Sabrina and Char that the idea had formed. It was a slow, rainy morning, and they were rolling silverware in napkins at a table behind him, close enough for eavesdropping. Char was telling Sabrina about Nantucket Chat, a place where people from all over the country posted messages on a variety of topics. Some posters were residents, others just people who'd visited and fallen in love with Nantucket's charms. Tucker had logged on a few times to see what people were saying about local politics or preservation of the island's ecology.

"That's a good idea," Char was saying. "You should write that on Nantucket Chat. I think a lot of people would be interested. It's free to join. Just log in and post it in the Nantucket Ecology discussion forum."

"I might do that," Sabrina said.

Tucker watched the forum for two days, waiting for a new name to appear. When it did, it was SweetpeaKS, and he recognized Sabrina's idea. He'd posted a couple comments himself, then emailed her privately to discuss her idea. The rest had been history.

A kid two tables over let out a piercing cry, drawing his attention from the past. The baby pounded his fists on the table, demanding more Cheerios from his mom, who was busy with two other kids. Several feet away, Char stopped Sabrina, two coffeepots grasped in her bony hands. "Hey, Sabrina, I had this family thing come up last minute and need to leave early. You think you could stay over a few hours?"

Sabrina pulled her order pad and pen from her apron pocket. "Sure, no problem."

She went to take an order from an elderly couple three tables away. Char must not know it was Sabrina's birthday. In fact, he hadn't heard anyone mention it. Between her hours at the café and working on his project, she wouldn't have a spare minute today. Maybe Sabrina needed the money.

He recalled their email conversation the evening before.

It's almost your day, he'd written.

Got big plans?

Are you kidding? she'd replied.

It's my twenty-fifth birthday.

Don't have too much fun without me, birthday girl.

It sounded at the time like she had something fun planned, but now he realized she'd never answered his question. She did that sometimes—changed the subject.

"Warm you up?" Sabrina's voice interrupted his thoughts.

He realized his paper blocked the mug, and moved it. Color bloomed on her cheeks as she realized her words' double meaning. His lips twitched with the urge to comment, but he stopped himself. "Thanks."

Oliver sank into the chair at his usual table. Sabrina turned over his mug and filled it. "Good morning."

"Morning, Sabrina." Oliver folded his sausagelike fingers on the table, leaning back. "You know, I'm feeling rather *edacious* this morning."

She set down the coffee and poised her pen over her tablet. "Great, then can I get you something more than coffee?"

Oliver pursed his lips, and Tucker smothered a grin as the man reluctantly ordered rye toast. Poor rascal. He tried so hard.

Tucker checked his watch. He had to gas up his boat before they opened. When Sabrina returned with the toast, she set his tab on the table.

He reached for his wallet. "See you tonight around six?"

She nodded once, no eye contact. Tucker watched her gather dishes a few tables away, her motions efficient and fluid.

"No way." Oliver glanced back and forth between them, gray brows crouching low over his eyes.

Tucker pulled out three bills and set them by the saltshaker.

Oliver lowered his voice. "You did not get a date with the Ice Princess."

Tucker stood, pocketing his wallet, taking one last peek at Sabrina as she put an order on the wheel.

"Is she going out with you, McCabe?"

Tucker pushed in his chair and adjusted his hat as he walked away.

"*McCabe?*"

A smile tickled Tucker's lips as he exited the café.

Harbormaster: My twin sister called tonight. What a mess. Her jerk of a husband cheated on her and now they're separated. If I see him again, I'm afraid what I might do to him. He deserves it for what he's putting Tracey through.

Chapter Seven

A large, teal envelope was waiting in Sabrina's mailbox when she arrived home. She hurriedly tore it open and skipped the card's flowery greeting. Her aunt had signed for both of them. *Love, Uncle Everett and Aunt Bev.*

She held the card a moment, then dropped it in the wastebasket and checked her email. Nothing. She reread the email Tucker sent early that morning.

Happy 25th birthday! I hope you have a great day. I'm thinking about you.

After she showered and dressed in modest shorts and a clean blouse, she gathered her hair into a ponytail and headed for Tucker's. Her palms sweated against the handlebars, turning sticky. Would she ever relax in Tucker's presence? Being with him was painful. Bad enough serving him at the café, but there was something intimate about being in his home. And the man would not leave her alone. If he didn't stay in the office, he peeked in every few minutes. She was constantly tense, waiting for him to materialize.

She wiped one damp palm at a time on her beige shorts. *You have got to relax. As far as he's concerned, he's only your employer. Do your job and forget about the relationship.*

It was the relationship that prevented her from relaxing. *It's not a relationship. It's just a—a correspondence.*

A daily, intimate correspondence.

He doesn't even know my name.

He knows who you are deep inside.

Sabrina's stomach tightened as she clutched the handlebars. It was true. Tucker did know her, better than anyone ever had.

Except Jared.

A pool of panic welled up in her. Had she made a terrible mistake in corresponding with Tucker? She'd thought the anonymity provided safety, but then, she'd thought Jared was safe, and she'd been wrong about that. How was she to know he'd hurt her when she'd met him under such noble circumstances?

It had been the second semester of her sophomore year at college when she met Jared. After high school she left Macon to study literature at Miami University in the quaint town of Oxford, Ohio. Putting distance between herself and her family had been both frightening and liberating. Without her beautiful and charming Southern cousins at her side, a seedling of confidence began to sprout.

One night she walked from her last class to her car, unlocked it, and slid inside, closing the door against the bitter-cold wind. She had twenty-three minutes to be at Bruno's, where she would serve pizza to a rowdy weekend college crowd until closing.

Vapor plumed in front of her face as she slid the key into the ignition, and she turned it, eager to get some heat going.

But nothing happened at the motion. Nothing except a clicking sound. *No, no, no.* She turned the key again, and the same noise greeted her. A dead battery, she was sure, but she had no cables. She glanced around the darkened parking lot through windows that had begun to fog with her breath. There was no one in sight. Besides, she wondered how many college students carried battery cables in their cars.

She could call her roommate, but by the time Zoe arrived, Sabrina would be late. She'd have to walk to Bruno's and worry about her car later. She grabbed her backpack and exited the car, locking it and hoping it wouldn't be towed in the dead of night.

The hum of an approaching engine startled her. It was a dark pickup truck, and the man behind the wheel was a stranger. But that wasn't unusual, given the size of the campus.

"Need help?" He'd rolled down his window and leaned out, the corner of his elbow poking from the vehicle. He had short, dark hair, but shadows masked his facial features.

Sabrina was suddenly aware of how alone she was in the massive parking lot. She clutched the keys in her palm, searching for her car key in case she needed to unlock the vehicle quickly. Just last month she'd overheard students discussing the latest sexual assault that had occurred at the victim's off-campus home.

"No." She hitched the bag higher on her shoulder, hoping he'd leave. "Thanks for asking though." Her words should've dismissed him.

He looked out his front window, then back to her. "Can I call someone for you?"

"No, thanks." She made her voice sound confident. Should she walk toward town or get in her car and lock the door? Maybe she should call Zoe and be late for work.

But the last person who'd been late for work had been fired. Bruno had no tolerance for irresponsible college students. He'd only hired her because of her shining references from her former bosses back in Macon.

"It sounded like a dead battery. If you have jumper cables, I can give you a jump."

"I don't have any."

"Shoot, I don't either. Listen, it's not safe to walk around at night, especially a pretty girl like you. If you don't have anyone to pick you up, I can give you a ride."

As if jumping in a car with a stranger was safer. "No, thanks, I'm fine." She turned in the opposite direction and began walking toward Main Street. Her legs wobbled as she navigated the maze of cars, huddled against the wind.

She was relieved when she reached the sidewalk, but the short distance to Main Street seemed to stretch out forever.

When she heard the hum of an engine approaching from behind, her legs pumped faster. Was the man returning? He seemed friendly, but she supposed that had been the rape victim's last thought before the guy violated her.

Her longer stride was no match for the vehicle. The truck pulled along the curb and kept pace with her.

The man rolled down the passenger window and called through it, "Hey, why don't you just let me give you a ride? It's too cold out there. You're shivering."

"I'm fine. I'm almost where I'm going."

"Have it your way." His voice had changed, and the kindness peeled off his face like a mask. He put the truck in park, and he reached for his handle.

Fear clawed at Sabrina's spine. She broke into a run. She heard footsteps behind her, rubber soles grinding on the pebbled cement. Then she ran into something hard.

Run! You've got to move!

But the hard thing she'd run into steadied her. The man released her and stepped around her. "Everything okay here?"

The truck driver stopped in his tracks ten feet away. His hard face slackened as he sized up the man in front of her and found himself on the short end. He stepped back. "No trouble, dude. Just trying to help the girl."

The new man looked over his shoulder. "You all right?"

Sabrina swallowed, her breath still caught like a bubble in her throat. She nodded.

"I've got it from here," he said. "Why don't you get back in your truck and call it a night?"

The truck driver's jaw twitched as he clamped it down, staring at her. Sabrina's gaze fell to his tennis shoes as she prayed he'd leave. He seemed to stand there forever before he returned to his truck. It roared away loudly.

The other man moved from her side, walking away, and she wondered where he was going. Then he stooped and picked up something. Her purse. She hadn't even realized she'd dropped it.

"Thanks," she said as he handed it to her, meaning the word in more ways than one.

"Are you sure you're okay?"

Her hands shook as she set her purse on her shoulder, and she wasn't sure if it was the cold or the belated terror kicking in.

"I'm fine," she said, feeling oddly safe for someone who'd nearly been attacked. Jared had walked her to Bruno's that night and had eaten there two nights later. Because of how they'd met, she'd thought of him as her knight. Thought it was safe to love him. It had been three years before she realized the foolishness of her thinking.

Sabrina shook the memories from her mind as she turned into Tucker's drive.

"Hey, neighbor!" She followed the sound of the voice to the porch next to Tucker's house. A blond guy leaned on the railing, smiling widely.

"Uh, hi. I don't live here, actually."

"Renting?"

"I'm just working here for a few weeks."

Blondie ambled down the porch steps and onto the lawn barefooted. "My friends and I rented this place for the month."

Sabrina slid off the bike and set the kickstand. "Hope you have a nice visit." She smiled in a dismissive way. She had enough on her mind with Tucker.

"Maybe I'll see you around."

"Maybe." She stepped onto Tucker's porch and rapped, conscious that Blondie was still standing on his lawn, watching her. *Keep your head in the game. Be professional. Do the job, and don't let it become personal.*

Tucker opened the door and ushered her inside. "Hey there." His voice was chipper, his smile engaging. There were tiny lines beside his mouth that made him look a little older than his twenty-nine years. And that little scar by his mouth . . .

Look away, you ninny.

"Something to drink? Iced tea?"

"No, thank you." She went straight to the office and settled behind his desk. He stood in the doorway. She could feel him staring into her back. "I'll go ahead and get started."

She'd hoped the words would dismiss him, but the quiet behind her made her think he hadn't gone anywhere, and the way the hairs on her neck stood on end made her sure of it. She opened the email program, then the folder where the messages were stored.

Go away. She couldn't think with him standing there.

She started where she'd left off, opening the letter and reading it. The messages became short and quippy, and she remembered it was a time they'd both been at their computers, exchanging emails for a couple hours.

She heard a shuffle in the doorway and felt that Tucker had left. Finally, she could concentrate. It took almost an hour to read one evening's messages. Opening each email for only a sentence or two was tedious and time-consuming. At some point she heard the phone ring, followed by Tucker's friendly greeting, then the sliding of the patio door as he continued his conversation outside.

Turning her attention back to her work, Sabrina saw that she'd finally reached the last emails sent that night. She remembered it well. She had opened it expecting another short quip, and had gotten the shock of her life instead.

This is me, he'd written.

Pasted into the email was a photo. Her breath caught and hung in her throat, choking her. The photo was from a distance, but she would've known Tucker McCabe anywhere.

It can't be. She stared at the photo, taken beside a boat. No, it was definitely him. The blue cap, the dark curls, the T-shirt with his company's logo. Tucker McCabe whom she waited on every morning at the café. How could it be? What were the chances?

What do I do? He was sitting at his computer, waiting for her reply. Did he—oh, for heaven's sake, no—did he expect her to send a photo of herself? *I can't do it.*

Sure, it was easy for him. He had nothing to hide with his dark good looks and muscular physique. What would he think when he discovered who he'd befriended? That it was the Ice Princess from the café? The plain, gawky one with a ponytail and sharp tongue? He'd want nothing more to do with Sweetpea, that's what. And maybe that was best, because a real relationship was not going to happen.

Her pulse began to pound at her temples.

I have to write back. What do I say? She cupped her forehead in her palms. Maybe if she didn't reply, he'd think she'd gone to bed. But that would be rude after he'd sent his photo. And they always said goodnight before they signed off for the night.

Another email appeared.

Hello?

She had to respond. She put her fingers on the keyboard.

I'm here.

She sent the message and waited. Finally a reply appeared.

Am I that ugly?

She closed her eyes, then forced her fingers onto the keys again. What to say? She bit her lip.

Of course not.

She hit Send.
A few seconds later another email appeared.

I'd love to see who I'm spending all these hours with. I want to picture you. ☺

She'd known it was coming. What should she do? If she sent her photo, he'd know who she was. It would be the end of their relationship, one way or another. At the very least, mornings at the café would become awkward. What if he wasn't repelled by the fact that Sabrina was Sweetpea? What if he wanted to start dating or something?

An email appeared in her inbox.

Are you there? Are you downloading a photo or fretting over it? I don't care what you look like (in case you're wondering).

Sabrina choked on a laugh. But of course he cared. He was a man, wasn't he? She'd learned early that a woman's looks were her currency, and Sabrina had been bankrupt from the beginning. If she hadn't known it before she'd moved in with her cousins, she'd learned it afterward. Arielle and Jaylee had no idea how lucky they were to be born with—

The picture. Arielle had sent a photo of herself the week before. Maybe she could send it . . .

That's not right, Sabrina.

But what did it matter?

She couldn't let him know who she was, so what did it matter if he thought she was beautiful? He probably already did.

She opened her cousin's last email, copied the photo, then pasted it into a reply to Tucker. She stared at the picture. Even at the beach, Arielle's face was artfully made up, her lips cherry red. The photo resembled a CoverGirl ad. Dread sank like a weight in her stomach. Before she could reconsider, she sent the photo.

Her fingers tapped on the desk while she waited. Had she done the right thing? *It's not as if you have a choice. He can't know who you are. What could it hurt if he thinks you're beautiful?*

It's not as if they were going to meet. Well, they *had* met, but it's not as if Tucker would discover her identity. And if he had to imagine her, why not picture a beautiful woman? If she'd refused to send a photo, he might assume she was homely. And what if he decided to discontinue their relationship? She couldn't bear the thought of returning to the lonely life she'd had before their email relationship. She couldn't lose him.

She shook her head, trying to connect the visual image of Tucker with the mental image of Harbormaster. He was the one who listened so carefully, who took her ideas and thoughts seriously, who never judged her regardless of what she said.

What was taking him so long to reply?

He was probably on his knees, thanking his lucky stars that she was so gorgeous.

The weight in Sabrina's stomach sank lower. She opened the email with his photo. She couldn't believe it was Tucker.

But he doesn't know it's you. Thank God for that.

A reply appeared in her inbox. She rushed to open it.

Thanks for the photo. You don't know how much I enjoy our chats.

Sabrina reread his words. He hadn't mentioned her appearance. She'd expected a compliment at least. It wasn't the first time Tucker surprised her, and it probably wouldn't be the last.

A knock at the front door snagged her attention. She closed out the email. So much for remaining detached. This was harder than she'd thought it was going to be. She opened a new one and began reading. *Stay detached,* she told herself. *You do not know these people. They are characters, like the ones in Renny's—*

Another knock sounded. She listened for Tucker's footsteps but instead heard the deep rumble of his voice from the deck outside. Still on the phone.

Sabrina went to the door and opened it. Blondie stood on the stoop, hands pocketed in his Hawaiian-print swim trunks. "Sorry to bother you—uh, didn't catch your name before."

"Sabrina."

She was rewarded with a bright smile. "I'm Cody. My friends and I are grilling steaks, and we forgot to get steak sauce. You wouldn't happen to have any?" He winced like he hated to ask.

She turned and saw Tucker sitting in the deck chair, his feet propped on the railing, the phone tucked against his shoulder. Surely he wouldn't mind. "Come on in. I'll check."

After riffling through the contents, she found a bottle of A1 Steak Sauce corralled in the fridge door behind a bulk-sized bottle of ketchup. She grabbed the sauce and took it to Cody. He was leaning against the door frame when she returned.

She handed him the bottle.

"Great, thanks," he said but didn't budge. Instead he asked her a few questions about the local beaches. After they covered that topic, he straightened. "Say, we made plenty of food. You want to come over for dinner?"

"She's working."

Sabrina turned at the sound of Tucker's voice. She hadn't heard him enter. His arms crossed his chest, and his jaw was set in a way she'd never seen.

Sabrina turned back to Cody. "He's right. But thanks for the invite."

"Maybe another time." His eyes swung to Tucker's, his smile smug. "Thanks for the steak sauce."

Sabrina shut the door, feeling like she was in trouble. "He'll bring it back."

Tucker pursed his lips, and she wondered what he was thinking. It was only steak sauce, for crying out loud.

"You were on the phone."

Shadows danced over his face as his jaw clenched and loosened. He turned toward the patio door.

Okay then. "I'll get back to work." She was almost to the hall when his voice stopped her.

"It's her birthday today," he said.

It took a moment for his words to register. "What?"

"Her twenty-fifth birthday. And all I can do is send a stinking email greeting."

Maybe that's why he was all moody. Then anxiety kicked in. Did he know it was *her* birthday? There was nothing to give her away. No card, no present, no bouquet of flowers delivered to the restaurant. She looked into his eyes. She wanted to soothe away his sadness. She wanted to lay her palm against his cheek and tell him it was okay. She wanted to—

She turned away.

"I need to find her." His tone was sobering. "I want to be with her."

His words filled a hollow spot inside her. Sure he wanted to be with her, she reminded herself. Because he thought she looked like Arielle. *Because he doesn't know who you are and what you did.*

Sabrina cleared her throat. "I'm working on that."

She could hear the water lapping the sides of the pier outside. The ferry horn sounded in the distance.

"Let's get out of here," he said.

She glanced at him, then looked away, resisting the pull of those eyes. "What?"

He stood. "Let's go for a ride in my boat."

"I'm working."

"You've read a lot of messages already. You've got notes. Bring them along, and we can toss ideas around."

Panic welled in her, rushing her words. "It's getting late."

"There's plenty of light. Come on, you're not afraid of a little water, are you?"

"Of course not."

"Then come on." He approached and reached for her hand, tugging. The contact felt good, his hand warm and strong around hers.

"All right, all right," she snapped, pulling her hand away. She turned toward the door.

"Don't forget your list." His eye held a sparkle of humor, but he blinked away the expression before she could fathom its meaning.

Sweetpea: My aunt entered me in a beauty pageant after I came to live with them. I felt like a fraud with layers of caked-on makeup and hair goop. After overhearing other contestants laughing behind my back, I purposely bungled the interview to assure I wouldn't final. Not that I would have anyway. My aunt never again entered me in a pageant.

Chapter Eight

They were miles from shore by the time Tucker cut the engine. She'd expected they'd take his large passenger boat, but instead he'd led her down the steps of his deck, where a smaller craft was roped to a piling. A much smaller craft. Instead of being spread out on a fifty-foot boat, they were side by side on pedestal seats. Miles from land. Miles from the nearest person. Alone took on new meaning.

A seagull flew overhead, its piercing cry echoing the panic building inside Sabrina.

Tucker swiveled his seat around. His cap removed, his curls were wind tousled. Wondering what the wind had done to her own hair, she smoothed it back toward her nape, feeling all the strands that had escaped the rubber band.

He looked more relaxed than he had earlier, his lips slack, almost grinning. He loved the ocean. He'd once said he never felt better than when he was on the water. He'd said even on his worst day at work, he never regretted giving up a career in law.

Watching him now, she believed it. He looked at peace with the world, his eyes closed, his head leaning against the headrest.

"So," he said without opening his eyes, "have you come up with anything that might help me locate her?"

Sabrina took the list from her bag. It had been tricky pulling details from the letters. She'd chosen facts that might mislead him and omitted details that pointed to her.

"I think she might be from the South," Sabrina said.

He opened one eye, peeking at her sideways. "What makes you say that?"

"She mentioned Piggly Wiggly once. She doesn't say she goes there, but she uses it in a metaphor."

He shrugged. "Could be. But everyone's heard of Piggly Wiggly, haven't they?"

"It wouldn't be the first thing to come to mind if she didn't live near one."

"She doesn't have a Southern accent."

Sabrina smirked. "You've never talked to her."

"It would come through in email, don't you think? 'Y'all' and 'bless your heart' and all that," he said with a country twang.

"No stereotypes there."

He grinned. "What else have you got?"

She perused her list. "Some of the same things on your list. Her allergies, the poetry, the food preferences."

"What about her ex-fiancé?"

She crossed her legs, tucking her feet under the chair. "What about him?"

"They met at college. Maybe if we can figure out which one, we could go from there."

"She mentioned being a literature major," Sabrina admitted reluctantly.

"What was Jared's major?"

Hearing Jared's name on his lips distracted her, and she opened her mouth, the words *political science* on her tongue. Then she realized she'd never revealed that. "I don't think she said."

"Hmmm." Quiet settled around them, filling the space between them.

He probably thought she wasn't earning her pay. She studied the list again. "If you combine the clues of her major and the fact that she seems to spend a lot of time at the computer, maybe she works in a library. Or maybe she's a journalist," Sabrina added, remembering her old ambitions.

"If only I knew her name."

Sabrina had been careful about that. She'd never revealed her initials, other than her original screen name on Nantucket Chat and, even then, they were backward. But he didn't know those were initials.

"Are there any Piggly Wigglys near the Gulf Coast?" she asked.

"Why?"

She jotted a note on the paper. "The photo taken at the beach. She's been careful about the details she's given, so I think we'll need to combine facts and draw conclusions."

He tipped his head back, and the setting sun cast a golden glow over his skin. His dark eyelashes brushed the top of his cheeks. She studied the Cupid's bow of his upper lip. She wondered how he'd react if she dipped her finger into the arch.

"Listen to that."

She startled, as if he'd caught her staring, but his eyes were still closed. "What?" she asked, then slowly became aware of the sounds around them. The gurgle of water lapping the sides of the boat, the cry of a distant seagull, the sound of the wind cutting across the water.

"I never get tired of this. I want to bring her out here," he said. "I want to share this with her."

The air smelled of salt. The taste of it coated her lips. The gentle rock of the boat lulled her. What would it be like if he knew she was Sweetpea? If he knew she was with him right now? Would he pull her close and kiss the salt from her lips? Would he hold her tenderly and tell her he loved her?

He opened his eyes, trapping her under his gaze.

Sabrina fought the ache in her chest. She had to say something. Something to break the spell he wove around her. "I'm sure she'd love it."

Something flickered in his eyes. She wanted to know what that emotion was, but to find out, she'd have to stare, and staring was dangerous. Staring sucked her in and held her captive. Staring made her careless. She looked away.

"Do you think there's any hope?" he asked.

Sabrina clenched her fist in her lap. Guilt pricked her conscience. How could she reassure him when she planned to fail? She let his question drift away on the wind. There was nothing she could say because he hoped for the impossible, and she knew how he felt. Hope was the fuel of life, and she'd been running on empty a long time.

Sweetpea: My cousins had a big white fluffy cat when I came to live with them. I sneezed ferociously for two weeks before my aunt and uncle finally got rid of Roxy. My cousins didn't speak to me for days.

Chapter Nine

"How's the schedule looking, Dorothy?" Tucker asked. The sixty-two-year-old woman was his part-time office employee. Her thinning gray hair was short, and she wore large-framed glasses that only helped minimally with her sight. Still, she was efficient and dependable. Even if she did have to sit six inches from the computer screen.

"Pretty full for the next week or so, especially with Nate being out for a couple days. You'll be run ragged."

"I'll survive." He sat at his desk to review the repairs estimate on one of his boats. Three grand. He sighed. Nothing he could do about that.

"Hey, boss." Nate poked his head in the door. Tucker had hired him three years earlier when the business outgrew one driver.

"How'd the Parkers enjoy their trip to the Vineyard?" Tucker asked.

"They had a blast. I have a family I'm taking around the island now."

Tucker checked his watch. Sabrina would be at his place in thirty minutes, and he needed a shower.

"You didn't forget about my two days off this week for my mom's surprise party, did you?"

"It's on the schedule," Dorothy said.

"It won't be a problem." Tucker stood and gathered the papers. Maybe he should get another estimate on the repairs. Three grand seemed steep.

Tucker put his cap on.

"Uh, I was wondering something." Nate shifted his bulky frame in the doorway, looking like a sheepish schoolboy.

"Beth had arrangements for Nickels while we were gone," he continued. "But they had a family emergency and can't keep him now. We, uh, were wondering if one of you might take him in for a couple days." He looked between Dorothy and Tucker.

The silver cat was notorious in the office, though Dorothy and Tucker had never seen the feline. Nickels had come into the marriage with Beth, and he and Nate had a love/hate relationship. Heavy on the hate.

Tucker wasn't fond of cats, and they weren't crazy about him either.

"I'm gone all day," he said. "I know Beth wouldn't want her baby orphaned."

"Count me out." Dorothy filed a thin stack of papers, leaning so close to the tabbed files she could've licked them. "I'm allergic to cats."

Nate turned pleading eyes on Tucker.

He envisioned his favorite recliner becoming a scratching post, litter strewn across his carpet, and that brought another thought: the smell.

"Just this once?" Nate scrunched up his eyebrows.

"Aw, come on. Can't Beth ask one of her friends?"

"She already tried. You're my last resort, man."

Dorothy smiled innocently, eyes widening behind her thick glasses. She blinked slowly. "You're his last resort."

Tucker glared at her, wishing he was the one with a cat allergy. *Very convenient, Dorothy.*

He remembered Sabrina's email from months ago. Something about her cousins having a cat that made her sneeze incessantly. There was his excuse. With Sabrina coming over, he couldn't have a cat around making her sneeze, making her eyes redden and her nose—

Or could he?

He wasn't supposed to know who Sabrina was. Wasn't supposed to know she had a cat allergy. What would happen if he suddenly had a cat? She wouldn't be able to hide her allergic reaction. Maybe it would flush her out of hiding. It had been a week since she'd started coming over. She was settled in, and maybe this was just the thing to get his plan started. Maybe—

"Just think about it?" Nate continued. "I promised Beth I'd find somebody, and she's gonna kill me if I come home—"

"I'll do it," Tucker said firmly.

Nate's chin tilted away while he stared suspiciously at Tucker from the corner of his narrowed eyes. "You will?"

"You will?" Dorothy's fingers stopped on the files, and she looked at him, doubt written all over her pale, wrinkled face. "You hate cats."

"Hate is a strong word," Tucker said.

"You hate cats," Dorothy repeated.

Tucker pulled his hat down firmly on his head. "What are friends for?"

He left the office and began the short walk home. *Sabrina, you'd better enjoy the dander-free air tonight, because when you come over tomorrow, no more Mr. Nice Guy.*

Sabrina tapped on Tucker's door.

"Come on in," Tucker called from somewhere in the house.

She turned the knob and entered. The house smelled like a mixture of Tucker's woodsy cologne and the remnants of his supper— something Italian, she thought, detecting the tang of onion and garlic.

Tucker rounded the corner from the kitchen. "Want some left-over spaghetti? I made plenty."

"No, thank you." She took a step toward the office, but stopped abruptly when a cat slinked from behind the chair and blocked her path. She pulled in a silent breath.

It stopped and stared up at her, its long, silver tail fanning the air gracefully like a fluffy flag, its back arched high. The cat rubbed against her bare leg.

"You got a cat?" She tried to tame the panic in her voice.

"Just temporarily." He scooped up the feline and cradled it.

"Nickels is going to be my houseguest for a couple days, aren't you, buddy?" The cat struggled for release, and Tucker set him down.

She opened her mouth to inform him of her allergy, then snapped it shut. He knew Sweetpea had cat allergies. She couldn't let him know she did too. It would be one more detail that linked them, one more piece of this two-sided puzzle. *You'll have to avoid that cat and hope for the best.*

How long would it take her allergies to kick in? The cat was new to the home, so the dander levels would be low. And he usually kept the office door closed . . . maybe the cat hadn't been in there.

"Nate from work asked me to take him while he and his wife are out of town."

"That was kind of you." She walked down the hall, her heart sinking at the open office door.

"I'm not much of a cat person, but Nate's a good friend, and he was in a bind."

She knew he had a distinct dislike of cats. When he was little, he'd rescued a stray cat from its high perch on a tree limb and had been rewarded with a scratch on his shoulder deep enough to require stitches.

Tucker followed her into the office. Nickels came along too. He jumped on her chair and sniffed the keyboard.

She had to get the cat out of there.

"Good day at the café?" Tucker propped his hands on his hips. He wore a white T-shirt that set off his tan, and a pair of frayed jeans that looked as if they'd been washed a hundred times.

"It was fine." Sabrina set her bag on the desk and looked at

Nickels, wondering how she could get him off the chair without touching him.

"Well, I'll let you get to work. I put your check on the desk." Tucker left, leaving a wake of yummy-smelling cologne behind. A moment later she heard him in the kitchen, washing dishes. Her paycheck sat beside the computer, a reminder of her deceit.

Never mind the money. She had bigger problems.

She glared at Nickels. She needed a decoy. She looked around for a toy to lure him away. Nothing but computer cords and boxes. Her eyes fell on the blind cord dangling against the window. Well, that would at least get him off the chair. Maybe.

She walked to the window and jiggled the cord. "Here, kitty, kitty," she whispered. Nickels roosted on the chair's edge, yellow eyes half-closed, looking like a king on his throne.

She jiggled the cord again, and the plastic weights bobbed up and down, knocking together. "Come here, Nickels!" she said quietly.

The cat seemed insulted by her attempt to lure him with something as juvenile as a cord. *All right, then, mister, have it your way.* Sabrina took hold of the chair's back and tipped it forward until the cat leapt off. He turned and stared her down.

"It's not as if you gave me a choice."

From the other room, she heard the patio door slide open. Nickels's ears twitched, then he slinked out of the room.

Finally. Sabrina closed the door, making sure it caught so Nickels couldn't wander back in. Already she felt itchy—or was it her imagination? Like this wasn't difficult enough without adding a cat to the mix. She sat on the chair, hoping there was a minimal amount of dander in the area.

She opened the email program, noticing the check beside her

hand. How was she going to take his money? What she was doing was no better than stealing.

What kind of person was she?

She couldn't keep it. Bad enough that she was wasting his time, getting his hopes up; she was not taking his money too.

She opened the next message. She could do something else with the money. Something Tucker would approve of. She could donate it to some cause or charity or even to his church. She remembered his first messages on Nantucket Chat about the island's ecology. He was passionate about protecting it. Maybe she could donate the money to Nantucket Soundkeeper. It wasn't ideal, but at least his money would be used for a cause he believed in.

She spent the next thirty minutes reading letters and jotting notes. She'd once written that she was going into the city, saying it facetiously at first because Nantucket Town was a far cry from the city, but she left the phrase in the email, thinking it would throw him off track.

She jotted down a note that Sweetpea must live near a big city. Of course, that still left it wide open. She needed to make this mission seem futile; otherwise, after she failed, he'd hire someone else.

She rubbed her eyes and opened the next email—the one where she'd told him about Jared. She'd vacillated about whether or not to tell him. In the end, she'd decided it couldn't hurt when he didn't know who she was. She read the end of the letter where she'd summarized her thoughts.

I know Jared and my cousin didn't set out to hurt me. Things are never that simple. People make their bad choices with a side of justification and a side of entitlement, never considering the pain their overindulgence might cause. Even if they had carefully considered the ramifications, they couldn't possibly have imagined what deep damage their selfishness would inflict.

"She has a way with words." Tucker's voice startled her.

She hadn't heard him enter the room. He stood beside her, too close. She felt his hand pressing on the chair's back near her shoulder.

"Almost poetic, don't you think?" he asked.

Sabrina cleared her throat. "She did say she enjoys poetry."

Something rubbed against her leg under the desk, and she remembered the cat. She sneezed, hard and sudden.

"Bless you," Tucker said.

Her nose started to run. She sniffed.

"Tissue?"

The cat curled around her leg. "I'm fine."

Her eyes started itching. She rubbed casually. She had to get that thing out of there.

"Turn up anything new?"

Sabrina nudged the cat with her foot.

"A few things." She handed him her list, hoping he'd take it and leave, cat and all.

Instead he sat in the chair beside her. *Great.*

"The city, huh?"

She sniffed again. A sneeze was coming. She could feel it. She breathed through her mouth, hoping to squelch it. "She mentioned going to the city," she said between silent gulps of air.

"She didn't say which one."

"True." Under the guise of shifting her legs, Sabrina knocked Nickels away from her feet.

"Do you know how many cities there are? And who says she even lives near it? I don't remember her mentioning it other than the one time."

She tried to blink away the itch in her eyes. Were they turning bloodshot? She needed to blow her nose.

She was surprised she was reacting so severely to a cat that had been in the house less than twenty-four hours. She turned away from Tucker to discreetly wipe her nose and saw something she hadn't noticed before.

A cat bed. Just then Nickels slinked toward the round sheep-skin-covered bed.

Oh, great. This is Nickels's bedroom. That explained why she was having such a—

"Uh-CHOOOO!" The sneeze sneaked up on her. She glanced at Tucker.

His brows hiked upward. "Bless you."

She had to get out of there. It would only get worse. "Goodness. I must be coming down with something." *Like allergies. Or insanity.*

"Can I get you anything? Tylenol? Orange juice?"

Beside the desk, Nickels curled into a ball and closed his eyes.

Another sneeze was building at the back of her nose. Her throat felt scratchy, and any minute her eyelids were going to swell.

Tucker was going to figure it out if she didn't get out of there. Quickly. "No, I—I think I need to go home and rest." She stood, grabbing her bag.

"Oh." His voice rang with disappointment. "Are you sure?"

She felt terrible, but what could she do? "I'll be fine by Monday." *Presuming that infernal hairball is gone.* The pressure at the back of her nose was building. *Get out of here, Sabrina.*

"Hope you feel better." Tucker stood as she walked toward the office door.

The sneeze was coming. *Breathe through your mouth.* She'd reached the hallway when she heard his voice again.

"Don't forget your check."

She returned and snapped the paper from his hand as the sneeze ripped through her, louder than the last one. She couldn't cover her mouth in time. "Sorry." She turned and rushed toward the door.

"Take care of yourself," Tucker called, but by then, she was out the door.

***

Tucker watched Sabrina pedal away on her bike until she rounded the corner and headed toward Main Street. He slapped the wooden door frame with his palm. *Way to go, McCabe.*

Not only had he succeeded in causing Sabrina pain and misery, but his plan to force her out of hiding had totally backfired. He'd accomplished nothing except chasing her away. He shook his head. *Brilliant.*

He turned into the house and shut the door. He'd been so close. It had been on the tip of his tongue after the second sneeze. *Maybe you're allergic to cats.* It would've been so easy, such a reasonable remark. It might've been the nudge she needed to admit who she was.

Maybe that one sentence would've helped. If only he'd been able to say it. He nearly *had*.

But then he'd seen the look on her face. The fear scrolled between her eyebrows, glazing her eyes. She had the look of a trapped animal, and he couldn't do it. Words she'd written months ago surfaced in his mind, words about people inflicting harm on others without thought to the ramifications. Maybe using the cat against her was a small thing when weighed against the actions of Jared and her cousin, but the fact that he was capable of this small infraction against her shook him, shamed him.

Nickels entered the living room and stared at him, eyes half-closed, and Tucker could have sworn they were full of reproach.

"What are you looking at?"

The cat lifted his pointy chin and exited as quietly as he'd appeared.

Tucker made his way toward the office. He had a bed to move and a room to vacuum.

Harbormaster: Growing up, I thought my sister and I would always be together. After all, we'd been in the womb together, shared everything all our lives. We grew up and went our separate ways, though we remain close. And one day I know I'll be married and my wife will be everything to me—even closer than a twin sister.

Chapter Ten

The next week Tucker was relieved that he'd successfully removed the cat dander. Sabrina didn't sneeze once all week.

That was the good news. The bad news was his plan wasn't progressing as quickly as he'd like, and he was running out of time. Sabrina was working through the emails all too fast. Maybe if they did something together. Something that didn't involve computers and lists. Something that would force her from her comfort zone and put them face-to-face.

But he'd already taken her out on his boat, and what had come of that? Nothing.

It was time to raise the stakes. He wandered into his office and

sat where Sabrina had been an hour earlier. He picked up the tablet with her notes. She was careful, including only innocuous details
that were so broad as to be useless, or things he'd already listed.

Can't whistle

Takes a daily walk

Likes her steak well-done

Reads mysteries

Has an aversion to bees

He smiled at that one. Sabrina had been stung on the eyelid
when she was five and had been terrified of bees since.

Imagine a chicken flapping her wings and running in circles,
and you have an accurate picture of me in the presence of a
bee. Not rational, I know, but I can't seem to help it. I once
spilled a glass of fruit punch all over my cousin's favorite
pashmina scarf in my hysteria.

He opened the email program and checked his inbox. It was
empty. She wasn't writing as often as she had before she'd started
working for him. But then, she had less time. He missed her. How
could he miss someone who sat right next to him? Because the
Sabrina he loved was honest and vulnerable, but the Sabrina who
worked for him wasn't sharing that part of herself yet. He missed
that intimacy.

He opened a blank email and started a letter. Right now he
didn't want to trick her or corner her, he didn't want to manipulate
her. He just wanted to talk with her.

I miss you, Sweetpea. Work's been hectic, but you must be busy too.

I took in a friend's cat last week. Yeah, I know, I'm a glutton for punishment. The thing did not like me. I have several scratches to prove it.

Read any good books lately? I got another novel at the library, but couldn't make it past page twenty. You can't say I didn't try. I'll leave the fiction to you and stick with the newspaper.

Tucker paused, his fingers hovering over the keyboard. He wanted to say so much more. *I miss you. Even when you're here, I miss you. Why won't you open yourself to the possibility of us? Every time you're near me, I want to touch you. But if I did that, I'd scare you away. You're like a doe in a field, so beautiful and proud and strong. But at the slightest hint of danger, off you go. What are you so afraid of?*

Tucker scowled at his thoughts. He couldn't say any of that. He'd nearly scared her off for good when he'd mentioned meeting in the first place, and he wasn't going to risk losing his only contact with her after she finished this job. Or rather, failed at finishing this job. He knew that was the plan, and it frustrated him, but that's what he deserved for backing her into a corner.

Did I do the wrong thing, God?

It was too late for that question, wasn't it? But it was never too late to ask for help. He whispered a quick prayer, then sent the email.

He wondered if she was home. Maybe she'd get his message and reply. It had been a while since their last exchange.

The house was quiet except for the hum of the dishwasher. He'd offered Sabrina a slice of the roast he'd slow-cooked that day, but she'd turned it down as always. He wondered if he could convince Sabrina to stay for dinner after she finished. He could cook while she worked, maybe grill a couple steaks on the deck, serve her the corn he knew she wouldn't eat, couldn't eat, ever since she'd gotten sick on it in the seventh grade.

He fantasized about sharing a candlelit meal on the water with a salted breeze ruffling her hair. Sure, she wore it scraped back in that ponytail, but it was his fantasy; he could imagine her hair down if he wanted.

If only they could have a normal date. The kind where he picked her up and took her someplace quiet, where she could let down her guard and let him in a little. But he couldn't ask Sabrina out. She knew he was in love with Sweetpea, and he wasn't supposed to know she and Sabrina were one and the same. How would it look to her if he put the moves on her?

Well, you've got yourself a quandary, don't you?

The computer chimed as a message appeared in his inbox. Sabrina.

I can't believe you took in a cat. That's above and beyond.

I haven't had time to read lately, but am hoping to get back into a good book soon. I still think you need to keep trying until you find what you like. There's a genre for everyone. I haven't given up on you. ☺

I got a wedding invitation from Jared and my cousin.

That was the end of her message. His thoughts spun like a whirlpool. How had the news affected her? Was she still pining for Jared? She hadn't seemed upset at the café or at his house.

He replied, hoping she hadn't left.

I'm sorry. When?

Less than a minute later, her response arrived.

About a month ago. :-/

A month ago? He'd wanted to know when the wedding was, but she must mean it had been a month since she'd received the invitation. And she was just now telling him? It must've hurt if she hadn't told him sooner. And if it hurt, maybe she still loved Jared. Tucker was hurt now too. Hurt that she still had feelings for Jared and that she hadn't confided in him sooner. He poised his hands over the keyboard and typed.

When's the wedding? I really am sorry. ☹

At least she was telling him now. What did she need from him? He wished he could do more than type a few words of encouragement. He wanted to hunt Jared down and beat him to a pulp, but that's probably not what she needed from him. He wished that he could at least wrap his arms around her and tell her he loved her, that Jared didn't deserve her anyway.

Another email arrived.

Twenty-second of August.

He typed a response,

Are you doing okay? Want to talk about it?

A few moments later another message arrived.

No, thanks. I'm coping. Just wanted to tell you.

'Cause I could beat him up, if you want, he replied, then sat back, waiting for her response. It arrived seconds later.

<g> Good to know. I'll let you know if I need to call in my manpower.

Tucker grinned. He wondered if her family had given her any warning. But she didn't want to talk about it, so he refrained from asking. Instead, he asked the obvious question.

Are you going?

He pushed Send.
Before he could lean back, she replied,

Going where? :-P

He smiled.

To the wedding, goofball.

No.

When the sinking sensation hit his gut, he realized he'd been hoping she'd go. To avoid the wedding meant she was still angry with her cousin. And if she was angry with her cousin, she still had feelings for Jared, didn't she?

Coward. Just ask.

Before he could stop himself, he typed the words.

Do you still love him?

After he hit Send, regrets of all sizes and shapes crowded into the room. What if she did? She still wore that infernal bracelet, and he was sure it was a gift from Jared. Why would she still wear it if she was over him? He considered writing back. *Never mind*, he'd say. But before he could act on the thought, another message appeared. Maybe he should delete it without reading.

Who was he kidding? He wanted to know. Needed to know. He felt sick as he opened the email.

Why do you ask?

Well, duh. Wasn't it obvious he had feelings for her? Maybe he'd never come out and said he loved her—she might think it was weird or pathetic.

Why didn't you answer my question?

He tapped his fingers on the keys, waiting. It had been over a year since she'd seen Jared. Could you love someone that long from a distance? Could you even be certain of your feelings?

A new message arrived.

My aunt and uncle seem to have given up on reaching me. Part of me is relieved, but I admit the victory feels a little hollow.

She was changing the subject. Not a good sign. He replied,

Maybe they haven't given up. They're probably distracted by the wedding.

He hated the loneliness her words implied. She knew he was there for her, didn't she? A message appeared.

Maybe.
And no, I don't love Jared.

Relief filled him. If she didn't love Jared, there was room in her heart for him, wasn't there? Feeling renewed, he changed the subject to current news events, secure in the knowledge that, while her heart may not fully belong to him, it didn't belong to someone else either.

Sweetpea: I got the name Sweetpea from my mom. I don't remember much about her, but she was always working in our garden. I can still hear the soothing sound of her voice as she whispered "Goodnight, Sweetpea" from my bedroom door.

Chapter Eleven

A week later Sabrina was grabbing her bag from the kitchen counter when she noticed the blinking light. Checking the time, she decided she could spare an extra minute before leaving for Tucker's. Char had been queasy when Sabrina left the café. Maybe Gordon needed her to finish Char's shift. Truth was, she'd welcome the opportunity to avoid Tucker.

The stress was eating her alive. Sitting there, pretending to work, desperate to escape before she did something stupid, like grabbing the man and kissing him full on the mouth. One of these days, her facade was going crack wide open and she'd find herself chin deep in a pit of humiliation.

She pushed the machine's button and listened.

"Hey, Sabrina! It's Arielle. I left a message last week, but you didn't return my call. A-hem! But my feelings aren't hurt. Really. Not hurt at all.

Anyway, call me back, okay? For real this time. I'll keep pestering you until you do. You know I will . . . Bye!"

Sabrina deleted the message and headed out the door. She wouldn't return this message either. And yes, her cousin would continue leaving messages and sending emails. Sabrina knew what Arielle wanted, and her cousin wasn't getting it.

She pushed up the kickstand, hopped on her bike, and began pedaling down the lane. The incident with Jared and Jaylee had drawn a line between Sabrina and her family. And Arielle stood on the line, trying to pull everyone to the middle. Arielle had always been the mediator, but never had her job been so impossible. Maybe that skill served her well in class, but they weren't three-year-olds fighting over a canister of red Play-Doh. Sometimes there was no good resolution.

When she reached town, she stopped to let pedestrians cross. Town was packed when the summer people arrived. She couldn't fathom having a vacation home and six free weeks to spend at it. If she did, she would put up a hammock on her back porch and read all day. But the summer people seemed to prefer sunning at the beach, spending money in the boutiques, and being waited on in the restaurants. Sabrina would rather learn to cook her own gourmet food. But what was the point when she was only feeding one?

Two black Labs were leashed to the bench outside the Even Keel Cafe, and a little girl stopped to pet them. Her parents nudged her along; then her dad swooped her into his arms, and the girl wrapped herself around him. The mom laughed at something the girl said. They looked like the all-American family.

Had she ever had that? Her mom had died of ovarian cancer when Sabrina was five. All she had of her mother were a few foggy memories and a handful of photos. Her dad had seemed like a ghost in the house after her mom died, and then he was gone too.

A horn blared, and she saw that the pedestrians had cleared. She pressed on the pedal and accelerated through town, passing the quaint shops and milling tourists, the wheels of her bike bumping along the cobblestone streets.

When she arrived at Tucker's house, Cody was sitting on his porch, reading a book.

"Hey, Sabrina."

"Hi, Cody." She stopped by Tucker's stoop, swung her leg around, then set the kickstand with the toe of her tennis shoe.

"Invitation for dinner's still good. We're grilling chicken fajitas, and my buddy Ron is making his famous homemade salsa."

Tucker was at the door, on the stoop really, glaring in Cody's general direction. "She's working tonight."

Sabrina tossed Cody a smile of consolation, though by the cocky look he was giving Tucker, he didn't need it. "Guess I'm on the clock," she said.

Tucker followed her to the office. The house didn't smell like supper as it often did, but maybe he'd been in a hurry and had grabbed takeout. Instead of savory scents, she relished the familiar woodsy fragrance of his cologne.

"You should be nicer to the tourists," she said. "It's good for the island economy."

"What am I, the welcome committee?"

Sabrina shrugged, then, settled at the desk, checked her notepad to see where she'd left off.

"How far along are you in terms of the emails?" Tucker asked from the doorway.

She opened the program and compared the date of the one she'd last read with the date of their first letters. "About five months from the time you began writing."

The tablet with her notes was open on the desk, so she started with the next email, hoping Tucker would leave.

"I was thinking we could have another brainstorming session. I have some steaks that I need to cook. How about I grill and we can have dinner while we chat? We can eat out by the water."

A working supper. It was on the tip of her tongue to say she'd already eaten. But she'd been in a rush after staying a few extra minutes to help Evan bus tables and hadn't had time. The last thing she wanted was to sit face-to-face with Tucker. She'd rather be next door with Cody and company.

That's not true, and you know it.

Truth be told, Tucker was just tempting. To know him so well and pretend as if she didn't . . . to care so much and pretend as if she didn't. It was too hard. She needed to get through these letters faster.

"Sabrina?"

If he wanted to use the time to brainstorm, who was she to argue? He was paying for her time.

"That's fine." She could do this. She'd done it on the boat; she could manage supper alone with him. All alone, on the tiny, secluded square of his deck.

"Great. How do you like your steak?"

She started to say well-done. But she'd put that on the Sweetpea list a few weeks ago. Plenty of people liked their steaks well-done, but the fewer similarities between her and Sweetpea, the better.

"Medium well," she said, grimacing on the inside. The thought of pink meat nauseated her.

"Give me half an hour?"

"Sure."

With that, he was gone, allowing Sabrina to work. Now she had a supper and an uncooked steak to endure. She wondered how she was going to control herself and her wayward thoughts through a romantic supper for two.

Shaking the thought, she delved into the next batch of messages. They were full of banal tidbits, so she noted the details on the sheet. How could she sidetrack him later? Sweetpea had made few comments regarding her residence, but now Sabrina had no way of misleading him.

She settled back in the chair and opened the next email. She remembered receiving the original message, and her heart tripped at the memory. They'd been exchanging emails late one night about mundane things, joking around, and then he'd sent this message:

Do you ever think about meeting in person?

She'd frozen in response to the words. What should she say? She had to answer. He was waiting.

Not really, she typed, and sent the message. Would he press her further? What would she say if he asked more about where she lived?

Why not?

Fear curled inside her, thick and hot. Her fingers poked at the keys.

What's with the twenty questions?

Her mouth was as dry as the sand at Jetties Beach. She didn't have to wait long for his reply.

I really want to meet you.

And there it was. Tossed out like a water bomb from a second-story window, and just as unrescindable.

Suddenly their correspondence didn't seem safe at all. It felt immediate and threatening. Like waking from a dream to find it was real after all. Her heart knocking against her rib cage, she'd closed the message, closed the program.

The next morning a message had been waiting in her inbox.

I'm sorry if I overstepped a boundary. Let's forget I said that, okay?

He changed the topic, telling her about a customer who'd been terrified of the water. Sabrina had been relieved at his change of heart, and he hadn't mentioned meeting again until months later.

"Dinner's ready." Tucker leaned against the door frame, arms crossed, as if he'd been there a while. She'd been so absorbed in the emails, she hadn't heard him. So much for remaining detached.

Shaking the remnants of trepidation, Sabrina followed Tucker down the hall and out the sliding door. Three stairs led down to a water-level porch where a plank deck nestled against the back of his house. A wooden railing was the only barrier between them and the boat-dotted harbor.

He gestured toward the round wicker table, set for two. A terracotta pot with a cluster of purple pansies graced its center.

"I hope you like iced tea," he said after they were seated.

"That's fine." A steaming baked potato accompanied the steak. And beside it, corn. Her stomach turned. She retrieved her fork and knife and cut into the steak, then felt like a heel when he bowed his head in prayer.

"I think I may have overcooked your steak," he said when he finished praying. "The timer for the potatoes went off, and I got distracted."

The steak was brown throughout. "It's perfect." Thank God for distractions. What was she going to do about the corn? Everyone liked corn. Everyone except her. It only took her right back to seventh-grade gym class, where she'd vomited her lunch on her favorite Nikes in front of everyone.

"So, tell me about yourself." Tucker stabbed his meat. "You work at the café, do some editing and research for Renny Hannigan. What else is there to know about the mysterious Sabrina Kincaid?"

She took her time chewing the meat, then sipped her tea. "There's no mystery. I grew up in the South and went away to college. I visited Nantucket on my—vacation—and decided to stay. I guess you could say the beauty of the island lured me."

In truth, it had been weeks before she'd come out from her

depression enough to notice the beauty. Slowly, she'd noticed the sweet scent of hydrangea, the rugged, scraggly brush, the beauty of the marina. Initially her only reason for staying was she hadn't wanted to return to Macon. The island felt isolated from the rest of the world, an incubator, and she'd been in sore need of the respite.

He was waiting for her to continue.

"I saw a Help Wanted sign in the window of the café for a server and got the job." She wondered if he thought that was a lame job for someone with a college degree. But he'd quit law school to follow a less lucrative passion.

"I'd intended it to be temporary until I found something more fitting with my degree, but the tips were good, and then I found Renny. My work with her is fulfilling, and it could turn into full-time eventually." She regretted mentioning her degree and hoped he wouldn't inquire further. "Either way, I've enjoyed working with her and have even considered getting into editing someday." See, she had ambitions.

"Tell me about your work with Renny. We attend the same church, but I didn't know she was an author."

"She has an agent, but she's not published yet." Sabrina eyed Tucker. "I thought we were going to brainstorm."

"Are you in a hurry?"

She shrugged, then wiped her mouth. "It's your dime."

"That's right, it is. About Renny . . ."

His eyes twinkled. Why was he curious about her boring life? For a man so rushed to find his lady friend, he was sure taking his time.

"I struck up a conversation with Renny at the café when she was reading a book I'd recently read. We started talking about plots and characters; then she invited me for supper to pick my brain about her work in progress. When my ideas worked for her, she asked if I'd be interested in exchanging room and board for help on her stories."

"But she's not published?"

Sabrina shook her head. "She should be though. She just finished her ninth manuscript, and it's superb. Frankly, I'm shocked her work hasn't been picked up yet."

"She told me you have of way of inventing complicated plots and twists."

Sabrina salted her potato and stirred. "I read a lot. I guess it becomes intuitive after a while." *Change the subject before he asks what you read.* She didn't want to lie, and he knew Sweetpea read mysteries.

"You have a beautiful home." The sun, low in the sky, glowed behind a swath of pink clouds. Somewhere nearby, a boat knocked against the rubber sides of a pier.

"Thanks."

They ate in silence a few minutes. She should ask about him, but couldn't bring herself to inquire about things she already knew. Besides, the sooner they got on with this, the sooner she could leave.

She finished her potato and began poking at the corn. She had to get rid of it. Her stomach gurgled in response to the thought.

She drained the last of her iced tea. "Could I bother you for another glass?"

"Glad to."

When he was out of view, she scraped the corn into the water.

Great. Corn floats. She helped it toward shore with her hand and was in her seat before Tucker returned.

"Thanks." Now that the corn was gone, she could focus on laying the groundwork for the inevitable conclusion that Sweetpea was unfindable.

"I have to say," she started, "most of Sweetpea's clues are vague."

A bee hovered around the porch railing behind Tucker. Sabrina tensed. *Go away, bee.*

"She's been careful not to reveal important details," he said.

The bee passed the railing and entered the porch, flying toward the table. *No, no, no. Go away.* Sabrina set down her fork, keeping a close watch. It flew over Tucker's shoulder and headed toward her.

She pressed her spine against the wicker back, barely breathing. Everything in her wanted to jump up and run into the house.

It's just a bee. It's. Just. A. Bee.

"I keep thinking there must be something there, though," he said. "With so many messages, surely there are enough clues to get us close."

The insect stopped over the pansies, hovering. It caught Tucker's eye. He moved his hand off the table as if to shoo it away, then reached for the saltshaker instead.

Don't panic. It's not going to hurt you. It's just investigating the flowers. She should say something. Her mind couldn't seem to formulate a thought. The bee nearly settled on one of the petals, then moved on to the next.

She glanced at Tucker. He was studying her, one eyebrow higher than the other. *Say something.* "Maybe I'll find something as I get through the rest of the letters."

The bee hovered higher, seemingly bored with the flowers. It flew toward her. She held her breath as it floated in front of her. A red shirt! She'd worn a red shirt. *I'm not a flower, stupid bee!*

"Are you okay?"

Breathe, Sabrina! The bee closed in. She could hear the buzz of its wings. She grabbed her napkin from the table and swatted it away, trying to appear calm despite the fact that her insides were as volatile as a shaken can of coke.

Tucker reached out and waved his hand until the bee retreated. It flew over the railing and around the corner.

"Don't like bees?"

She wasn't hiding it as well as she'd thought. "Not so much."

She reached for her fork. She was trembling, for heaven's sake. She darted a glance toward the corner to ensure the bee wasn't returning for the giant red flower.

"You were saying?" Tucker said.

Sabrina had no idea what she'd been saying. She sucked in a cleansing breath. Where was she?

Oh, yes, that it was time to lay some groundwork. She sipped her tea. "I just read the message where you asked about meeting her."

Tucker's eyes fell, his lashes hooding his blue eyes.

What was he thinking? Was he reliving the moment when she'd ignored his question? How long had he waited that night for her reply? How had he felt when he realized she didn't want to meet? If only she could've explained.

"Why did you ask her?" The question escaped before she could stop it.

"When you really connect with someone, it's a rare and valuable thing. I'd come to care about her." He gave a half grin. "It might seem crazy that I feel so strongly about a woman I met online, but it's not. It's real."

The passion in his eyes mesmerized her. "Why do you care so much about her?"

"Why do you ask?"

She froze for a second, then took a sip of tea and picked up her fork. Was she wrong for keeping him at a distance?

What if? What if she let it happen? What if she told him she was Sweetpea and let the cards fall where they may? She looked at the familiar planes of his face and wondered what it would be like if she had the privilege of running her hand along his jaw, of kissing his eyelids closed, of tucking her face in the crook of his neck, and breathing in the scent of his skin.

What would it be like to come home to him, his smell, his touch, rather than a skimpy email?

She set her fork down and laid her napkin on her plate. She wasn't Arielle, with long, blonde hair and stunning good looks. She was Sabrina, plain and awkward. *Imagine what he'd think if you told him who you are. Imagine the disappointment. The confusion.* And that was just for starters. Eventually he'd find out what she'd done and the relationship would be set on a course for disaster.

She couldn't tell him. To do so would risk everything. She swallowed against the ache in her throat. "It's obvious she doesn't want to meet," she said as gently as she could.

"I've never been one to give up easily."

He was downright stubborn about some things. "What did she say the next time you asked?" The words escaped before she realized her mistake. How could she know he'd mentioned it again? "I'm assuming you asked more than once."

"She insisted she wanted to keep the relationship the way it was. She said it worked for her that way."

"But it doesn't work for you." *What are you doing, Sabrina?*

He pushed back his plate and folded his arms on the table. "I want more."

Her eyes locked on his. She couldn't pull them away if she tried. And truth be told, she didn't want to try. He was looking at her as if . . . as if he *wanted* to look at her.

You're misreading the signal.

He was looking at her like Jared had when he walked her to her apartment at college. When the night was over, but he didn't want it to be. Tucker was looking at her the way Jared had right before his lips found hers.

Ridiculous! Tucker had feelings for Sweetpea, not her. So they were one and the same—he didn't know that. He couldn't be making eyes at her when he thought he had feelings for someone else.

Could he?

"Why do you think she doesn't want to meet?" Vulnerability weighted his eyes.

What could she say that wouldn't hurt him? "Maybe, for whatever reason, she's comfortable with the status quo. Maybe she can't risk losing what she has for the mere possibility of something more."

"Isn't it worth the risk?"

"Not to her, maybe." She was getting perilously close to the cliff's edge. She tore her gaze away, twisted the watch on her wrist. "Or there could be some other reason. Who knows?"

"You think she's married, don't you?"

Sabrina looked up, surprised. "What? No."

"'Cause she's not."

"I never said she was."

"What, then? Locked in someone's attic? In a women's penitentiary? What possible reason could she have for not meeting?"

"I doubt her reasons are so concrete. People are motivated by numerous things, many of them internal and intangible. We could sit here and speculate all day and still not come close. In the end, what does it matter?"

"It matters to me."

"Why? What if you find her and she didn't want to be found? What if she's not who you think she is? How would that affect your relationship? What if it changed everything? What if it ruined what you have now?"

He took that in, staring over her shoulder. The sun had disappeared and the sky had darkened as if someone had twisted a dimmer switch. "It won't."

"You can't know that."

He looked at her, his eyes glittering. "It's a risk I'm willing to take."

"Well." Sabrina clasped her hands tightly in her lap. "Maybe she's not."

Chapter Twelve

Sabrina's feet pounded the vacant cobblestone street. In the distance, dawn's fingers curled around the horizon, nudging the sky awake with shades of midnight blue and periwinkle.

She liked this time of day, before the island awakened, before the chatter of birds roused the tourists. This time of day she could be alone with her thoughts and enjoy the quiet island sounds that were swallowed by the daytime bustle. The whisper of sea oats brushing together, the sound of the leaves shimmying in the wind.

When the street opened to the wharf, she turned and made her way toward Brant Point Lighthouse and Jetties Beach, where her calves would get a good workout on the sand. Her breath came in shallow puffs, and she welcomed the salt-laden breeze that blew in off the harbor.

Her thoughts turned to the message Arielle had left on her voice mail the day before. How many phone calls would Sabrina have to ignore before her cousin would give it up? Maybe after the wedding, things would settle down and everyone would go back to their lives and leave her alone.

She turned onto Easton Street, realizing her feet had carried her to the route she tried to avoid. She picked up her pace; the sooner she passed it, the better. The White Elephant stood to her right, the hotel's lights still glowing in the early morning hours. But she didn't look. Wouldn't look.

Her lungs protested the sprint, but she kept on. Sweat trickled down her neck and between her shoulder blades. She pushed herself harder, lengthening her stride until she was past the property. Only then did she slow her pace, letting her speed taper to a walk as she neared the end of the road where the beach met the pavement. Her lungs worked to keep pace with her pounding heart. She drew her wrist across her forehead, across her eyes, trying to wipe away the sweat, the thoughts. But still the memory came. The memory of the night that had started it all. Had started a cataclysmic chain of events that changed her life forever.

The restaurant had been slow, and her boss let her go home halfway through her shift. "You've been working so many hours, kiddo. Besides, I'm sure you have last-minute wedding things to do."

Sabrina was grateful. She'd been unprepared for the hundreds of details involved in planning a wedding, and even though Aunt Bev had helped, Sabrina wanted everything to be perfect. She smiled, checking the date on her watch as she drove home. Six more days. She considered stopping at Jared's apartment, but she needed to decide on seating arrangements for the rehearsal dinner, wrap the wedding party gifts, and start packing for their honeymoon. Neither of them had been to Nantucket, but she'd heard it was the perfect honeymoon destination. Quiet and quaint, slow paced. She and Jared could rest after the hectic months leading up to the wedding. She needed to remind him to confirm their reservations.

She pulled into her apartment's drive. Jaylee was home, no doubt resting after a long day studying for her bar exam. Sabrina had been helping her between the hours at the restaurant and the wedding preparations.

She grabbed the bag from the passenger seat. She'd finally found something blue and wanted to show Jaylee. She found the silver pendant earrings with tiny light-blue stones in a small boutique that afternoon, and they were perfect.

The parking lot light buzzed overhead and cast a faint yellow tint on the graveled lot. On the second floor of the building, her apartment was dark behind the thin sheers. She entered the building, dashed up the carpeted stairs, then fished for her keys in her bag. The smell of garlic and onion filled the hallway, and she knew Mr. Figliono had fixed a big batch of lasagna again.

She shifted the bag to her other hand and unlocked the door, stepping through it and closing it behind her. Country music blared from the speakers, a male voice crooning about lost love.

Already Sabrina was considering the rehearsal dinner and wondering what she would do about Aunt Linda and Aunt Cathy. They didn't get along and, in fact, had not spoken since Christmas two years prior when Aunt Cathy bought presents after agreeing on no gift exchange. Words had flown, loud ones. A door had slammed; then tires had peeled from the drive, leaving a roomful of awkward silence.

It hadn't been the first family argument between them, Aunt

Bev had said. Sabrina couldn't imagine anything significant enough to divide two sisters.

Since that Christmas, holidays had been comprised of one aunt or the other, but not both under the same roof, and certainly not in the same room. Sabrina wondered how she could arrange them in a room with a U-shaped table. Maybe one or the other wouldn't show, but they'd both agreed to come.

She set her bag on the foyer table and kicked off her shoes, setting them out of the way. Her middle toe poked through a hole. Time for new socks. One more thing for her to-do list. It could wait until after the wedding. She would only need sandals on their honeymoon.

She rounded the corner where the hall opened to the small living room, her hand reaching for the light switch. But a noise, a groan, sounded over the country crooning. Through the sheers, the parking lot light shed a yellow glow over the space. Two people embraced on the couch. A man was half on top of Jaylee. Sabrina wondered if she should grab a blunt object or call 911. As her eyes adjusted, she realized her cousin was stroking the back of his head, not fighting him off.

Jaylee didn't have a boyfriend, and she didn't sleep around. Sabrina felt like a Peeping Tom standing there, watching. She stepped backward, wondering where she could go.

Her foot connected with the tall metal pail holding a cluster of artificial sunflowers. It scraped backward on the wood floor and clanged against the wall, an awkward percussion over the slow country verse. Jaylee and the man jumped apart.

Sabrina felt her face warming the instant before she saw his face.

In the dark, his features were obscured. It was his silhouette against the pale wall behind him. It was the way he hunched slightly, the way he cleared his throat.

Her fingers felt for the light switch on the wall and stumbled across the protrusion. She flipped it up.

Jared blinked against the glaring overhead light.

Jaylee jumped to her feet. "Sabrina!" She straightened her shirt. The top two buttons of her favorite pink blouse were undone.

Sabrina looked at Jared. His hand covered half his face, his elbow protruding outward.

Jaylee took a step toward her, reaching out.

Sabrina moved away. "Don't touch me." Her voice was a deep snarl.

Jared stood, looking at her, uncertain. "I'm sorry. I'm so sorry, Sabrina."

Sorry? She looked at the two of them. Their expressions, a mixture of shock, horror, and guilt, might have inspired laughter if the lump of pain in her throat hadn't choked it out.

"We didn't mean for it to happen," Jared was saying.

"We were going to tell you," Jaylee said.

How long had this been going on? "After the wedding?" She turned on Jared. "We're getting married in six days! *Six. Days.*" How could he do this to her? How could he sit—no, *lie*—with her cousin on her couch? The couch she'd bought and paid for with her own money.

"We didn't mean for it to happen—didn't mean for you to find out like this," Jaylee said.

"How did you mean for me to find out? And when? Why are

you doing this?" Sabrina turned, disinclined to see them standing together like a—like a couple. Jaylee and Jared weren't the couple. Sabrina and Jared were. They were engaged.

"I'm sorry." Jared's voice sounded from behind her, close. The picture on the wall blurred in front of her. It was just like high school. Just like when Ethan Sterling had pretended to like her only to get invited to her house so he could be near Jaylee. Just like when David Ellenburg had befriended her only to pick her brain about Arielle. Just like all those times. Only worse. Much worse.

Jared's apology felt impossibly inadequate. How did an apology rectify the damage her heart suffered? How did an apology justify the pain they'd caused?

Was it only physical? Jaylee was so beautiful. She'd won most of the pageants she'd entered for a reason. Had she been too much for Jared to resist? Could Sabrina bring herself to forgive him?

"I'll leave you two alone," Jaylee was saying. She slid past Sabrina and slipped out the door. She didn't want to think about her cousin right now. One betrayal at a time.

The music died midsentence. Jared must've turned it off. The quiet was alarming, because now she could hear her heart thudding in her head, hear Jared's ragged rasps. Was he winded from the make-out session or from the distress of Sabrina's appearance?

"Come and sit down."

"I don't want to sit down." If he was going to beg her forgiveness, he could do it with her standing, face-to-face. She turned around and met his gaze.

He looked at the floor. "We need to talk."

"You think?" Was this the kind of man Jared was? The kind who was seduced by a pretty face? It was so contrary to her previous convictions it made her head spin. She couldn't have been more surprised if she'd arrived home to find her apartment upside down.

"We didn't mean for it to happen."

We. It was a couple word. But they weren't a couple. Sabrina and Jared were a couple. If she said it enough, it would be true.

"I should've told you. I'm sorry you found out like this."

A weight hung heavily in her middle, sagging downward, dragging her with it. She fought to keep her legs under her. "Should've told me what?" She nearly put her hands over her ears. Instead she steeled herself for his answer.

"It's over, Sabrina."

What was over? He and Jaylee? It was a quick, cold-feet thing, right? One last escapade before he settled down.

"What's—" She cleared her throat. "What's over?"

He looked at her now, but she wished he hadn't. His eyes were laden with guilt and pity. "Us."

She looked deeply into his familiar green eyes. There was nothing familiar about them now. She'd never seen this expression. Never wanted to see it again.

"We're getting married in six days." They had two hundred and forty-six RSVPs, two thousand dollars in flowers, and a three-thousand-dollar dress to prove it.

"I'm in love with Jaylee."

Each word was a nail in her heart. Everything in the room stopped. Everything in the world came to a screeching halt. Everything but the pain.

"What?" *You need to hear it again for torture's sake?*

"We didn't mean for it to happen."

"So you keep saying!" She ran her hand over her face. It was wet. She pushed at his chest with the palm of her hand. "How long?" she demanded.

He looked away, color blooming in his cheeks.

She shoved him again. "How long?"

His eyes glazed over. Good. She was glad he was hurting too. He deserved to hurt.

"I thought it would go away," he said.

"How long?" She needed to know the truth. All of it.

"A few months."

Her mind went back to the week before, when they'd gone to the beach for the day. To the week before that, when they'd shopped for a dress for the rehearsal dinner. To the time they'd gone bowling and laughed when she'd gotten five gutter balls in a row. All the memories from the past few months filed through her mind. All of them lies.

And now she'd lost Jared? Lost him to her cousin? The betrayal bit hard. It was too much. Too overwhelming to bear all at once. "Get out."

"Sabrina." He reached for her.

She flinched away. "Get out!" Her breath came hard and fast.

He stood, unmoving, hunched, for a moment. Then he walked away, toward the door. She heard the soft click of the latch settling into place.

The next six days had been a blur of pain, humiliation, and darkness. Aunt Bev had made most of the cancellations. Jaylee had made herself scarce, going to stay with her parents.

Now, a seagull called, landing a few paces away in the sand. A wave washed up, and the gull scurried up the beach. The sky was filling with golden light. She had to get home for a shower. Sabrina quickened her pace, falling into a swift jog. But she wondered if she'd ever run fast enough to escape the memories that haunted her.

Sweetpea: I don't like surprises. I know a lot of people say that, but I really mean it. I do not like surprises.

Chapter Thirteen

A week later Sabrina was halfway up the stairs to her apartment before she saw the woman blocking her door.

"Surprise!" Arielle spread her arms wide.

Her cousin wore white shorts that set off her tan, and her long hair was captured in a sleek ponytail.

"Arielle." Sabrina walked up the steps, taking in her cousin's floral suitcase, which looked large enough for a wardrobe or two.

Arielle embraced her, rubbing Sabrina's back. "Oh, it is so good to see you, cuz."

Sabrina had missed the Southern accent. "This is a surprise." An understatement.

A sudden thought sent a shiver of panic up her spine. What if Tucker saw Arielle? He would think she was Sweetpea. How long was Arielle staying? Sabrina had to keep her away from Tucker.

Arielle leaned back, propping both fists on her slim hips. "Well, it wouldn't have been if you'd returned my calls."

"Sorry about that." Sabrina unlocked the door and flipped on the lamp. "Come in."

Arielle rolled her suitcase over the threshold and shut the door. "Nice setup you got here, right on the beach. I met Mrs. Hannigan, but she didn't feel right letting me in without your knowledge, and I didn't want to call you—wanted it to be a surprise . . ." She struck a ta-da pose.

"Well, it certainly is." Sabrina set down her bag and offered her cousin a drink.

"How's your summer break going?" Sabrina asked after they were seated in the tiny living area.

"It's half over already. I miss those little rug rats." Arielle was born to teach preschool.

"You'll be back to school before you know it." A silence gathered between them. There was a white elephant in the room, and Sabrina was doing her best to ignore it.

"I guess you got the wedding invitation," Arielle said.

So much for denial. "Of course." Sabrina stood under the guise of turning on another lamp. "I'm not going, Arielle, so you can save your speech."

Arielle started to speak, but Sabrina put her hand up, palm out.

"I know you mean well, but I've made up my mind. I'm glad you've come for a visit, but let's be clear about this up front: I'm not going to the wedding."

"We don't have to talk about it today."

"Or tomorrow or the next day. Because it's futile."

Arielle studied Sabrina's face. Seeming to recognize her resolution, she turned and surveyed the room, running her hand along the back of the couch.

Sabrina perused the room with a fresh eye. She hadn't done much to the place since she'd moved in. It looked barren and void of personality.

"Did you pick the wall color?"

Sabrina had never liked the dark green, but hadn't cared enough to paint it. "It was that way when I moved in."

"Depressing, don't you think?" She peeked in the dining room. "I like the wood floors. Maybe I can help you with furniture placement while I'm here. The room lacks harmony. We'll have you feeling better before you know it."

"I feel fine."

"Aren't you going to ask about the family?"

"How's the family?"

"You don't have to be sarcastic." Arielle's smile softened her words. She squirmed on the sofa, clearly bothered. She seemed to shake the notion and continued, "Mom is wrapped up in the Miss Georgia Teen pageant. She's on the board again. Dad's traveling a lot still, but seems pretty happy with his work." She paused, as if wondering if it was safe to bring up Jaylee. "And, well, you pretty much know the rest. I'm moving up to the four-year-olds next year, so I'll have the same kiddos I had this year."

What Sabrina really needed to know was how long Arielle was staying. She was glad to see her cousin. She just didn't want Tucker to see her. Sabrina checked her watch. She was due at Tucker's in a couple hours.

"Am I keeping you from something? I don't want to rearrange a thing while I'm here—except maybe your furniture. I did just drop in, after all." Her jaw relaxed slightly, her lip dropping. "It is okay that I'm here, isn't it?"

Even with the pouty frown, Arielle was adorable. Sabrina wondered if she had any idea how lucky she was. "Of course it's okay."
She'd missed Arielle. Hadn't known how much until she'd seen her
in front of the door. "I do have a part-time evening job though, so
I won't be home much. How long can you stay?"

Please not long, she thought, then felt guilty.

Arielle shrugged her tanned shoulders. "I'm free as a bird for
another month. I booked a flight back in about four weeks—I hope
that's okay."

A whole month? Sabrina pasted a smile on her face. How would
she keep Arielle out of town that long? Nantucket wasn't that big,
and she didn't want to consider what would happen if Tucker recognized her.

Sweetpea: I'm a little bit stubborn.

Harbormaster: No kidding.

Chapter Fourteen

Sabrina didn't notice when the rain began. Her eyes glued to Tucker's computer screen, she'd been absorbed in the messages that had flown between them several months ago. Focused on her new plan.

Only when a clap of thunder pealed did she glance out the office's bay window and see the sheets of rain pouring into the harbor.

Ordinarily, she loved a good downpour, loved the smell of rain, the sound of it on the roof. But today she'd ridden her bike to Tucker's, and the rain didn't look like it was letting up anytime soon.

Deciding to call it an evening, Sabrina shut down the program and gathered her things. When she entered the living room, Tucker was in the corner, carving a piece of wood that didn't yet resemble anything. He smiled as she entered the room, lowering his tool.

"I'm finished for the night," she said. "Can I use your phone?" If she could call a cab before Tucker offered her a ride, she wouldn't risk him seeing Arielle. Why hadn't she brought her cell phone?

"Something wrong?"

A crack of thunder sounded in the distance. "I need to call a cab."
Don't offer. Please don't offer. She picked up the phone, then realized
she'd have to look up the number. The phone book sat on the table
under the phone.

He set down the block of wood. "I'll give you a lift."

She flipped open the yellow pages. "No, don't worry about it."
While she waited for the cab, she could initiate her plan.

He stood. "Really, I don't mind."

There were too many cab companies to choose from. She picked
one and dialed. "It's okay." She imagined him pulling up to her
apartment at the same time Arielle arrived home. The thought sent
a shiver of dread through her.

He took the phone from her and turned it off.

Why'd he have to be so persistent? She glared at him. "Why'd
you do that?"

"It's pouring rain. Every tourist in town is calling for a cab, and
you'll have a two-hour wait." He grabbed his keys from the table,
then turned, giving her a look she couldn't decipher. "Unless you
want to hang around for a couple more hours."

The thought was more tempting than he'd ever know. What
choice did she have now?

Huffing, Sabrina headed toward the door. Anyway, what were
the chances he'd see Arielle? It was pouring rain. She was probably
taking a warm bath by now, or snuggled on the couch, watching
the latest chick flick.

As soon as Tucker packed her bike in the trunk and backed the
car from the drive, the rain let up. Naturally.

"How far are you with the letters?" he asked.

She'd just come to the one where she'd confided about her dad's death. He was the only person other than Jared whom she'd told. But she didn't want to talk about that. "Lots of back-and-forth stuff."

"She's fun to dialogue with." Sabrina could hear the smile in his voice. "Has a great sense of humor, don't you think?"

No one had ever told her that before. But then, she didn't let loose around just anyone. "You think?"

He propped one hand on the console between them, inches from her thigh. "She has a sarcastic streak a mile wide. A dry sense of humor."

Sabrina shifted away. "I suppose." The wipers arched across the windshield.

"She's witty and intelligent, has a great vocabulary . . ."

He was hitting too close to home. "I didn't notice." Her throat was dry as dirt.

He grinned, stealing her breath with that crooked smile. "That's because you have a great vocabulary."

In town there were tourists clustered under awnings, waiting for the rain to stop.

Tucker braked as a man and woman darted across the road. The man slung his arm around the woman, and they laughed as they ducked through the rain. Sabrina wondered if the couple was as happy as they seemed.

She remembered how it felt to be wrapped in a man's arms. To feel secure and loved. She missed that.

"I contacted the host of Nantucket Chat," Tucker said. "Did I mention that?"

"What for?"

Tucker accelerated through the crosswalk. "He knows the identity of all the members. When you sign up to participate, you have to give your name and contact information."

Why hadn't she thought of that? "What did he say?"

"He said the information is confidential."

She started breathing again. "That's too bad."

"I haven't given up yet. You still have a few months of messages to wade through, and there's always the chance she'll change her mind, right?"

She folded her arms around her stomach. "Actually, I think I may have found some significant details."

"Really?"

"The clues are spread apart, but I think she might be from Ohio."

"Really?"

Why was her heart beating so fast? "She mentions being a Reds fan, and she said something about the Cincinnati airport being in Kentucky. Most people wouldn't know that, right? And she mentions a pretzel festival. I looked it up online, and there's one in Germantown, Ohio, every September."

"There are probably pretzel festivals in other states."

"Maybe, but like I said, it's the cumulative factor. The Reds, the airport, the festival. There are other tidbits that go along with the Ohio theory, too, and nothing to contradict it so far." Of course, Ohio was plenty big, and there weren't enough clues to pin down a particular city. When she was finished, he'd see they were at a dead end.

"There's the beach photo," he said.

She was ready for that one. "It may have been a lake. The waves were small. It could be Lake Erie or any number of lakes. It could also have been taken while she was on vacation."

He pulled into her drive. "I guess you're right."

"So we should definitely focus on Ohio. Maybe I can pin it down to a city as I read further." Sabrina looked at her apartment window. The blinds were up, but the living room was dark except for the faint glow of the TV. *Stay away from the window, Arielle.*

The gravel popped under the tires as Tucker pulled the car to a stop and put it in Park. She reached for the handle. The sooner she got him out of there, the better.

"Wait." He set his hand on her forearm.

She turned and faced him. His palm was warm on her wrist, the heat of it sizzling a path up her arm. She waited for him to say something, afraid and eager at the same time.

"Thanks for what you're doing. I appreciate your help and your confidentiality."

"No problem." She glanced at her apartment. So far, so good. The rain was merely a drizzle now.

He was still holding her arm. She wondered what he'd do if she turned her hand over and twined her fingers through his. She itched to do it. Would he return the touch? She longed to be connected to him. Letters only allowed so much intimacy. She missed the personal contact. The touching. The security of an embrace. Would it be so awful to take the risk and see what happened?

But even as the thought formed, a memory rose, unbidden. A foreign touch, the smell of alcohol, the chill of a cold sheet.

Sabrina knotted her hand into a fist.

Tucker's hand slid down to hers, and he squeezed her closed fist. "You okay?"

She nodded, finding her voice. "Just tired." She glanced up at the window. A light came on. She looked at Tucker, but he was studying her hand. Thank God he hadn't seen.

"You always wear this." His fingers found the *S* charm on her bracelet.

The bracelet had once been a symbol of love. Now it was a reminder of loss. A tangible warning that some risks weren't worth the cost.

Sabrina pulled her hand away. "It was a gift." She pressed her lips together. She needed to get out of there before she said too much. Before she ruined what progress she'd made tonight. She reached for the handle and opened the door.

"I'll get your bike."

She followed him around to the back of the car, and he set the bike at her feet.

"Well, regardless of how this turns out, I've enjoyed getting to know you."

He was sounding as if this project was winding down. He must be buying her Ohio theory. "There goes my mysterious air."

"Oh, you got plenty of mystery left, don't you worry."

"Who's worried?" She reached for the bike's handles.

He laughed, deep and throaty. "Goodnight, Mystery Woman."

"Goodnight," she called, wheeling the bike toward the garage. Even as she scurried through the drizzle, she couldn't stop the smile that formed on her lips.

Tucker pulled from the drive, still smiling. So she hadn't admitted who she was . . . But she was still coming over every night.

Ohio. He shook his head. Well, at least he was spending time with her. She was opening up a little. Okay, so it was a minute amount, but it was something. Ten more years and she'd be an open book.

He breathed a laugh. He had time. He still had a few tricks up his sleeve, and she had four months of letters to wade through. Plus, the list of messages was getting longer every day as they continued to write. In fact, he'd write her when he got home. After all, the more they wrote, the longer she'd be around.

Harbormaster: After my sister's accident, I took her to physical therapy for months and tried to distract her from the pain. Once I got really stupid and stuck a Tic Tac up my nose. An ER tech had to remove it. Good news: It did get a laugh from my sister. What's the stupidest thing you've ever done?

Sweetpea: Go on my honeymoon alone.

Chapter Fifteen

"I'm going for a jog," Sabrina called to Arielle the next evening.

"Run a mile for me." Arielle changed the channel to a house-flipping program and settled into the sofa.

Sabrina trotted down the steps and walked down the lane at a brisk pace, warming her muscles. She couldn't stay home tonight. The emails she'd read earlier brought back too much, and it would drive her crazy to sit around dwelling on it.

When she reached the street, she turned toward town and settled into a slow jog. She felt guilty leaving Arielle home alone, but she needed to run tonight like she needed oxygen.

The heat of the day hadn't yet given way to the evening coolness, and the warm air burned her lungs as it came and went. When she reached town, she set a punishing pace, turning down Pleasant Street, hoping to avoid the worst of the traffic.

Daylight was fading, and the summer people were exiting rented homes, clicking down sidewalks in their heels toward their supper reservations. She navigated around such a couple as she crossed Main Street. The woman wore a filmy ivory dress, and the man matched her in his linen suit. They looked like they belonged in a Nantucket ad.

Sabrina hitched her sleeves up her shoulders, thankful for the breeze that whispered across her skin, even if it was warm. She wondered what Tucker was doing right now. Was he on his deck, enjoying the same breeze? Enjoying the way the evening light danced on the surface of the water?

She couldn't get out of there fast enough tonight. It had been disturbing to read that email, the message that had sealed her fate. The message that ensured Sabrina and Tucker could never be more than online friends. Even now, it replayed in her mind, words committed to heart, not by will, but by sheer repetition.

Tracey called today. She wasn't this despondent even after her accident, and I feel helpless to do anything about it. She's divorcing Sebastian.

Her mind flashed back to the first time she'd read the email, her heart skipping in response to the memory. It was the first time he'd mentioned his brother-in-law's name. The first time she'd realized that the terrible mistake she'd made had consequences that reached further than she imagined.

Her thoughts washed back farther in time to the night she'd arrived on Nantucket. To the night she'd met Sebastian.

She'd never felt more alone than she had upon entering the cavernous honeymoon suite at the White Elephant. The room featured a giant bed with puffy pillows, a fireplace, and an ocean view. On the table by the door, a bottle of champagne chilled in a bucket. Everything about the suite said "romance."

Her suitcase hit the floor with a thud, and she sank into the first chair she reached. She should've called ahead and told the hotel she was alone. Even with her aunt's help, there'd been so many things to do in the six days since she'd found Jaylee and Jared. Cancellations, phone calls, gifts to return. She hadn't realized how drained she was, how utterly empty, until this moment, sitting in the darkness in her honeymoon suite.

The amount of money her aunt and uncle had lost was mind-boggling. Sabrina tried not to feel guilty. It was Jaylee and Jared's fault, not hers. Both of them had tried repeatedly to contact her, but after one phone call with Jared, she was done with them both. What could they say to change things now?

Sabrina curled in the recliner, tucking her feet under her. The big bed loomed across the room. The big, empty bed. She and Jared were supposed to be here together. They should be celebrating the beginning of their life together, yet here she was. Alone. How could everything have changed so drastically in a week?

She wanted to curl up in that bed, draw the covers over her, and never come out. She shed her shoes and crawled under the covers, clothes and all. It wasn't quite dark out, she hadn't washed her face, hadn't brushed her teeth, but she didn't care.

Maybe she could spend the next seven days under the blankets. She could hang up a Do Not Disturb sign and disconnect the phone.

But regardless of how she spent the coming week, eventually it would end. And then what? She'd have to return to Macon and face them again. Her family, her friends. Jaylee. Jared.

Sabrina pulled the duvet over her head. She hadn't felt so alone since her father killed himself. Like it was yesterday, she could see his lifeless body on his bedroom floor the way she'd found it after school that day. She'd been nine then, in the third grade. She'd thought he was playing a game.

If her aunt and uncle hadn't taken her in, she would've spent the remainder of her childhood in a foster home. They'd made her feel like a sister and daughter. But the past week had shown her clearly who their daughter was. Blood was thicker than water, and Jaylee had more of their blood than Sabrina did.

She turned over and stared at the lit face of the clock. Were Jared and Jaylee together right now? Were they lying together in each other's arms? Were they glad she was gone so they could be together without having to hide their feelings?

The betrayal had carved an aching hollow spot in the middle of her stomach. She was tired of the ache. Tired of the pain. She wanted it to go away. But the truth was, the betrayal was only now hitting her fully. The busyness of wedding cancellations, she realized, had distracted her. And while all she'd wanted the last six days was to escape, she hadn't realized that being here, that being idle for seven days, would allow her full exposure to the pain.

Why did she lose everyone she loved? Her mom, her dad, now

Jared. Was she unlovable? Was there something about her that was so terribly flawed?

The ache grew, spreading, swelling, devouring her. Is this how her dad had felt before he killed himself? Had he suffered some heartbreak or had her mother's death been too hard to recover from? Still, he'd had Sabrina. Why hadn't that been enough?

You're not enough, Sabrina. You weren't enough for your dad, and you weren't enough for Jared.

Maybe thoughts such as these had driven her dad to that ultimate act of selfishness. Maybe she wasn't so very different from him. Maybe things like suicide were hereditary.

She rolled over and clutched her hands to her chest, feeling the bracelet Jared had given her all those months ago. It had been Valentine's Day and the bracelet had only held a single heart. Every special occasion after that, he'd given her another charm. A pearl birthstone pendant for her birthday, a key charm for their anniversary, a book charm, an *S* charm, and a ring for when they got engaged. Sabrina wrapped her hand around the bracelet, holding it close to her skin as if by grasping it she could keep a tiny piece of her life with Jared.

She closed her eyes against the throbbing ache. She was so tired. Tired of thinking, tired of hurting, tired of breathing. *Don't think. Don't think about anything except the sound of the water outside. The sound of it lapping the shoreline.*

Eventually she fell asleep, but when she awoke, she wished for sleep again, for oblivion. She spent the next day in her room, telling the maids she didn't need her room serviced. She ordered food only when her gnawing stomach became unbearable, took a long bath, watched TV without seeing it. When the phone rang, she disconnected it.

The next day, when the maids came to the door, she went outside and walked down the beach, listening to the lonely cries of seagulls and the shushing of water lapping the shoreline. When the maids finished, she was relieved to return to the cocoon of her room. The maids had replaced the tepid water in the champagne bucket with fresh ice.

Day three was a duplication of day two. The loneliness was getting to her, and the realization that she'd lost not only her fiancé, but her best friend and family, was weighing hard on her. She missed feeling wanted, feeling needed. She missed feeling normal. She'd never felt so unwanted. Not even in high school when she hadn't exactly shone like a star next to her beautiful cousins. Not even in the beauty pageant her Aunt Bev had entered her in.

Near the end of the week, when evening arrived, she felt suffocated by loneliness. The air in the room seemed thick and impossible to pull into her lungs. Two more days and she would face Jared and Jaylee. She didn't want to go home, dreaded the thought. Visions of her dad lying on the floor haunted her.

Her eyes fell on the champagne still nestled in the bucket. She picked up the bottle and went to work. The cork popped off. She poured the liquid into a fluted glass and made a toast.

"To life alone. May I never be so stupid as to love again." She drained the first glass. Then, feeling somewhat better, Sabrina poured another.

She wondered why she hadn't drunk the champagne earlier. To

think she'd suffered needlessly when a reprieve had been nearby all along.

This was better than lying around depressed. Better than contemplating the similarities between herself and her dad. She wasn't like him. Would never do something so horridly selfish and destructive.

Again, that vision of him on the floor, his denim-clad legs crumpled, his oval glasses askew on his ashen face.

She sprang to her feet.

She needed to leave this depressing place. Go someplace fun and lively. She'd stared at these four walls too long.

The only dress she'd brought slipped easily over her head. The waist hung loosely, so she tightened the belt, then went to run a brush through her hair. By the time she was ready, she almost looked like she fit in with the elite summer crowd.

The Nantucket air was mild at night, a warm breeze blowing in off the harbor. She walked toward town, her sandals clicking on the sidewalk. Main Street was lively. People on their way to supper, dressed in fine linen and suit jackets. There were a lot of couples, she noticed suddenly.

She looked around, from the cars on the cobblestone streets to the tourists milling on the sidewalks. She didn't see anyone alone. Only her. And where was she going to go? Supper reservations were necessary here, especially on a weekend, and she couldn't see herself dining in some exclusive restaurant anyway, certainly not alone.

Music and chatter poured from a doorway as she neared it. A shingled sign beside the canopied entrance read "Cap'n Tully's Tavern." She wouldn't feel out of place there. The sound of laughter pulled her inside. She could count on one hand the times she'd entered a bar. Her feet crunched over peanut shells as she made her way to a darkened corner and took an empty table, a low one with two stools.

The effects of the champagne were wearing off, and the idea of losing herself again held some appeal. She took in her surroundings. A pool table crowded the opposite corner, surrounded by four college-aged men. A few singles sat at the bar, nursing drinks, but even in here, there were couples. She felt like a wallflower, stuffed into the corner of the room, invisible, wilting.

I used to be half of a couple, she reminded herself. What a fool she'd been to think it might last forever. She'd never had Jared, not really. She wondered again what was inherently wrong with her. There had to be something.

Enough, Sabrina. These thoughts were only digging her deeper into the hole of despondency. Keep going and she would end up at the very bottom, where her dad had no doubt landed just before he took his life.

She was not like that. She was not.

When a young male server stopped at her table, she ordered a snakebite. She'd never had one, but there was no time like the present. Now that she'd found her drug of choice, why not take the shortcut to oblivion? It was better than sitting around, writhing in her pain. At least she was *doing* something. It felt good to have a little control back.

She tapped her stubby nails on the tabletop. They'd been long only a week ago. She'd taken exquisite care of them in the two months before the big day, and they'd been longer than ever. She'd had an appointment for a manicure the day before the wedding—another cancellation she'd made. But the six days of stress had taken their toll, and now the edges were short and ragged. She must have gnawed on them, though she didn't remember doing so.

A few minutes later, her shot and a wedge of lemon arrived. *Okay, here we go.* She licked the webbing between her thumb and index finger, salted it, then licked it again. Before the taste faded, she downed the tequila and bit into the lemon wedge. The sourness of the lemon puckered her lips, and she gave a shudder.

Jared's words from that night rang in her head. "*I'm in love with Jaylee. We didn't mean for it to happen. It's over, Sabrina.*"

"*It's over, Sabrina.*"

Were there sadder words in the English language? "*It's over.*" He didn't want her, was rejecting her, discarding her like yesterday's newspaper.

Stop it.

Sabrina ordered a second snakebite, and when it arrived a few minutes later, she repeated the process. She was starting to feel it.

Jared's words were fading like a dream sequence, and a warm, fuzzy feeling was taking their place.

Her gaze collided with a man across the room. He had dark, neatly trimmed hair, and a loosened tie. He was staring at her, or at least she thought he was. She was sitting in a corner, so there was no one behind her. But the room was dim, and maybe she was mistaken. A second glance proved her suspicions. He was at a high table, his hand wrapped around a fancy goblet. His lips turned up at the corners, and she realized she'd been staring.

Sabrina pushed the empty shot glasses past the flickering candle to the table's edge. Across the room, the bartender slid a full mug across the bar to a woman with short blonde hair and a long, ballerina neck. The bartender was flirting with her, smiling. He said something, and she tossed her head back and laughed.

Sabrina was feeling better. Almost giddy. She should've come here days ago instead of locking herself in that depressing suite.

The server approached, blocking her view. He set another snakebite on her table. "From the gentleman over there." He gestured to the corner, where Tie Man dipped his head and raised his goblet in a mock toast.

The server left, and Sabrina lifted her own glass toward Tie Man before she salted her skin and downed the shot. He hadn't taken his eyes off her. His white shirt almost glowed in the dimness of the room. He was broad shouldered and handsome. And he was interested in her.

The sudden knowledge flattered her, emboldened her. She stood. Her legs felt light, as if they were filled with helium, as she approached him. He watched her every step of the way, and when she stopped at his table, his eyes swept down her body to her bare knees, then back up again.

"Thanks for the drink," she said.

"Have a seat." He pushed out the empty chair.

Her body felt weightless as she sank into it. Her thoughts were pleasantly fuzzy. She leaned her elbow on the table and propped her chin in her palm. "I like your tie." It was red with white dots that played tricks with her eyes if she stared at it.

"I like your eyes."

She smiled coyly. "These old things?"

"They're like warm caramel in this candlelight."

Warm caramel. She liked the thought. She liked this man. He was handsome in a Wall Street kind of way, though his loosened tie made her think he was ready to kick back and relax.

"What's a pretty girl like you doing all alone tonight?"

She laughed, though she wasn't sure why. "Looking for company, what else?" It made sense suddenly, why she'd left the hotel, why she'd wandered toward town. It was company she sought. And it looked like she'd found it.

"What's your name?" he asked.

"Sabrina."

"Sabrina." He seemed to taste her name on his tongue. "Sexy."

He made her feel good. Or maybe it was the tequila. He took a drink from his goblet and it left his lower lip wet.

"What should I call you?" Sabrina reached across the table and drew her thumb across his lip.

He let out a quiet curse. "Whatever you want."

She laughed, tossed her hair aside. The movement made her dizzy. "Come on, I told you mine." She tugged his tie, enjoying the flirtation, feeling less like a wallflower and more like Ballerina Neck at the bar.

He smiled lazily. "Sebastian."

He looked like a Sebastian. "Well, Sebastian. What's your story? What do you do for a living?"

He grazed his index finger along the curve of her palm. "Do you really want to know?"

The way he looked at her with those mesmerizing gray eyes made her even dizzier. She realized she didn't care who he was or what he did. "Not really," she replied. His touch was warm and pleasant, making her tingle. He wanted her. The thought empowered her. Made her heady with excitement.

"Why don't we go someplace quiet?" The meaning in his eyes was clear, and suddenly Sabrina wanted that more than she wanted her next breath.

"Lead the way," she said.

He fished his wallet from his pocket and set two crisp bills on the table, hardly taking his eyes from her.

He pulled out her chair, and her head swam as she rose to her feet.

"Okay?" he asked.

She smiled. "Oh, yeah." She followed him through the maze of people and into the cool night.

"I'm parked around back."

She reached for his hand, but he ushered her in front of him, looking around. She drew in a deep breath of tangy sea air, letting it fill her lungs, then blew it out through her mouth. The gravel crunched under her sandals when they reached the parking lot. He opened the door of a low, sleek car, and she slipped inside.

Her skirt rode up high as she tucked her legs in. She laughed. "Whoops."

In the car, his hand found her leg, and she returned the favor. She felt so good. *This* felt so good. She leaned over the console and kissed his neck. He smelled like soap and alcohol. His face was rough, and she scraped her lips across his jaw.

He pulled her closer. She wished she could make the console disappear. It was a barrier, digging into her ribs.

By the time the car stopped, she was desperate for more. She followed him through the back door of a house, and she tripped over an empty suitcase. He steadied her, then pulled her into the darkness. She followed blindly, her needs propelling her.

Sabrina woke to a distant thud. She opened her eyes, then shut them against the bright light pouring into the room. Maybe the thud had been her brain pounding against her skull.

Even closed, her eyes ached. The bed under her felt odd. Soft and not like her bed at all. Then she remembered. Nantucket. The hotel. But that didn't explain the sun streaming into the room.

She forced her eyes open in time to see the door to the room open. Where was she? She'd gone to a bar the night before.

An attractive brunette appeared in the doorway just as a body moved beside Sabrina. A man, bare chested, was awakening.

Sabrina felt a chill sweep over her and realized she was unclothed beneath the covers. She clutched the cool sheet to her chest.

The woman froze in the doorway, her ice-blue eyes widening. She looked back and forth between Sabrina and the man.

The bar. She'd been in the bar. Tie Man. He'd bought her a drink.

"Tracey!" Sebastian sprang up. He stared at Sabrina as if he wasn't sure how she'd gotten there.

"That's *it*, Sebastian. It's over!"

Sebastian jumped from the bed, tugging the sheet with him, wrapping it around his waist, leaving Sabrina exposed.

She grabbed the pillow, clutched it to her.

Sebastian cursed. "It's not—I'm sorry, baby!" He followed the woman—his wife? His lover?

Sabrina wasted no time finding her dress, lying haphazardly on the hardwood floor. Her head throbbed as she leaned over to retrieve it. She shrugged into her dress, sliding on her sandals even as she tugged the dress over her hips. She hopped on one leg, finding balance as she slipped on her second sandal, then scanned the room for her bag.

Then she realized he had driven her there. How would she get back to the hotel? She didn't even know where she was.

The woman was screaming now. "How dare you bring that tramp here! Sleep with her right under my nose!" Her voice wobbled erratically.

She had to get out of there. The voices were coming from across the house somewhere. She crept down the hall. Sebastian was apologizing, pleading. "Come on, Tracey—"

"Don't you touch me!" the woman said.

The back door was within sight. The voices were coming from the living room just beyond the kitchen. She could slip out without being seen. Her feet moved quickly across the linoleum. She opened the back door and escaped into the bright morning.

She walked almost an hour before she came to a main road. She'd asked a bicyclist for directions to town and had walked until her feet were blistered. By the time she'd returned to the hotel, the aftereffects of the tequila and her night of shame put her in bed for the day.

She'd known that night had been a terrible mistake, but she hadn't known until much later that it would ruin her chance with Tucker.

Now, Sabrina turned up the hill and blew out a shuddery breath before setting a punishing pace. If she ran hard enough, fast enough, maybe she could chase the memory from her mind.

Harbormaster: I love the way we talk about nothing.

Sweetpea: I love that I can say anything I want to you. I've never had that freedom with anyone else.

Chapter Sixteen

The next night, Arielle went shopping for some things to perk up the loft, giving Sabrina a chance to write Tucker. After she'd sent the first message, he'd replied, and they'd been chatting since.

Are you kidding? she wrote. Name one good movie in the eighties. Just one.

She sent it and leaned back, anticipating his answer. She realized she missed being with him on the weekends. She'd gotten accustomed to going to his house, to being with him physically.

She shook the thought, reluctant to spoil her good mood.

His response appeared.

Back to the Future. E.T. Raiders of the Lost Ark. Honey, I Shrunk the Kids . . . I could go on and on.

Honey, I Shrunk the Kids?, she replied.

He knew she wasn't a movie buff. Give her a good book any day. She wasn't even sure how they'd gotten on the topic, but that's how it was with them. They'd leap from one topic to another, and before she knew it, hours had passed.

"Ooooh, who's Harbormaster?" Arielle's voice made her jump.

"Don't sneak up on me like that." Sabrina's heart raced from the scare.

"I wasn't sneaking. You were just distracted." Arielle wiggled her eyebrows. "Is it a maaan?"

Sabrina closed the program before Arielle could snoop. "Yes, it's a man, but he's just a friend."

"A friend, huh?" Arielle tugged Sabrina's ponytail, then set a bag on the floor and sank onto the sofa, still panting from her trip up the stairs. "Does he live on the island?"

She supposed the truth couldn't hurt. "Maybe." She regretted closing the program without saying goodbye to Tucker. She'd write him when Arielle took her bath.

"So, are you, like, dating? Come on, tell all. How long has this been going on?"

"There's nothing going on. We're just writing each other. What did you buy?" Why did her cousin have to be so meddlesome? But then, maybe if Arielle saw she'd moved on from Jared, she'd stop pushing her to attend the wedding.

"Stop changing the subject. When did all this start? I know I'm being nosy, but give a single girl a break. I haven't had a date in months."

Sabrina couldn't imagine that was by anything but choice. "We've been writing a year or so."

"A year! And he hasn't asked you out?"

How could Sabrina explain without revealing everything? "I told you, it's not like that."

"Ha! I saw that look on your face when I came in. You were totally absorbed, and you had this goofy smile on your face."

"I did not have a goofy smile—"

"Did too. Completely goofy."

"Whatever. Don't you need a bath?"

"Changing the subject again?" Arielle raised an eyebrow. Finally, she jumped off the couch. "Fine, fine. Be all mysterious and secretive," she tossed over her shoulder, walking down the short hall.

"I will, thank you very much," Sabrina called after her.

The next week Sabrina had to admit that Arielle had livened up the quiet loft, and coming home to someone was nice, even if it did mean the TV was on too much. She'd bought a new rug and a giant oval mirror that she hung in the hall. That was coming down the instant Arielle left. Sabrina didn't need to see herself every time she came and went.

If only Arielle would stop pressing her about the wedding. If she had a dime for every time Arielle had said, *"But the family will be so disappointed . . ."*

"Order's up, Sabrina," Gordon called from the grill. She hadn't heard the bell. It was unlike her to be so distracted, but Arielle's arrival had discombobulated her. It was as if her two worlds, past and present, had collided. As much as she enjoyed Arielle, she couldn't help worrying that her path would cross with Tucker's. For that reason, Sabrina was eager for her cousin's departure. But she was beginning to think Arielle wasn't going anywhere until Sabrina agreed to attend the wedding.

Well, that wasn't going to happen.

Sabrina set the loaded plates on a tray and delivered them to table fourteen, a four-top by the front window. Outside the glass pane, the morning sun wakened a sky that promised to be clear and blue. The door's bell chimed, and Oliver shuffled in, nodding at her from across the room. She wondered what word he had up his sleeve today.

She went for the coffee carafe, and when she returned to fill Oliver's mug, Arielle was seated at the table diagonal to his. She looked flawless in a pastel-pink T-shirt. Her blonde hair framed her face, and pink lip gloss highlighted her trademark smile. Arielle waggled her fingers at Sabrina.

Panicked, Sabrina glanced at the clock above the door. Nine minutes after seven. Tucker would arrive in three minutes.

Three minutes. She had to get Arielle out of there. Quickly. He'd think he'd found Sweetpea, and then what? Everything would be ruined. And just when she was so close to convincing him that finding her was hopeless.

Sabrina made a beeline to her cousin, watching the smile slide from Arielle's face.

"You've got to leave," Sabrina whispered. She should've told Arielle not to come here. Why hadn't she just said it? Now look what was happening.

Arielle opened the menu. "What? I came for breakfast."

"I know. I can't explain now, but you can't stay." She checked the clock. Ten minutes after seven.

"Sabrina," Oliver said, tapping her arm. "Yesterday I gave one of my employees a vituperation. What do you make of that?"

She glanced in his direction. "Not now, Oliver."

Arielle perused the menu. Sabrina took it from her hands, watching her cousin's eyes widen. "You have to leave. Now. *Please.* I can't explain, but can you just trust me?"

Seeming to read Sabrina's desperation, Arielle eased back from the table and stood. "All right, but you are acting awfully weird, cuz, and I expect a full explanation later."

"Okay, okay." Sabrina ushered her toward the door, praying Tucker was running a minute or two late for once. The clock read 7:11. Her heart was in her throat, a solid lump that pulsated wildly.

The kitchen bell dinged. Table five's order.

Sabrina pulled the door for Arielle, but her cousin stopped on the threshold, coming face-to-face with Tucker.

No.

No, no, no. Her mind spun in a hundred directions as she watched the emotions flicker across Tucker's face. Surprise at nearly bumping into Arielle. Recognition. Confusion. One emotion faded into the other, slowly, as if time was wading through molasses.

Then his eyes found hers. Two furrows crouched between his brows. Something dimmed his eyes. Hurt? Disappointment? But that made no sense.

Tucker looked at Arielle. "What's going on?" he asked finally.

Say something. Think, Sabrina!

Arielle was looking at her, too, her eyes searching for answers Sabrina didn't have.

"Excuse us," a man behind Sabrina said.

They were blocking the exit. Sabrina and Arielle moved outside, letting the man pass.

What could she say? She was caught. There was nothing she could do but introduce them. Her eyes begged Arielle to play along.

She swallowed hard. "Tucker, I'd like you to meet Arielle. I was—I was going to surprise you, but, well, here she is. The woman you've been writing to all this time." In her stomach, an aching hole opened, wide and gaping. The smile on her face felt frozen and stilted. Plastic.

Arielle studied Sabrina a moment, then turned a dazed smile on Tucker.

Tucker looked between them. Finally, as if remembering his manners, he extended his hand. "Nice to meet you." He cleared his throat. "In person, I mean."

Arielle shook his hand. "You too."

Sabrina shrank inside as they touched. What had she done? What was going to happen now? Now that Tucker thought he'd met the woman of his dreams? *You're going to lose him for good, that's what.* The thought awakened an old wound.

A tap on the café window snagged her attention. Char motioned toward Gordon, who gave an exaggerated shrug from the kitchen window. His brows were pulled low in a deep V. It was the same look he had right before he'd fired their last server. The couple at table five was glaring at her. She had to get back in there.

Tucker gave his cap a sharp tug, then stuffed his hands in his pockets.

"I have to get back to work and—uh—Arielle has to be somewhere else . . ." Sabrina looked to her cousin for a confirmation.

"I do. I have to be somewhere else."

"So, maybe you two can catch up later?" Sabrina eyed Arielle, who took the hint and started walking away.

"Sure, later," Arielle said.

Tucker nodded once. "See you."

As he entered the café behind her, Sabrina could swear he was burning a hole through the back of her head. She needed a moment alone like she needed oxygen. She didn't even look at Gordon as she passed the kitchen and headed to the employee restroom. Just two minutes. She closed the metal door behind her and bolted it shut, leaning against it. Her legs quaked. Her entire body had become the epicenter of some horrific earthquake.

What now? What was going to happen? Could she get Arielle to leave? But then Tucker would wonder why she'd come at all.

There had to be some way out of this. *Think!*

She remembered the look on Tucker's face. Not the response she expected from someone meeting the woman he'd been desperately searching for. But then, he'd come to the café expecting coffee and had gotten the surprise of his life instead. Maybe he'd been in shock.

Well, he wasn't the only one. And Arielle must be totally perplexed. But she could deal with her cousin later. Right now, she had to face Tucker, had to seem pleased that she'd located his Sweetpea.

Sabrina closed her eyes and banged her head against the door.

Okay, maybe she could fix this. Maybe she could convince Arielle to spend a day with him and then go home. Then Sabrina and Tucker could continue writing, and everything would return to normal.

Normal. The word had such a nice ring.

She drew a deep breath, let it fill her lungs, then exhaled, feeling in control now that she had a workable plan. Of course, she'd have to convince Arielle to cooperate. And she'd have to endure the knowledge that Tucker was with her cousin. The notion made her stomach twist.

One bridge at a time, Sabrina.

A tap on the door startled her.

"Sabrina . . ." Char's voice called. "You okay in there?"

She straightened. "I'm fine."

"Well, Gordon's not, honey. You've got three orders up, and he wants to know why you're MIA."

"Be right out." Sabrina splashed cold water on her face and tidied her ponytail. *Just go out there and do your job. You'll be too busy to chat with Tucker. Tell him you'll talk to him tonight. No, scratch that. There's no reason for you to go to his house tonight since you've already found Sweetpea.*

The realization hit her fresh, and her spirits deflated. No more evenings at Tucker's. No more impromptu suppers or boat rides. No more sitting close at the desk while he read over her shoulder.

You ninny. That's what you wanted. All these mixed feelings were making her crazy. But she couldn't worry about that now. *Get through the next half hour. Once Tucker leaves, you can figure out everything else.*

She exited the restroom and collected the plates of food. "Sorry about that," Sabrina told Gordon when he glared at her through the window.

She delivered the food to the tables, then took the orders of two new customers. Next she went for the coffee carafe and stopped at Tucker's table first. No sense delaying the inevitable.

"So," he said as she poured the coffee, "you found her, huh?"

Sabrina drew up her lips and hoped for the best. "Surprised?"

He leaned back in the chair. "You could say that."

He was looking at her oddly. Staring. Studying her as if he'd ordered oatmeal and she'd served a bowl of wet sand.

"Well, Sabrina . . ." Oliver said from behind her. "What do you think about that? You know, about my giving an employee a vituperation yesterday?"

"Oliver, I—"

"So, how'd you do it?" Tucker asked. He adjusted his cap, crossed his arms over his chest. His arm muscles bulged against his fists.

A man across the room caught her eye and raised his empty mug in the air expectantly.

Sabrina nodded his direction, then looked at Tucker. "How did I . . . ?"

"Find her," Tucker said. "How did you finally find her?" His words sounded like ice chips, chiseled from a thick, heavy block. His chin rose. He tilted his chair back on two legs.

"I—"

Oliver hooted. "I stumped you, didn't I?"

She turned a glare on Oliver. "It means reprimand," she said just to shut him up.

"She from Ohio, like you thought?" Tucker asked.

Why didn't he seem happier? "Uh, no. Georgia."

The bell dinged as Gordon put up another order. She had to get it together. "I have to get back to work. I'll explain later." Maybe by then she would actually have an explanation.

Harbormaster: Women are so complicated. What do you people want?

Chapter Seventeen

Tucker steered his boat into the harbor, relieved his last tour was over. The bow sliced through the water, parting it effortlessly. A wind had kicked up from the east, blowing in angry gray clouds that reflected his mood more accurately than the cumulus clouds that dotted the sky earlier.

Every customer annoyed him that day. The forty-something woman whose coiffed hair required them to move at a snail's pace, the dad who let his kids riffle through the boat's cubbies and compartments, the couple who couldn't keep their hands off each other all the way to the Vineyard and back . . .

Even Dorothy's bluntness had annoyed him when he'd returned to the office between customers. *"Boy, you're in a snit today."*

No kidding. What man wouldn't be when the woman he loved was foisting him on some other woman? And that's what Sabrina was doing.

He recalled the moment that morning when he'd come face-to-face with the phony Sweetpea. He'd relived the nightmare a hundred times, and each time it left him more irritated than the time before.

It stank, and that's all there was to it. How much could Sabrina care for him if she pushed him on some other woman? Didn't the thought of him with someone else make her want to hit something?

And who was this woman, anyway? Some longtime friend of Sabrina's here to play a part? How long would she stay, and was he supposed to see her again? Take her out?

He pounded his fist on the steering wheel, feeling it vibrate under his hand. He didn't want to be with this woman . . . Amber? Arielle? He couldn't even remember her name. He wanted to be with Sabrina. But now that she'd supposedly found Sweetpea, he wouldn't be spending time with her at all. There was no excuse for her to come over now.

So much for Operation Sweetpea. Instead of forcing Sabrina out of hiding, he'd forced her to find a stand-in.

Now he'd be back to stealing moments at the café during coffee refills. Back to pretending to read the paper while he watched her every move. Back to being his old, pathetic self.

Only now he had a new girlfriend to amuse. He prayed she wouldn't stay long. What if she remained the rest of the summer? What if she was moving here?

Please, God, no. His thoughts took every disastrous detour, and by the time he finished ruminating, their old online relationship didn't seem so terrible after all.

Arielle was waiting inside the door when Sabrina returned. "Okay, spill it."

Sabrina closed the door and set her bag down. "Nothing like being bombarded the moment one gets home."

"Nothing like being pawned off on some stranger at seven o'clock in the morning."

"Touché." Sabrina went to the kitchen and poured a glass of iced tea. Her head pounded. All she'd wanted was to come home, curl up in bed, and pretend today never happened.

Arielle had followed her to the kitchen. "Out with it. Who's this Tucker guy, and why did you say I've been writing him for a year?"

Sabrina sighed. "Let's sit down."

"It's that bad?"

"Unfortunately, yes."

They sat at the kitchen table. Sabrina looked out the window, where dark clouds hung low over the ocean. The water chopped and churned beneath them, an angry, moving canvas. Despite the day's beautiful start, a storm was brewing. She hoped Tucker was off the water.

"You're Sweetpea," Arielle said. "Why did you tell that guy it was me?"

"I'll get to that. Sheesh. Let me start at the beginning." It was the only way to make her cousin understand the importance of what she was about to ask.

"This should be good." Arielle crossed her arms and cocked her head.

Not a great start. *Just get it over with.* Sabrina stalled with a sip of tea, then told Arielle about the start of her relationship with

Harbormaster. She told Arielle how stunned she was to discover Harbormaster was Tucker from the café. And then came the first hard part.

"After he sent his own photo, I didn't know what to do," Sabrina said. "I couldn't send my photo or he'd know it was *me*."

Arielle's face softened. "What's so bad about that? He probably would've been delighted. You could've started dating."

Sabrina shook her head. "You don't understand."

"Then explain it."

"I'm not like you. He wouldn't have been delighted. He would've been disappointed."

Arielle started to interrupt, but Sabrina waved her off. "And I didn't want that anyway. I *don't* want that."

"Don't want what?"

"A relationship. I'm done with that."

"You can't be done with relationships, Sabrina. They're part of life."

"Well, they're not part of my life. And I like it that way." *Liar.* Well, maybe *like* was too strong a word. It was safer that way, that's what she'd meant.

"But you have a relationship with him, whether you call it that or not."

"A relationship at a safe distance. I can handle that."

Arielle shook her head. "We'll get back to that later. So he sent a photo and you didn't reciprocate. What happened next?"

Back to that. How could she say it? It seemed so harmless at the time. She never intended for Arielle to know or be involved. How was she to know that—

"Sabrina?"

"Well, I couldn't send my picture, and he wanted a photo and . . ."

"And . . . ?"

Sabrina licked her lips, gone suddenly dry, like someone had sucked all the moisture from the air. "Remember that photo you sent me? The one of you on the beach in Florida . . . ?" Her voice got smaller as the sentence dragged out.

Arielle's countenance changed. Her eyes widened; her jaw went slack. She sucked in a breath and held it, frozen. "You didn't."

"It gets worse."

Arielle's eyes slowly narrowed. "Could it possibly?"

She slumped in her seat. "Unfortunately." How could she have deceived him like that? And yet, wasn't she planning to cover her deceit with another lie? Her Aunt Bev's words danced through her mind: *"What a tangled web we weave, when first we practice to deceive."*

"Go on." Arielle was glaring now.

This wasn't looking good. Not good at all. What was she going to do if Arielle refused to cooperate? What possible reason could she give Tucker for bringing the woman here only to have her disappear again?

One step at a time. "About six weeks ago, Tucker approached me after work and asked if he could hire me to find the woman he's been writing."

"What? Why would he ask you?"

"He'd been talking to Renny, and she was raving about how intuitive I am. Of course, she was talking about her stories and how

I help her with the clues. Tucker thought if I read the letters, I could piece together enough facts to locate this woman."

"How ironic."

"I tried to dissuade him for all the obvious reasons. I tried to convince him that if she didn't want to be found, it was best to leave it alone. But he was determined. And I thought—well, if I could pretend to try and find her—me—and fail . . ."

"And he's paying you for this?"

Sabrina felt heat creep into her face. All right, it was wrong. But he'd backed her into a corner. "I've been donating his money to Nantucket Soundkeeper."

"Oh, that makes it all right."

"I know, I know!" Did Arielle have to beat her with it? She already felt like slime. "I didn't know what else to do. He was going to hire someone else if I said no, and I couldn't risk that."

"I don't understand."

"You couldn't understand, Arielle."

"Does this have something to do with Jared and Jaylee?"

"I don't want to talk about that." Sabrina took a swig of tea.

"Everyone gets hurt sooner or later. You have to pick yourself up and have some hope."

Sabrina wasn't going there. She'd already hashed it out a hundred times in her own mind, and it was settled. Besides, there was a far more compelling reason that prevented her from telling Tucker the truth now, but she couldn't tell Arielle about that.

"You don't have to understand," Sabrina said. "Just try and understand that this relationship is special to me. Too special to lose."

"Then let it become all it was meant to be. Tell him who you are."

Sabrina stood, her chair scraping against the ceramic. "No." Her breath caught at the thought of him knowing. At the thought of him realizing who she was and what she'd done. Eventually he would introduce her to his sister, and everything would be ruined.

Arielle took her hand. "What are you so afraid of?"

She had to get back on topic. She wasn't going into this with her cousin. "I've already set the plan in motion. I've nearly finished reading the messages, and I was going to inform him next week that it's hopeless, that there aren't enough clues for anyone to locate her."

Sabrina walked into the living room and plopped on the couch that Arielle had moved against the wall. "I didn't anticipate you coming here, and I certainly didn't anticipate Tucker seeing you."

Arielle approached, sitting on the edge of the sofa next to Sabrina. "I'm sorry for that." Her voice gentled, "But maybe this was God's doing. Maybe this will force you to do what you should have done to begin with."

How did God get in the middle of this? "I'm not telling him who I am." She drove the words home with her eyes. Arielle needed to understand how adamant she was. She wouldn't lose this relationship.

"We write every night. Usually about nothing, but sometimes we talk about serious things. About politics and previous relationships and our deepest fears. I depend on him. I never meant to let that happen." She begged her cousin to understand. "If I tell him who I am, I'll lose him. And I can't bear that. I just can't." Her eyes burned, and she felt tears welling up.

"Oh, honey." Arielle embraced her, rubbing her back.

Sabrina blinked back the tears. She wouldn't have to lose Tucker. She could still salvage this mess if only she could convince Arielle to do this one tiny thing for her.

Sabrina pulled back and wiped the corner of her eye with her knuckle.

"So, what now?" Arielle asked.

Funny you should ask. Sabrina folded her hands in her lap. "I was hoping you'd agree to see him."

Arielle leaned back. "You are not asking what I think you are."

"A few dates and it'll be time for you to leave."

"A *few* dates!"

"It won't be hard. You know me well. Just pretend to be me." Sabrina tried for a grin. "It's not like he's hard on the eyes."

"That's hardly the point!"

Arielle's indignation resurrected the guilt in Sabrina. Not only had she fabricated a lie, but she was asking her cousin to perpetuate it. Arielle had always had a high code of honor. So had Sabrina before all this. Before Nantucket. Before Jared. What had happened? How had her life spun so far off track?

"I know it's a lot to ask," Sabrina said.

"I don't leave for two and a half weeks. How can I go out with this guy and pretend to be something I'm not? I can't do it."

Why couldn't her cousin see how much it meant to her? What had Sabrina ever asked of Arielle? "You mean you *won't* do it."

Arielle stared, eyes wide. "I'm not the one who started this charade."

"And I'm not the one who showed up here uninvited." Sabrina regretted the words the moment she said them.

Arielle's eyes turned down at the corners, a mirror image of her mouth. She slowly stood.

She should say something. Maybe she should apologize, but she was still angry. It was selfish of Arielle not to do this one thing for her. She had to know how important it was.

"I'm going for a walk." Arielle headed out the door, shutting it hard.

Sabrina heard her cousin's sandals thudding down the wooden steps. Across the room, the logo on the screen saver darted across the computer screen. Tucker would expect to hear from her, expect to see her—Arielle. She checked her watch. He'd be home soon. What should she do? What if he called—or worse, came over?

Why did this have to happen? Why did Arielle have to come? Why did she have to show up at the café just when Sabrina was ready to wrap everything in a nice, tidy bow?

Sweetpea: Have you ever felt like you just weren't enough?

Chapter Eighteen

Sabrina turned and pulled the blanket over her shoulders. A thick wedge of moon brightened the sky, illuminating the tree outside the window, and a gentle breeze ruffled the sheers. The air smelled of rain and salt from the storm. How long had she been lying here? An hour? Two? She refused to look at the clock for confirmation.

Her only consolation was the squeak of the sofa bed in the living room as Arielle tossed and turned. At least Sabrina wasn't the only one kept awake by the argument. Then she felt guilty for the thought. Really, what had Arielle done wrong? She'd inadvertently stepped into Sabrina's mess.

But would it kill her to help me?

Tucker must be wondering why she hadn't called or written. But if he'd been so eager to meet Sweetpea, why hadn't he contacted her? Surely he was eager to see Arielle. *Especially now that he's seen her in person.*

Maybe she could fabricate a family emergency that called Arielle away. Still, that wouldn't prevent him from wanting to know where she lived. And if she'd come to the island for the express purpose of meeting him, why wouldn't she disclose her address?

She turned again, tugging at the sheet that had bunched around her legs and tangled with her feet. Arielle's words haunted the corridors of her mind. *"Everyone gets hurt sooner or later. You have to pick yourself back up and have some hope."*

If only it were so simple. There was no hope where Tucker was concerned. Not when it came to a real relationship. She'd sealed that fate her first week on the island.

"Sabrina?"

Her eyes snapped open. Arielle stood in the doorway, dimly lit by the moon.

"Are you awake?" her cousin whispered.

Sabrina rolled onto her back and checked the time. She'd been awake for two hours. "Yeah."

Arielle entered the room, and Sabrina scooted over as she eased down on the bed's edge.

"I can't stand for things to be like this between us," Arielle said. She'd stayed out past dark, and by the time she'd returned, Sabrina was in bed.

"Me either."

They sat quietly, listening to the wind rustle through the leaves. Somewhere in the distance, a dog barked. Sabrina loathed the guilt that pricked her conscience, but she deserved it. She'd created this mess. Although she wished Arielle would help, it wasn't her cousin's responsibility.

"I'm sorry I got angry," Sabrina said. "I didn't mean what I said about you being uninvited."

"I'm sorry too."

Thunder rolled in the distance, and raindrops hit the roof, first in loud dollops, then in a steady patter. Sabrina got up and pulled the sash until it clicked in place, then crawled back under the covers.

"I don't know what I'm going to do about Tucker," Sabrina said finally. "But it's my problem, not yours." Maybe it was going to blow up in her face. If she told Tucker Arielle had to leave the island, maybe he'd give up on the relationship. Maybe she'd never hear from him again.

She envisioned coming home to an empty inbox, no letter asking how her day had been. Tried to imagine her evenings without their back-and-forth conversations. Could she go back to that kind of life? That kind of loneliness?

"The thing is, I have an idea," Arielle said.

Hope sprouted a tiny seed. At least someone had an idea. "Let's hear it."

"I don't think you're going to like it."

"Like I have so many appealing options."

"True." Arielle shifted toward her, pulling her feet onto the bed and wrapping her arms around her knees. "The way I see it, we both want something. I was thinking we could make a deal."

It didn't take a genius to figure out what Arielle was saying. "The wedding."

"If you agree to go to the wedding, and *be nice* . . . I'll go out with Tucker."

They'd both have to don some serious acting skills. Sabrina would have to pretend she approved of Jaylee and Jared's relationship, and Arielle would have to pretend to be Sabrina.

She didn't want to go to the wedding. Didn't want to see Jaylee. And she especially didn't want to see Jared.

But what about Tucker? *Is it worth losing him over? Can't you bury your pride for one event? Just hold your head up and stick it out?* Fear was such an ugly thing.

"What do you think?" Arielle asked.

"You know this doesn't change anything. My going to the wedding—"

"I know."

She knew what Arielle was thinking. That if Sabrina saw their family, everything would fix itself. Maybe it would. Maybe that's why Sabrina was afraid to go home.

But in all fairness she was asking Arielle for a huge favor. It was a fair trade. "You'll be here for another two and half weeks. Tucker will expect to see you a lot." As it was, he'd wonder why she hadn't called tonight. "Maybe six or seven dates?"

"*Six or seven?* It's only one wedding."

"It's an entire weekend."

Arielle tilted her head and pursed her lips. "Three dates."

"Four."

The pause between them was filled with the pitter-patter of rain. Finally Arielle extended her hand. "Four."

Sabrina put her hand in her cousin's, and they shook on it. "Deal."

Harbormaster: When I can't sleep, I work.

Sweetpea: When I can't sleep, I write to you.

Chapter Nineteen

"Why are you here so early?" Nate asked Tucker as he ducked into the office, out of the rain.

Tucker wiped his face dry and pulled his schedule for the day.

"You look awful."

"Thanks." Tucker had a grand total of three hours sleep. He'd worked until eleven and risen before dawn. He was avoiding the inevitable phone call or email from Sabrina. He'd had his cell phone off since his run-in with the Sweetpea imposter the morning before and hadn't checked his email since. Sabrina must be wondering what was up.

"Something going on?" Nate scanned the schedule. "Business all right?"

If only it were that simple. "Business is fine." Why did relationships have to be so complicated? He'd pursued Sabrina for over a year, and he was farther than ever from winning her.

"Must be a woman." Nate chuckled.

Tucker scowled.

Nate sank into Dorothy's chair and spun around, lacing his hands behind his head. "Women are complicated, man. I'm just glad you've moved on to a real, live relationship."

Tucker had recently confided in Nate about Sweetpea, but had never told him it was Sabrina. She was as real, live a woman as you could get. Unfortunately, she didn't want a real, live relationship.

"You *have* moved on . . ."

Tucker pulled a file and looked over the bills. "Not exactly."

"You're still mooning over some woman you don't know?"

"I do know her." He knew her better than he'd known any woman. Maybe that was why it hurt so much.

"Dude. She could be a man."

"She's not a—" Oh, for crying out loud. "I mean, I really know her. In person."

Nate's eyebrows scrunched under his hairline. "I'm confused. This is that email chick we're talking about, right?"

He made it sound cheap and meaningless. "She's not an email chick."

"Well, when you don't know her name—"

"Sabrina." What could it hurt? Nate didn't go to the café, and there must be a dozen Sabrinas on the island.

Nate smiled. "Ah, she does have a name. So you know who she is. What's the holdup?"

"The holdup is she knows who I am, but she doesn't know I know who she is."

"Come again?"

Tucker exhaled hard. "Stay with me here. I met her . . . where she works. I wanted to get to know her, but she was kind of stand-offish." More like a brick wall, but why put a nasty spin on things. "I found out her email and started writing her anonymously, and that's how this whole thing developed."

"But you said she knows who you are. At least, I think you did."

Tucker clenched his jaw. Thinking about it still caused a jolt of humiliation. "After we wrote awhile, I sent her my picture."

Nate smirked. "Pretty gutsy."

"Pretty stupid. She didn't own up to knowing me."

"Ouch."

"She sent me a photo of some other woman, passed it off as herself."

Nate leaned back in the chair until it bumped the desk. "What, is she, like, homely or something?"

Tucker narrowed his eyes. "No, she is not homely." She just thought she was.

"Just asking."

"She's very attractive. I don't know why she sent some other woman's picture."

"She doesn't want to meet you."

"You think?" It wasn't something he liked to dwell on. He was a decent guy who just wanted to love her. Having that love rejected wasn't the best feeling in the world.

Tucker explained how he'd devised a plan to spend time with Sabrina and how they'd spent the past six weeks working together.

"You're paying her, and she's pretending to help you find her own self."

"Basically."

"You're both nuts."

He was beginning to think so too. "It wasn't going too bad until the other woman showed up yesterday."

"What other woman?"

"The woman from the photo. Sabrina said she'd found my friend and, *voilà*, here she is."

"Dude. That's bad."

Uh, yeah. He checked his watch. Should he go to the café as usual? Would the imposter be waiting for him? He didn't know what to do.

"Who's the woman from the picture?"

"No idea."

"This Sabrina chick must have some reason for not wanting you to know. You sure she's not, like, married?"

He was tired of defending her. "She's not married."

"Well," Nate set his arms on the armrests, smiling. "What's this other chick look like?"

"I don't care what she looks like. It's Sabrina I care about." And he'd been so close to a breakthrough. That last night when he'd driven her home. The way she'd looked at him, her defenses crumbling down to her feet. He felt it. He'd been certain he was making headway. That it was only a matter of time before she admitted who she was.

And then she'd gone and found an imposter to play her part. Had the moment in the car scared her? Made her retreat even further? What was it that kept her away?

"What are you gonna do?" Nate's voice pulled him from his thoughts.

There was the question. So far he'd avoided any possibility of seeing or hearing from Sabrina, but that couldn't continue forever. He'd have to do something. He needed to figure it out soon, though, because Sabrina expected him at the café in fifteen minutes.

"Don't know," he said. "I don't know."

※

Sabrina topped off Oliver's coffee, then bussed table six for Evan, who'd spilled milk down his apron and gone for a fresh one. Business was slow that morning, the drizzling sky keeping most of the tourists in their hotels.

She checked the clock and saw it was time for Tucker. He hadn't responded to the message she'd sent first thing that morning. She'd awakened early and spent forty-five minutes writing one paragraph while Arielle hung over her shoulder. What was he thinking? Surely he was eager to see Arielle.

The bell above the café's door jingled, and Tucker entered, dripping wet from the rain. From the corner of her eye, she watched him navigate the tables and seat himself in his usual spot.

She grabbed the coffee and headed his way, her heart speeding in anticipation. *Keep your cool. He doesn't know anything.*

He flipped his cup as she arrived at his table. "Morning," he said, then cleared his throat.

She forced a smile. "Good morning." She poured the coffee. "Did you get Arielle's email?" *Well,* that *was abrupt.* She bit her lip, wishing for a little tact.

He sipped the coffee. "No, actually. I got in late last night, and I was at work before dawn this morning."

Oh. She hadn't figured on that. *Well, don't just stand here with the coffeepot like an idiot.* "She wants to see you, of course."

"Funny, she didn't before."

Sabrina panicked, speechless. *Think of something!* "You're right. I—I had to do some fast talking, and you were right all along. She was afraid of taking the relationship to the next level. But she can explain all that to you later."

He nodded once. "Right."

He didn't seem eager. He hadn't even asked why Arielle hadn't contacted him yesterday.

"She's staying with me."

"Really." His cap was pulled low over his eyes. When he looked down, she couldn't see them at all.

"So you can reach her there. Or email, whatever." At least if he wrote, she'd still have contact with him. *You truly are pathetic.*

"I'll do that." His smile didn't reach his eyes. Why didn't he seem happy? Why were his eyes as dim as the harbor on a moonless night?

The kitchen bell dinged. Table four's order. "Great."

An awkward silence bloomed. "I'd better fetch that order."

"Sure." He snapped his damp paper open to the front page.

She turned toward the kitchen before she realized she hadn't refilled Oliver's cup and he hadn't said a word. How was she going to survive the day? How would she survive the next two weeks knowing Arielle and Tucker were together?

And what if Arielle and Tucker . . .

No. She wouldn't even consider it. Wouldn't allow herself to remember what had happened the last time the man she loved connected with one of her cousins.

Harbormaster: Where were you last night? I missed you. I kept imagining you were out with some hot guy, and he was whisking you off to some fancy restaurant in his convertible. I almost came over there and beat him up when you came home. Oh, wait. I don't know where you live.

Sweetpea: Smart aleck.

Chapter Twenty

Tucker turned down the collar of his polo and fastened the bottom button. He'd found Sabrina's email when he returned from work.

I'd love to see you tonight. It doesn't matter what we do.

She'd suggested he email or call to set up a date. He'd replied and suggested dinner out. At least a restaurant would offer distractions, and he wouldn't have to worry about awkward silences.

His cell phone rang, and he snatched it off the table, along with his keys.

It was Tracey. "Hey, sis, how's it going?"

"You're on your way out the door, aren't you?"

"How the heck did you know that?"

"I have my ways. I just called to chat. Want me to call back?"

Tucker got into his car and started the engine. Tracey sounded better than she had the week before. She was going to get through this. "I can talk on my way there."

"Your way where?"

"On a date." That was going to invite the questions.

"Oooh, I'm so happy for you. You're finally getting somewhere with Sweetpea. I think I hear some wedding bells in your future."

He gave a wry laugh. "Not exactly. The date isn't with Sweetpea."

"What? I thought for sure she was the one you'd finally bring home to Mom."

He turned onto Main Street, already crowded with summer people heading to dinner.

He didn't feel like talking about Sabrina and her stand-in. "It's a long story. I'll fill you in later. How's your new job going?" He worried about her starting over in a big city like Atlanta. But if the accident several years ago had revealed anything about Tracey, it was her iron-core strength. He'd never seen anyone fight so hard through rehabilitation.

"I really like it. The people are friendly, and I feel useful—which I needed."

They chatted a few minutes about her job.

"You been eating?" he asked when there was a break in the conversation.

"Yes, Mother."

"Someone has to keep you in line." He turned onto Sabrina's street. "Speaking of which, have you heard from Mom and Dad lately?"

"Only every other day. Sheesh, you'd think I was suicidal or something."

He thought of Sabrina's dad and all the pain his selfish exit had caused. "Don't even joke about that."

"Sorry. You know what I mean though. I am starting to feel like I can breathe again. I found a good church too. I'm thinking about joining the choir."

"That would be good for you."

He pulled into Sabrina's drive and turned off the ignition.

"You're there, I'll let you go."

He smiled. "Am I on hidden camera?"

"Have fun on your date."

"Not likely."

Tracey laughed. "Lucky girl."

They said goodbye, and Tucker pocketed his cell, exiting the car. He was so not looking forward to this.

His good shoes crunched on the gravel of Sabrina's driveway as he approached the steps to her loft. Would Sabrina answer the door? If only he were going out with her. He'd wondered a hundred times if he should call an end to this absurdity. If he should admit he knew who Sweetpea was. But he was in too deep now. To do so would, at the very least, embarrass her, and, at the worst, anger her to the point of excluding him from her life. He was, after all, guilty of gross deceit. Then again, so was she.

In the end, he'd convinced himself to get through the dates.

How long could Arielle possibly stay? A few days? A week at most? Sabrina hadn't said in the email. At least, he assumed it was Sabrina who had written. But maybe not.

He shook his head, frustrated, as he approached the door. *Get it together, McCabe.* He raised his hand and knocked.

A few seconds later, Arielle appeared in a white dress. "Hey there!" Her smile was Julia Roberts wide. "Let me grab my bag, and we're good to go."

As she reached somewhere to the side, he peeked inside, hoping for a glimpse of Sabrina, but the interior was dark and empty.

"All set." Arielle slipped the thin strap of a wallet-sized bag over her bare shoulder.

He led the way down the stairs, opened the car door for her, then slid behind the wheel. He wasn't sure what to say, how to act. Maybe he should save them both a lot of trouble and tell her he knew she was an imposter. Before he could weigh the thought, she spoke.

"It's a gorgeous night, oh, my goodness. Even the rain was nice last night. I love the smell of rain, and the sunshine today . . . I could stay here forever."

She had a soft Southern twang that sounded nice. Comforting. "Summer's nice, but it gets pretty cold in the winter. We year-round residents have to take extra precautions to preserve heat in our homes. Especially the homes on the shore."

"Still, the summer is to die for, and the whole place has great energy. How many people can say they live on an island? It's awfully romantic."

He turned out of the drive, wishing she hadn't mentioned the *r* word, because now an awkward silence filled the car. He turned up the air. If only he'd thought to turn on the radio before he'd arrived. It would've filled the silence, but to do so now would be rude. Would she expect him to hold her hand? To kiss her good-night? His palms grew sweaty and sticky on the leather steering wheel.

"Well," she offered, "I guess since we already know so much about each other, we can skip the small talk, huh?"

"Guess so." He pulled his lips upward and hoped for the best. "Though I don't know what you do for a living or where you live. You've been a little secretive about that." He spared her a quick glance.

She laughed, nervously, he thought. "I live in Georgia, but you probably guessed that by my accent."

"Where 'bouts?"

"Macon. Born and raised there. I teach preschool, which I love. Not for everyone, I know, but those little rug rats are a hoot."

Even if he hadn't known Arielle wasn't Sweetpea, he would've been suspicious by now. She had too much energy, and she talked more and faster than his friend did. It hit him that her job gave her summers off. Still, surely she couldn't stay long on a preschool teacher's salary. Though since she was staying with Sabrina, there weren't many expenses involved.

Arielle related a story of a boy in her class who'd gotten a LEGO stuck up his nose. His mom took him to the ER to have it removed. She chuckled at the memory.

"Reminds me of when I got that Tic Tac stuck up my nose. But you already know all about that." Wasn't *he* feeling ornery tonight.

"Right, right." She fidgeted with her fingernails. "Those kids. Oh, my goodness, the things they say. I could fill a book. One day in the spring, I went home early because I'd developed a fever, and Mia, this adorable little girl, told her mom I went home with a temper! Can you imagine?"

"Must be pretty entertaining." She was nothing like Sabrina. Not that she wasn't nice. She seemed sweet, but she wasn't Sabrina.

He pulled alongside DeMarco's clapboard building and parked, then helped Arielle from the car. The shingled sign over the front windows swung in the wind.

"This looks so quaint. I love Italian."

Tucker opened the door for her, and the host greeted them.

"Hey, Tucker." Brant Morgan shook his hand.

Tucker introduced Arielle, then Brant seated them at a table for two by the front window. The restaurant smelled of seafood and garlic, and Tucker's stomach gave a rumble.

Across the room, he recognized an older man he'd taken to Martha's Vineyard a couple days before, along with the man's wife. The Wescotts were old money—he'd seen all the signs—and Mr. Wescott was a semiretired attorney.

Mr. Wescott caught his eye, a quick look of recognition followed by a crease on his forehead. Before the man could look away, Tucker nodded his chin upward. The guy probably wondered how a boat driver could afford a place like this. Tucker's lips twitched.

Arielle opened the menu, but her eyes took in the restaurant's atmosphere. "It's like a cozy country inn, very intimate. And it has nice flow, which is unusual for a restaurant."

Tucker opened the menu and perused the items, though he knew what he was ordering. "Are you interested in decorating?"

"It's a hobby. I've already rearranged Sabrina's loft. The furniture placement was all wrong. She needs to change the wall color, but I haven't quite decided on a color."

"Well, you just got here."

Her smile seemed to freeze for a minute. "That's true. I've got plenty of time to decide. That olive green is so dark and depressing."

He wondered what she meant by "plenty of time." "How long can you stay?"

She closed her menu. "A little over two weeks. We'll have plenty of time together."

He tried for a smile. "That's great." Over two weeks. How many dates would he have to go on? He'd figured on two or three tops. This was getting worse and worse. Maybe he could email and say the spark just isn't there in person. That was a thought.

The server arrived to take their drink orders, but since they'd decided what they wanted, they ordered their food as well. He wanted the date to be over, and the sooner they got their food, the sooner he could take her home. *Relax. You don't want her thinking you're eager to get rid of her.* He felt a moment's pang at the thought. It wasn't that she wasn't nice, but he was tired of feeling uncomfortable. And it wasn't the stiff shoes.

While they waited for their food, Arielle more than held up her end of the conversation, but service was slow, as was typical for a fine-dining establishment. His faking skills lacked, and he didn't have it in him to try harder. Still, she didn't seem to notice.

"Oh, my goodness, this looks delicious," she said when the server set their plates down. She stabbed a small chunk of spinach leaves and slid it into her mouth.

Tucker placed the white cloth napkin in his lap, said a quick silent prayer, then dug his fork into the capellini. He ate here regularly, and the shrimp-and-pasta dish was his favorite, but tonight his taste buds seemed numb.

"This place is hopping. I'm surprised you were able to get a table on such short notice."

"Fine dining is huge here, especially during the summer. This place books up a week in advance, but Brant's an old friend, so he squeezed us in."

"Is Nantucket the kind of place where everyone knows everyone? The island's not awfully big."

"Yes and no. In the summer the place swells with tourists and summer people. A lot of them own homes and come back year after year, so you get to know them. I have a lot of repeat customers that I've gotten to know pretty well."

They talked between bites of food, her mostly. When the server brought their bill, he tucked the cash inside the leather folder and set his napkin on his plate.

He didn't want her to feel rushed, but she'd finished her salad and refused dessert. Maybe she was ready to call it a night too. Or maybe she'd suggest they go somewhere else. Dread parked itself at the curb and fed the meter.

"You probably have to get up early in the morning," she said. "Maybe we should call it a night."

He exhaled quietly. "I do have an early run. Would you mind?"

She set her napkin on her plate and scooted her chair back. "Not at all. We'll have plenty of time to catch up."

That's what he was afraid of. Tucker walked her to the car and helped her inside, then slid behind the wheel. The evening was warm and dark, the stars dotting the cloudless sky.

"Thank you so much for supper. I haven't had a salad that tasty in years, truly."

"You're welcome."

They talked about his job on the way home, and he told her stories he'd repeated a dozen times to other people. Before he knew it, he was pulling into Sabrina's drive. A light shone from the window, and he thought he saw the movement of a shadow. He put the car in park, turned off the ignition, and helped Arielle out.

As they ascended the steps, his mind spun. Would she expect a kiss? Should he shake her hand? Hug her? Nothing seemed appropriate. None of it appealed.

They reached the small landing, and she faced him in the circle of porch light. Her skin glowed golden. "Would you like to come in for a few minutes?"

His eyes went to the window. He wanted to see Sabrina, but not under these conditions. "Not tonight, thanks. I should get home and to bed."

She touched his arm. "Well, thanks so much again for a wonderful supper."

"You're welcome." Should they make plans to meet again? She probably expected him to, but he couldn't bring himself to do it. He only wanted to get home and write Sabrina.

Sweetpea: When Jared left me for my cousin, I couldn't help but think of my dad and the pain he went through when my mom died. I even wondered if suicidal tendencies were hereditary. Is that crazy?

Chapter Twenty-one

Sabrina pressed her face to her bedroom wall and peered through the sliver between the drapes. It seemed Tucker and Arielle had been gone an eternity. She tried to stay busy with last-minute research for Renny's new manuscript, but her mind hadn't left Tucker and Arielle all night.

A glance at her digital clock proved they'd been gone less than three hours, not long for a date. But, oh, those hours had crawled.

When Arielle and Tucker came into view, her mood deflated like a punctured party balloon. They looked perfect together. Arielle in her gauzy white dress that displayed her long, lean legs, and Tucker in his crisp white polo that showed off his broad shoulders. Her sleek blonde hair was the perfect foil for his dark curls. They looked like a couple. Like the wealthy summer people who sunned in the afternoon and dined in the evening at the exclusive restaurants.

They stopped on the landing, Arielle too close to the door to be visible from her position. Tucker was in full view, the cone of porch light a mellow spotlight on him. Would he kiss her goodnight? *Please, no.*

She didn't think she could bear it. The image of Jared and Jaylee flashed like a blinding beacon in her mind, the memory so fresh it stole her breath.

She turned, pinning her eyes to the opposite wall, to the shadowed painting of a meadow she'd bought at a Nantucket gallery the summer before.

Arielle wouldn't let him kiss her, would she? Then again, she'd asked her cousin to play the part. And wouldn't Tucker find it odd if she turned away? *Why didn't I have this conversation with Arielle?*

Unable to resist, needing to know the truth, no matter how much it hurt, Sabrina peeked through the slit. She heard Arielle's voice, muted, then Tucker's. Why hadn't she thought to crack the window?

Her cousin reached out and touched Tucker's arm. Sabrina pressed her lips together. Was touching really necessary? She waited to see how Tucker responded.

But after a small smile, he was turning away, and then she heard the click of the front door closing.

Tucker's footsteps thudded down the stairs, and a moment later his car started.

"It's safe to come out now," Arielle called.

Was it? Did she want to hear about the date? *It's not like you have a choice. You're going to write him, and he's going to find it a little odd if you have date amnesia.*

A tap sounded at her door. "Sabrina? I know you're awake."

"Come in." She plopped on the bed as Arielle entered and flipped on the lamp.

Arielle's dress flared across the bed as she sank down. "Aren't you going to ask?"

"Ask what?"

"You know very well what. He didn't try to kiss me goodnight— not that I would've let him."

Sabrina didn't know how to respond. Admit she'd been worried? Pretend she didn't care?

"In fact, I have to say it was nice to go out with a gentleman. He didn't so much as touch me all night."

Relief flowed through her. Then a second later, she wondered why he hadn't. If he felt as strongly about Sweetpea as he claimed, wouldn't he want to touch her? Hold her hand? Maybe he was taking it slow, afraid of rushing after it had taken so long to find her.

"Did he ask how I found you?" Sabrina asked. They'd invented a story about Sabrina finding Sweetpea on another chat site, just in case.

Arielle frowned. "Actually, he didn't. So much for all that planning and rehearsing."

"Well, he might ask next time." The whole idea of a next time made her want to vomit. "Or the time after that."

Arielle spread out beside Sabrina and rolled to her side. "We went to DeMarco. Have you been there?"

"Not a restaurant I can afford on my salary, but I've heard it's good."

"Oh, my goodness. That salad was heavenly. They brought around this dessert tray, and the panna cotta looked so yummy, but I knew you were waiting with bated breath, so I said I was full, but truth be told, I could have *so* tied into that thing."

Sabrina felt a stab of guilt for the jealousy she'd felt moments ago. "I appreciate that. So, what did you talk about all night?"

"A lot of nothing, really. I told him about teaching preschool and that I live in Macon. You said that was okay, right?"

He would've been suspicious if Arielle had kept her occupation a secret. "Right." Sabrina turned to face Arielle, propping her head on her palm.

"So, let's see, we talked a little about his job and about Nantucket. I told him I'd be here for two more weeks."

He must've jumped for joy. Maybe the whole kiss thing had worked out for tonight, but did she really think a red-blooded man was going to keep his hands off a woman like Arielle for two weeks?

"That was kind of odd, come to think of it. He didn't seem overjoyed, but maybe he's not the expressive type."

"Did you make plans to go out again?"

"Not really. We just said we'd chat on email and left it at that."

They were quiet for a moment, and the hum of the air conditioner filled the gap. Would he write when he got home tonight? Would he say he enjoyed her company?

"He's a good listener. I think I talked too much, but it was so refreshing to be with someone who actually listened, you know?"

He *was* a good listener. Why did it hurt that Arielle appreciated the same quality? No, not hurt. Made her feel threatened.

Tucker is not Jared. And Arielle is not Jaylee.

Yeah, but Tucker thinks Arielle is you.

She squeezed her eyes closed and wished this were over, for time to fast-forward two weeks. She longed for simpler times when she was just Sweetpea and he was Harbormaster.

It had gotten so complicated.

"I wish you'd tell him the truth." Arielle disrupted her thoughts.

"You just want to bail on our agreement."

"I just want you to find happiness."

"Trust me, telling him the truth won't bring either of us happiness."

"Maybe you're not giving him enough credit. He seems like a nice guy."

She'd been through this. But even a man like Tucker had his limits. She couldn't expect Arielle to understand, because her cousin didn't know the whole truth. "Just keep your end of the bargain, cuz, and I'll keep mine."

Arielle sat up and shrugged. "Fine by me. He's not exactly an ogre." She scooted across the bed and bounded onto her bare feet. "Well, I'm going to grab a bath before bed."

"Goodnight." Sabrina lay in bed until she heard Arielle shut off the water, then went to check her messages. Tucker had been home long enough to write. She opened the program, half hoping he'd written, half terrified of what he'd say.

In the end, all the emotions were for nothing, because there was no letter from Tucker at all.

Chapter Twenty-two

When Sabrina returned from work the next day, Renny was pruning the rosebushes by the front walk. She hunched over a bush of pale pink buds, examining the petals of a rose in full bloom. The sun beat down on her back, and beads of sweat had popped out on her forehead.

"Afternoon, Sabrina." She straightened from her crouch, swiping the dirt from her red Hawaiian shirt.

Sabrina pulled her mail from the box and approached. A warm breeze blew in off the ocean, stirring the loose hairs by her ear and carrying the fragrance of roses. "*Gan Eden* is looking lovely. But you picked a hot day to garden."

"Well, the muse always visits while I'm pruning, and after last night, I need a visit."

"Didn't go well?" Sabrina leafed through the mail, bills and junk.

"I wrote two pages in four hours."

When Renny was on a roll, she could write two chapters in four hours. "Sorry to hear that. I'm sure it'll come to you. It always does. Have you heard anything on *Danger in the Night?*"

Renny stretched her back, then swatted a fly. "No, no, nothing good, I'm afraid."

It was early yet. Surely they wouldn't reject that one. Renny's stories were better than many of the books she bought. She shook her head. "It's only a matter of time."

Renny laughed, her leathery skin creasing at the corners of her eyes. "You're good for my ego, that's for sure. How are you doing, *amita?* Having a nice visit with your cousin?"

"She sure livens up the place."

Renny laughed. "I'm glad she came. She's good for you—full of *simchah!*"

"*Simchah?*"

"Joy, full of joy! You need more joy in your life. Your cousin's a believer?"

"How did you know?"

Renny tapped her temple. "I know these things."

Sabrina shook her head and made her exit. Returning to her apartment, she was glad she had no plans. Tucker hadn't written that morning, and she was eager to see if an email awaited her.

The loft was empty, and a hot-pink Post-it was stuck to the computer monitor. *Went for a walk.*

Sabrina set down her bag and opened the email program. Tucker had been quiet at the café. A couple times she'd caught him staring at her with a strange expression, but when she caught his eye, he looked away.

One message waited in her inbox, the one she'd hoped for. She clicked on it.

Hey there. Hope you had a good night's sleep. I checked my schedule when I got home last night and it's pretty full today. Saturdays are crazy this time of year. Would you mind if we didn't get together tonight? My schedule is lighter tomorrow. Maybe a picnic or something? Your call. If you're up late tonight, maybe we can chat awhile.

Sabrina stared at the words until they blurred. He hadn't mentioned their date. Hadn't said what a wonderful time he'd had, hadn't told her she'd looked beautiful. But then maybe he told Arielle that last night.

Not something she wanted to dwell on.

At least he and Arielle wouldn't be together tonight. It was something. Her cousin would be relieved.

She hit Reply and stared at the blinking cursor. He wouldn't get the message until late, but maybe when he returned they could get a conversation rolling.

Before she could formulate her thoughts, Arielle returned, her skin glistening from the hot sun, her hair pulled into a high ponytail. "What a gorgeous day! I think I'll put on my suit and go for a swim. How was work?"

"Okay." She closed the email, deciding to put supper on first. She wondered if Arielle had gone to the grocery for fruit and vegetables. Having a vegetarian in the house changed mealtime.

At least Arielle would be home for supper, though she didn't know yet. "I have good news," Sabrina said.

Arielle rummaged through her stack of clothing, a lumpy pile she'd shoved into the hollow recess of an end table. "You're telling Tucker the truth?"

Sabrina tilted her head and glared at the back of her cousin's head. She refused to give credence to the comment. "You're free for the night. Tucker wrote and said he was booked until late."

Arielle pulled her bathing suit from the pile and stood, frowning. "Oh. Well, okay."

"I'll put something together for supper," Sabrina said.

"I already made a fruit salad for you. I guess I'll be having that too."

Sabrina watched Arielle shut the bathroom door. Not the reaction she'd anticipated. Not that her cousin had seemed disappointed, but for someone set on avoiding dates with Tucker, she sure hadn't seemed relieved.

Harbormaster: I talked to Tracey again today. Divorce is for the birds. I'll spare you the sordid details, but I still want to beat the guy to a pulp. Does that make me a bad Christian? There's all that "turn the other cheek" stuff, but it's hard when the person who got slapped is your sister. She's already been through so much.

Chapter Twenty-three

Tucker couldn't stand the thought of faking it today. He had to pretend to some extent, but after his long day yesterday and another restless night, the thought of entertaining Arielle, running into people he knew, introducing them, was too much to stomach.

Which was how he came to be standing at his grill, flipping steaks. He checked the underside of the T-bones, then flipped them, hoping Arielle would arrive before he singed them. The potatoes were done, resting in their foil skins on the table. The broccoli was keeping warm in the steamer.

He'd offered to pick up Arielle, but she'd replied, saying she'd walk over. He'd been certain it was Sabrina at the keyboard. It had been her short, snappy sentences. When he envisioned Arielle's emails, he imagined long run-on sentences, punctuated with "oh, my goodness."

Now he wondered if Arielle had gotten lost between Sabrina's house and his. She was twenty minutes late. The sun was low on the horizon, but there was plenty of daylight left. She didn't believe in cell phones—he'd learned that on their last date—so he couldn't call. He should call Sabrina and see when she'd left. The idea gelled, an excuse to talk to her more than anything.

He turned the grill to low and dialed Sabrina. She picked up on the second ring.

"Hey there," he said.

The pause lasted so long he was about to identify himself, but then she responded.

"Tucker. Is something wrong?"

He smiled at her immediate assumption. "Does something have to be wrong for me to call?"

"If past experience is anything to go by."

"Come on, now. Isn't it possible I just called to see how your day went? To see if Oliver stumped you with a word yet? To see if—"

"When you're on a date with my—with Arielle—not so much."

Tucker sank into the wicker deck chair. "Okay, you got me. I called to see when Arielle left. She's not here yet." At the moment, he wouldn't mind if she had taken a detour. A very long one.

"Oh. I was out getting groceries, so I'm not sure when she left. I wouldn't worry though—she gets distracted sometimes and tends to run late."

Interesting observation for someone she'd supposedly just met. "You seem to know her well."

"Not really. She just—well, she's been staying here, so you get to know a few things about a person, that's all."

"Right." He didn't want to talk about Arielle. "So, are you going to keep me in suspense?"

"Am I supposed to know what you're referring to?"

He smiled. "Oliver. I believe he'd dropped the word *propinquity* as I was leaving this morning." He'd been late for his first run or he would've stuck around for pure entertainment value.

"It means nearness or proximity."

"You subscribe to Word of the Day or something?"

"Something wrong with that?"

Tucker laughed. "There is such a thing?"

The doorbell pealed. A pang of disappointment ricocheted through him. He wished he hadn't planned this date with Arielle. He wanted to talk with Sabrina all night. Maybe if he ignored her, she'd go away.

"Was that the doorbell?" she asked.

Busted. He entered the house through the sliding door. "Actually, yeah. I guess Arielle made it."

He stopped by the recliner, delaying the inevitable, not wanting to hang up just yet. *Just say it, Sabrina. Tell me the truth, and trust me to handle it, whatever it is.*

"Well," she said. "Have fun."

Not likely. "Talk to you later." He hung up, disappointed and frustrated. *Get it together, McCabe. You're going to scare the poor girl if you open the door with a snarl on your face.*

He took a deep breath and opened the door.

"Hey!" Arielle looked fresh and energized from her walk, her cheeks flushed.

"Come in."

"I love your house. It's so cozy and, oh, my goodness, right on the water. And I do mean *on* the water. Sabrina said you had a boat tied up outside, but I didn't know she meant *right* outside."

He smiled at her enthusiasm. "You can look around if you want while I get the food on the table."

"Sure."

Tucker dished up the broccoli and brought it outside. By the time he had the grill off and the steaks on the plates, Arielle was opening the sliding screen. Her hair was down, and it swung around her shoulders as she turned.

"Your house is so gorgeous. I could help you with the—" Her eyes seemed to stick on the plate of food.

He pulled out her chair. "What's wrong?"

The wicker chair crackled and creaked as she sank into it. "Nothing. I—I was just saying I could help you with the flow of your room. If you want, that is."

He studied her as he sat down. Something was wrong, though she was trying to cover with a smile.

"Yours is well-done, the way you like."

"Thank you."

He handed her the A1 sauce, but she hesitated before taking it. "I have Worcestershire if you prefer."

"No, no. I—I think I'll enjoy it plain."

Tucker dropped his napkin in his lap, breathed a quick prayer, then dug into his steak. It was juicy with a nice tang from the spices he'd used. He remembered when he'd grilled for Sabrina. Had it only been a few weeks ago? He'd had her right there in his house. What if he'd told her the truth? Would she be sitting here now instead of Arielle? Had he missed his opportunity?

He and Arielle made small talk, but conversation became stilted after ten minutes. Tucker wondered how he was going to survive the rest of the night. What had Sabrina been thinking? Arielle was nothing like her. In fact, they were complete opposites. Did Sabrina think he could be fooled so easily?

When they finished eating, he carried their plates to the sink. Upon his return, Arielle's face seemed pale. But maybe the pretense was wearing on her. It was certainly wearing on him.

Her lips turned up as he sat down.

"I didn't know what you might like to do," he said. "I could take you out in the boat. You might enjoy the sunset."

Her face fell.

"Or we could go for a walk or watch a movie. I have a pretty extensive collection—"

"A movie sounds great."

"Good. I'll stick the dishes in the dishwasher while you peruse the selection."

She followed him inside, and he pointed her to the DVDs. He wondered if she'd select a mystery or suspense like Sabrina, or if she'd choose based on her own preference.

When he returned to the living room, she'd chosen *Witness*, one of Sabrina's favorites.

"Ah, an old favorite, huh?"

"Why not?"

He put in the DVD, started it, then settled on the couch, close enough to Arielle but not touching. He fast-forwarded through the previews, and they watched the movie's opening.

Having seen the movie twice before, his mind wandered. Would Arielle expect him to make a move? How many dates could they go on before she realized something was wrong? A man who had feelings for her would've kissed her by now or would at least be looking for the opportunity.

He studied her from the corner of his eyes. Her arms were wrapped around her stomach, and she wore a grimace.

"You okay?" Her skin looked pasty.

"I—I'm not feeling so good." She swallowed, panic lacing her eyes.

He paused the movie, and Harrison Ford's face froze. "Can I get you something?"

Before she could reply, she sprang from the couch and ran down the hall. The bathroom door slammed shut. Two seconds later, he heard her hurling.

In the kitchen, he filled a glass with water, wet a washcloth, then tapped on the door. "Arielle? You all right?" Maybe she had a stomach virus, though it was an odd time of the year for that.

"Yeah." Her voice shook on the word. She vomited again.

He wanted to do something, but what? He felt helpless. Maybe she had food poisoning. Couldn't be the steaks, too soon for that.

Poor girl. Here she was, pretending to be something she wasn't, and now she was ill on top of it. Maybe the stress of pretending was getting to her. What a disaster. All of it avoidable if he'd just admitted the truth to Sabrina when he'd had the chance.

Maybe it's not too late.

A flush sounded; then the water ran. A few minutes later, she opened the door. Her pallor was even worse, a greenish cast ringed her mouth, and smudges of black stuff underlined her eyes.

He handed her the water and washcloth.

Her hands shook as she took them. "Thanks. I'm sorry—"

"Nothing to be sorry for. Come sit down."

"I must have a virus or something . . ."

"I'll take you home as soon as we're sure you're okay." He hoped Sabrina didn't catch whatever Arielle had. Looking at her now, wobbly and shaky, he wondered if she was going to make it through a car ride.

"If you don't feel up to going home, you could stay here."

He helped her to the recliner, and she ran the washcloth under her eyes. "I'm a mess." Her eyes filled, spilling over.

He hovered, uncertain. "Are you feeling worse?" Maybe a trip to the hospital was in order.

She sniffed. "No." But the tears flowed faster.

Maybe it was stress. What if he told her the truth? It would ease her worries about his expectations. It occurred to him belatedly that she may have taken his offer to stay as more than he'd intended.

Her breath wavered on an inhale. "I'm not her." The words shook on release.

She seemed rooted to the seat, so he sank onto the sofa. He wondered if she was aware she wasn't making sense.

"I can't do this anymore." She put her hand on her stomach, her eyes finding his again. "I'm not feeling so good."

He stood. "Why don't you—"

She darted past him, down the hall, into the bathroom. *Slam.*

He grimaced at the violent sound of her stomach emptying its contents. His own gut tightened in response. What if she *was* sick from the pretense? What if it was getting to her? His offer to stay the night hadn't helped.

A few minutes later the toilet flushed and the faucet ran again. This had to go down on record as his worst date ever. He'd never actually made a woman sick before. *Way to go, McCabe.*

The door opened. He helped her back to the living room, a sick sense of déjà vu filling him.

She was weaker and shakier than before. He wondered if this was going to continue all night.

"I feel better," she said after she settled in the recliner. She picked up the washcloth and wiped her eyes again. "That's what I get, eating steak after four years meat-free."

"You're a vegetarian?" He thought back to the night at DeMarco. She'd ordered salad, but that wasn't unusual. If only she'd said something. No wonder she'd eyed the food with horror. He felt like a heel.

"You must be confused, and I don't feel well enough for tact, so I'm just going to say it. I'm not your Sweetpea. I'm not her. I'm Sabrina's cousin from Macon, Georgia, and that's all I am. I didn't write all those letters. I'm sorry."

Sabrina's cousin? The one cousin was marrying her ex-fiancé, so this must be the other one.

"You don't seem awfully surprised." Arielle licked her lips. "Or mad." She was looking better, getting her color back.

"I'm not. I know you're not Sweetpea."

She stared at him. Emotions flickered across her face, starting with confusion and ending with anger. "What?"

"I guess it's my turn to say sorry. I know Sabrina is the one I've been writing."

"You *know*?"

"I know."

She let her head fall against the recliner's back. "If you know and she knows, what in creation am I doing here?"

Tucker folded his arms. "She knows and I know, but she doesn't know I know."

Arielle closed her eyes. "I am not well enough for that."

He explained how he'd fallen for Sabrina at the café and tried to get to know her anonymously online. He explained how he'd hired her in order to get her to open up. He explained his disappointment when Sabrina had brought Arielle instead.

"That's not what happened, just so you know," Arielle said. "She didn't know I was coming."

"She didn't bring you here to pretend to be Sweetpea?"

Her head rolled back and forth against the chair. "She tried to keep us apart, but that one day at the café . . . she just—did what she thought she had to do."

The realization comforted him. At least Sabrina hadn't been trying to pawn him off on someone else. She was a victim in this charade too. Sort of.

What a mess I've made of this, God.

"She's going to kill me for telling you," Arielle said.

Maybe if Arielle knew all this, maybe she knew what Sabrina was hiding from. "Why?" he asked. "Why won't she tell me who she is?"

"Why haven't you told her that you know who she is?" she countered.

Ah, the protective cousin had arrived. She was feeling better. "I'm afraid of scaring her away. She—she means a lot to me."

He looked at the TV screen, gone blank from being paused too long. "Look, I know it might seem like I've strung her along, pretending I don't know who she is. But it's not like that. I—I love her, okay? All those letters . . . hearing her heart, night after night. She's special to me. More special than anyone I've ever met."

Would he ever get to tell her in person? Now that Arielle knew, she'd probably tell Sabrina everything. And where did that leave them? Sabrina would be furious that he'd known all along. *Furious* wasn't the word. She might feel he'd played her for a fool. He'd probably get a lap full of hot coffee in the morning.

"Do you know why she won't admit who she is?" he asked again.

Arielle sat up straighter. "I don't think it's my place to say. Oh, my goodness, she's already going to kill me."

Tucker frowned. "Not going to be too happy with me either." Any chance he'd had with her was gone. She might stop writing him. What was he thinking? Of course she'd stop writing. What was he going to do if he'd lost her for good?

Once again he tried to imagine how Sabrina would feel when Arielle told her the truth. Furious wouldn't be the half of it. Add humiliation to the mix, and you had a concoction that spelled "The End." Done. Finished. *El finito.*

Though he loved Sabrina, he wasn't blind to her faults. She was stubborn as a bull. Look how long she'd harbored anger toward her ex-fiancé and cousin and her whole family for that matter. If she felt Tucker had betrayed her trust, she'd never forgive him. Why hadn't he considered that before?

The dishwasher kicked into a different cycle. A boat engine roared to life outside.

"Unless . . ." Arielle started. Her brows puckered, and she chewed on her lower lip.

"Unless . . . ?"

She locked her gaze on his. "Unless we don't tell her."

The idea didn't sound as fabulous as she apparently thought it was. It would get them both out of trouble, but what good would it do otherwise? At least they could dispense with the date pretense. That was something.

"I probably shouldn't tell you this, but Sabrina cares about you a lot. Maybe you already know that."

Something warm and pleasant swelled in his gut. He'd hoped. He'd even been pretty sure at times. But hearing it confirmed was euphoric. "She hasn't said it in so many words."

"Well, this hasn't been easy on her, watching us go out."

"Really?" It shouldn't make him feel so pleased.

"She was peeking out the window the other night when you brought me home."

She did care. She cared a lot. It must be eating her alive to see him and Arielle together. Especially after losing one man she loved to a cousin. "You're not suggesting we make her jealous."

Her face fell a bit. "That would be kind of mean. Especially after what Jaylee did."

"It's still pretty fresh."

"Oh, my goodness, she would hate me."

It would be cruel to stir up those feelings of betrayal. It might not even work. He imagined Arielle flowing in the door from one of their dates, raving about him. He imagined the letters he could write, the things he could say about their time together.

The look of hurt on Sabrina's face.

"I don't think I can do it," he said.

"It's for her own good. I don't think you'll get anywhere with her unless she's forced into it. She needs a big push."

But Jared had hurt her deeply. He didn't want to do the same. He couldn't believe Arielle was willing to risk her relationship with her cousin.

"I love her, too, you know," Arielle said. "Besides, maybe we can get you some time alone with her."

Now, *that* idea appealed. "How?"

"I don't know. We'll figure out something."

It would be worth it if he could get time with her. He missed having her over. He longed for time alone with her. If Arielle could arrange that, maybe he could show Sabrina how much she meant to him, how special she was.

"Deal?" Arielle asked, her brows disappearing under her bangs.

What did he have to lose? "Deal," he said, hoping he hadn't made another mistake in what was beginning to look like a long string of gross miscalculations.

Sweetpea: Life is so confusing.

Chapter Twenty-four

Sabrina read the first lines of Tucker's email, her chest muscles squeezing the oxygen from her lungs. Arielle had said little when she'd returned from Tucker's. Only that he'd served steak and she'd gotten ill.

She hadn't looked ill when he'd brought her home. Her makeup was faded, but she had a natural glow and a mysterious smile hovering on her lips. *I'll bet Tucker kissed her,* Sabrina thought, her knees going weak.

Arielle took a quick shower and lay down on the couch. She was asleep within minutes, and Tucker's message arrived shortly afterward.

She reread the first lines.

Hey there. Hope you're feeling better. You had me worried. I hope you're not coming down with something—talk about bad timing, huh?

When you're feeling better I'd like to take you out on my boat. Maybe we can have a picnic on the water and watch the sunset. I always wanted to do that with you, did I ever tell you that? There's something romantic about twilight on the water. The colors are unbelievable.

Write soon and let me know how you're feeling, okay? Until then, I'm thinking about you . . .

Was he really? Or was he thinking about Arielle?

Of course he's thinking about Arielle, you fool. That's who he's spending time with. He's falling for her. Just like Jared fell for Jaylee.

And she had no one to blame but herself.

Her fingers hovered over the keyboard. She wanted to reply. Maybe he was still at the computer. But he thought she was Arielle. What if he went on and on about the date?

As hard as she'd tried to hang on to him, he was slipping away. The thought brought a tidal wave of fear. She poised her fingers over the keys and started typing.

I'm feeling better. It was probably something I ate for dinner—

She paused. Maybe it would be better if he thought it was a stomach virus. That would require a few days to recover. Three days of keeping him and Arielle apart. She deleted everything she'd typed.

I'm still feeling a little nauseated. I'm sure I'm fine. Probably just a stomach virus or something.

She sent the message, then tapped her fingers on the desk, waiting. Behind her, Arielle snored lightly on the couch. She'd thank Sabrina for buying her time. Of course, for all she knew, the effects of the steak might actually last a few days. She hoped not, for Arielle's sake.

After several minutes, she gave up hoping for a reply from Tucker. He must've gone to bed.

She changed into her pajamas and curled under the quilt, tucking the cover under her chin. If they could survive the next two weeks, everything could return to normal. Arielle would be gone, and she and Tucker could continue writing. She could revert to sneaking glances at the café while he sipped his coffee. That was all she wanted.

But if that were all she wanted, Sabrina wondered why the thought of returning to normal carved a hollow spot in the center of her chest.

Laughter was the first thing Sabrina heard when she opened her apartment door. She closed the door, tossed her bag on the desk, and followed the sound of Arielle's soft voice. She found her cousin on the balcony, the phone cradled between her cheek and shoulder.

"That's so true," she was saying. "Oh, hi, Sabrina." She pulled her bare feet from the railing. "Sabrina's home," she said into the phone. "Okay. All right." Another chuckle.

Sabrina went to the kitchen and pulled the pitcher of iced tea from the fridge. She wondered who Arielle was talking to. It could be Aunt Bev, or Uncle Everett, or Jaylee. But Sabrina had a sinking feeling it wasn't any of them. Through the mesh screen, she heard Arielle laugh again.

Sabrina poured a glass of tea and took a long drink. They'd been busy at the café. Evan had called in sick and they hadn't found a replacement, so she'd bussed her own tables.

She heard the beep of the phone being turned off, then the grinding slide of the screen door.

Arielle stopped inside the door, all signs of laughter gone. "You told him I'm sick?"

Sabrina tried to decipher the source of her cousin's anger. "You were puking at his house last night."

"I feel better today. I told you this morning."

"You said you still felt nauseous."

"I said I felt a *tad* nauseous, but much better."

What in the world? Her cousin set the phone in the cradle and passed her on the way to the fridge.

"He has tickets to the community theater tonight," Arielle said.

"And . . . ?"

Arielle tossed her a look. "And now I can't go because he thinks I'm sick. He said I needed to stay home and rest."

"I thought you'd be relieved to avoid a few dates. I thought you'd be pleased."

Arielle surveyed the contents of the fridge.

Cold air washed over Sabrina, raising gooseflesh. Clearly Arielle was not pleased about missing her date. Clearly Arielle wanted to be with Tucker. Sabrina tamped down the fear that perched on the stoop of her heart.

Arielle pulled out a bottle of organic juice and shut the door. "What's done is done, I guess." She passed Sabrina and called over her shoulder, "Oh, I told Tucker you'd accompany him to the theater tonight."

She *what*? Sabrina followed Arielle to the living room, where her cousin had plopped on the sofa and flipped on the TV.

"You told Tucker *I'd* go with him?"

Arielle took a swig of her juice, taking her time, then set it on the end table and smiled sweetly. "I thought you'd be pleased."

Sabrina's own words came back to haunt her, and Arielle seemed to enjoy the fact. "Why can't he just skip the dumb play?"

"His secretary has one of the lead roles, and this is the last night it's showing."

So what? Why did that require him to drag Sabrina along? Her heart was performing a traitorous show of its own. "Can't he go alone?"

"He has two tickets."

"Well, can't he find someone else?" Her voice crescendoed.

Arielle changed the channel, surfing with a calmness that made Sabrina want to throttle her.

"I told him you loved the theater," she said. "And there's no need for his money to go to waste. He's already underwriting the Nantucket Light Keepers," Arielle so kindly reminded her.

Soundkeepers. Sabrina clenched her teeth. That was beside the point. Arielle knew how hard it was for her to be with Tucker. Then again, it was hard to see Arielle with Tucker too. Which was worse? Waiting for Arielle to return from her date or suffering through it herself?

Come on, Sabrina. Suffering?

Okay, so she enjoyed being with Tucker. That was the problem.

"He's picking you up at five."

"Five?" The play couldn't start until seven or eight at least.

"You're going to supper first."

"Supper?"

"Are you going to repeat everything I say? He already had reservations."

Oh, sure, reservations. That made all the sense in the world. Sabrina glared at Arielle, but her cousin seemed oblivious to her distress.

Finally, Sabrina wandered toward her bedroom, seeing her own dazed look in the oval mirror Arielle had hung in the hall. That thing was so coming down.

She was going on a date with Tucker.

You are going on a date with Tucker.

It's not a real date. He doesn't even want to be with you. You're a substitute for Arielle. Keep that in mind.

If she remembered that, she'd be fine. The only question was, could she make herself remember it when she was staring into Tucker's eyes across a candlelit table?

Sweetpea: Little-known fact about me: I haven't worn heels since prom.

Harbormaster: Little-known fact about me: I haven't worn a suit since I dropped out of law school. Little-known fact number two: I have a special appreciation for people who wear choking neckties.

Chapter Twenty-five

Le Languedoc was a restaurant and inn located downtown on Broad Street. The building featured cedar shake shingles, white trim, and blue shutters that matched the awning outside.

Sabrina fidgeted with the wispy strings of her belt as Tucker pulled into a parallel parking space. She pressed her lips together, unaccustomed to the sticky feel of lip gloss. *"Just a little,"* Arielle had said when she protested. *"You already have those gorgeous thick eyelashes, but a little color on your lips will do wonders."*

Judging by Tucker's expression when she'd answered the door, maybe Arielle was right.

Tucker turned off the engine, then helped her from the car. They hadn't taken five steps when her heel caught in a crack on the sidewalk. She stumbled forward.

Tucker steadied her, his hands burning the skin on her arms.

Idiot! She couldn't even walk a few steps in these ridiculous shoes Arielle had loaned her. Why hadn't she worn flats? She felt like a little girl playing dress-up in her mother's clothes.

"I should've let you off at the door," Tucker said.

"I'm a klutz in heels."

He laughed, a deep and warm sound. "This from the server who balances five plates of food on a tray, skirting tables and waitstaff without a spill?" He smiled.

The host took them out to the terrace, a secluded garden covered with an awning. Over their heads, white lights twinkled.

They were seated at a blue checkered table in the corner of the patio. Patrons filled the other tables, their chatter creating a quiet clamor. They looked at home in this upscale restaurant with their expensive jewelry and name-brand handbags.

The evening was mild, and the patio shielded them from the ocean breeze. The delicious aroma of garlic and steak filled the patio.

"Have you been here?" Tucker asked.

"No, I haven't."

He looked so handsome in his crisp white shirt and blue tie that matched his eyes. *He's wearing a tie.* She opened the menu, more to occupy her hands than anything. He opened his as well, and when the server came, they placed their orders.

Before an awkward silence could settle, Sabrina spoke, "So, your secretary is in the play?"

He propped his arms on the table, and she noted the sturdy thickness of his forearms protruding from his rolled-up cuffs.

"Dorothy. She's sixty-something years old and half-blind, but she throws herself into whatever she's doing."

"So what's the play we're seeing?"

"*Cinderella*. She plays the fairy godmother."

"Oh, for a fairy godmother! I can see where that would come in handy." She cringed as the sentence ended and took a sip of water. She wished she knew what to say, how to act. It had been a long time since she'd had a date.

"You don't need one tonight. You look especially nice. I like your hair down."

After staring at Arielle, she probably seemed plain as a weed next to an exotic orchid. "You don't have to say that." She immediately wished she could recall the words. He was going to think she was fishing for a compliment.

"It's true."

She glanced at him. His eyes turned down at the corners. She picked at the tablecloth, deciding not to argue. She didn't need someone patronizing her, especially not Tucker. Even Jared had rarely commented on her appearance. She didn't expect flattery.

Sabrina checked her watch, wondering how long the food would take and what they'd talk about until it arrived.

"Bored already?" The corners of his lips turned up.

"No, I just—I just wondered what time the play starts."

"We have plenty of time."

Great. Just what she wanted to hear.

"How was work today?" he asked. "You seemed busy."

She was glad for the trivial subject. "Evan was sick, so we bussed our own tables, which made it pretty hectic."

"Do you like working at the café?"

She shrugged. "I'm good at it, and it pays the bills."

"What about your work for Renny?"

"I love it. I hope someday when she's published and writing a couple books a year, she'll want me full-time."

The server brought their drinks. Sabrina sipped her tea. She'd thought Tucker might question her about Arielle, but he seemed content with casual conversation.

She had a flashback of the night he'd driven her home when it was raining. That night replayed itself often with vivid accuracy. The warmth of his palm on her wrist, his deep, throaty laugh. The woodsy smell of his cologne a breath away. The way he'd looked at her, as if she mattered.

Had Sabrina read more into the moment than there was?

Did it matter? There was no future for her and Tucker. Nothing beyond an email relationship.

And what would happen if Tucker and Arielle fell in love for real?

Tucker escorted Sabrina into the United Methodist Church, placing his hand on the small of her back as they navigated the crowd. She looked beautiful in the elegant navy blue dress. Her hair spilled around her shoulders like a dark veil, and it was all he could do to keep from touching it, from running his fingers through it. It had been a task keeping his eyes off her.

He greeted a few people, nodding on their way past. Normally he'd stop and chat, but he wanted Sabrina to himself. They found seats near the middle of the room next to an elderly couple who held hands. He wished he could take Sabrina's hand, but he was supposed to be in love with Arielle.

When Sabrina set her purse on the floor, he sneaked a glance at her. Her hair swung forward, falling across her cheek. She sat back, tucking it behind her ear, and the fragrance of lilacs and something citrusy reached his nostrils. He inhaled deeply. This may be his one and only date with Sabrina. If only he could get her to confess what was holding her back. He couldn't even email the question now. He was supposed to think Arielle was Sweetpea.

"You haven't asked about Arielle," she said, as if reading his mind. Her hands were folded primly in her lap.

"Was I supposed to?" A woman squeezed by with her teenage daughter.

"I thought you might ask my opinion of her."

"What do you think of her?"

She tossed him a look. "She's awfully nice."

What could he say? He had to be careful. "She wears a lot of makeup."

"I thought men liked that." She reached over her shoulder, to toy with her ponytail, he thought, but when she found her hair unbound, she returned her hand to her lap, seemingly oblivious to the jingle of her charm bracelet.

"Some do, I guess. I always liked a more natural look." His eyes took in Sabrina's natural beauty. Sometimes nature couldn't be improved upon.

He cleared his throat. "But you're right, Arielle is nice. A little . . . flighty, but nice."

She frowned at him, as though she were trying to look inside him.

"What?" he asked.

"I thought you liked her."

Was he handling this badly? What did she want from him? Did she want him to want Arielle? Was he supposed to be singing her praises? "I do."

She faced forward, the picture of calm. He would've believed it, except her hands were clasped so tightly her fingertips went pink, her knuckles white.

Ah, it's getting to you, my little Sweetpea. He was torn between tweaking her jealousy and comforting her. He settled somewhere in between.

"She's not exactly what I expected."

"What do you mean?" Her voice sounded squeezed through a knot.

He didn't know how to respond and wondered why he'd said it. The lights dimmed, and Tucker breathed a sigh of relief as the audience quieted.

"To be continued," he whispered.

Sabrina's mind wandered through the play. What did he mean Arielle wasn't what he'd expected? Was that good or bad? Was he suspicious that Arielle wasn't Sweetpea?

"There's Dorothy," Tucker whispered in her ear a few scenes later. His breath tickled strands of hair and sent a shiver down her spine.

Onstage, his secretary had made her appearance to a disheveled-looking Cinderella. The godmother's sparkly silver dress hugged her thick waist, and she waved a magic wand as she talked. Her brunette wig matched her conspicuous glasses. As oddly casted as she was in the role, she played it well.

As the play progressed, Sabrina forgot the woman was sixty-something and wearing thick glasses. All the actors were talented and, by the time Prince Charming put the glass slipper on Cinderella's foot, Sabrina realized she'd lost herself in the story.

After the actors returned for a curtain call, Tucker and Sabrina followed the throng of people into the darkened night. He ushered her with his hand at her back, and Sabrina's pulse sped at his touch. She could feel the heat of his palm through the thin material of her dress.

When they reached his car, he helped her in, then slid in behind the wheel. "What'd you think?"

Sabrina clutched her bag in her lap. "Bravo. Your Dorothy seems pretty feisty."

"You don't know the half of it." He tossed her a grin.

His right arm rested on the console between them, inches from her own. If this were a real date, would he take her hand? Would he lift it and press his lips to the ridges of her knuckles?

"I realized halfway through the play I left my cell phone on my boat," he said. "Would you mind if I swung by the harbor and got it? They're calling for rain tonight."

"Not at all."

Once they left the theater traffic, the roads were deserted. He turned toward the wharf.

The thought of a few extra minutes with Tucker gave her more joy than was healthy. *Just a few extra minutes. What could it hurt? Tomorrow will be here soon enough, and he'll be back with Arielle.*

She didn't want to think about that. She wanted to live in the moment for a change and not consider the ramifications.

She laid her head against the headrest and closed her eyes. For now, right this minute, Tucker was beside her. If she concentrated, she could hear him breathing above the whir of the car's engine. If she inhaled, she could smell the woodsy fragrance of his cologne. If she tried hard enough, she could imagine the way his jawline would feel against the softness of her fingers.

"You look peaceful."

Her eyes snapped open. He was parked outside his office, the streetlamp shedding a pale yellow glow on his features. How long had they been there?

"What were you thinking?"

A hot flush climbed her neck. "I don't remember."

"You had a little smile."

Remembering the direction of her thoughts, her mouth went dry. He was looking at her like—like he wanted to look at her. Like there was no place else he'd rather be. Like there was no one else he'd rather be with.

Absurd. He was in love with Sweetpea. Or Arielle. She wasn't sure which. She wasn't sure who was who anymore.

She cleared her throat. "You'd better get your cell."

He looked away, out over the darkened water, and removed the key from the ignition. "Come with me."

"Why?" His boat was a short walk down the pier.

"I want to show you something."

In his boat? At night?

"Come on. Take a walk on the wild side. You don't have to get up early tomorrow."

He had her there. "True."

"Come on." He motioned toward the door with his head and exited the car.

Curious, she did the same, then followed him down the lit pier, careful of where she stepped. With her luck, one of her heels would catch between the boards and she'd fall flat on her face.

When they reached his boat, he helped her onboard. "Have a seat back there," he said. "Are you chilly?"

"Are we going somewhere?"

"Don't you trust me?"

"Do you always answer questions with questions?"

He smiled. "Only with you." He untied the boat, then retrieved a thick blanket from a cubby and wrapped it around her.

Tucker sat in the captain's seat, pocketed his cell phone, then started the boat.

Moments later, they were gliding slowly through the harbor, the lights from town growing distant. What were they doing out here? Why did he want to take her out on his boat when he should be eager to get her back to her apartment and see how Arielle was faring?

Why are you looking a gift horse in the mouth?

When they cleared the harbor, he accelerated and the wind kicked up, blowing her hair off her face. She drew the blanket tighter and closed her eyes, letting the cool air wash over her. What would it be like if Tucker were her boyfriend? What would it be like if he were her husband? If everything was different? If everything weren't so complicated?

She opened her eyes and watched him navigate the smooth water of the ocean. The moon lit his white shirt, and the wind tossed his hair. His shoulders looked sturdy and broad, wider than the seat back.

He looked back at her as if to confirm she was still there. They exchanged a smile.

Pretend everything is different. Just for tonight. What could it hurt? Just to be with him and relax and let whatever happens happen.

It wasn't like anything would happen anyway. Tucker was in love with Sweetpea. Or Arielle. Or whomever.

She shook her head, not wanting to work at the fussy knot her life had become. *Forget all that. Just think about now. Right now. Out here. Me, Tucker, and the open sea.*

A few minutes later he slowed the boat and the wind died down. It was dark out on the water. Only the glow of the moon lit their way. The boat drifted to a stop, and Tucker walked toward her.

"You look cute all wrapped up like that."

She was sure she'd never been called cute. Maybe she had a fairy godmother after all.

Tucker sat beside her on the narrow bench. "We're here."

She looked around them. There wasn't a soul or anything else around. Only a blanket of darkness that hid the world from sight. "Of course we are."

He smiled. "You're going to be just like Dorothy when you're about sixty, know that?"

"Alone and feisty?" The words slipped out before she knew they were coming. She didn't like how vulnerable it made her, and she wished she could snatch them back.

"The feisty's a definite."

She could feel him watching her. She didn't dare look. Her eyes fixed on the water off the port side where the moon shimmered on the surface.

"The alone part is up to you," he said.

Not so much, she thought. But what did he know?

You weren't going to think about that tonight, remember? Why was it so hard for her to relax?

Uh, because she had one hundred and ninety pounds of man flesh sitting beside her?

Not just any man flesh. Tucker. And he was looking at her again.

"Why are we here?" Her voice cracked on the question.

He didn't seem to notice. "The second show."

"Second show?"

"Up there." He pointed upward, and she followed the direction of his finger.

Overhead, the sky was a black canvas, smooth as velvet and dotted with what looked like a million fireflies. She'd never seen so many stars. Some as bright as the moon, others so faint she could hardly see them.

"There are so many." She looked up until her neck began to ache.

Tucker placed his arm along the back of the bench. "Lean back." His eyes glowed dark in the shadows. Her heart stuttered.

She laid her head in the crook of his elbow, the strength of his bare arm resting against her neck. Oh, how she'd missed this. Things email could never provide. *Security. Comfort.* She could list a hundred more.

She inhaled the scent of his cologne, not daring to tear her eyes from the night sky. *Smells.*

The boat rocked slightly, a cradle on the water. The wind hummed a lullaby and waves lapped the boat, a gentle percussion.

"Sabrina?" he whispered.

Voices. She swallowed around a dry lump in her throat. *Don't look.* Do. Not. Look.

"What?" she asked so quietly she wasn't sure if he heard.

"Look at me." His voice, low and deep, beckoned.

She turned her head. He was so close. His breath mingled with the salty air and cooled her cheeks. His eyes . . .

His eyes were a deep pool, the color of the ocean at midnight. Had anyone ever looked at her the way he looked at her now? What was there, shimmering on the surface? Longing? Devotion? Desperation? She soaked it up, every ounce.

"What?" she asked, needing to know. Needing words, not trusting herself to interpret his expression.

And then his hand was on her face, his palm cooling her flushed cheek. His thumb grazed the ridge of her lower lip, and she thought her lungs might explode. *Touches.*

He drew closer, and then his lips were on hers, the merest of touches. A butterfly's wings, a baby's breath. It shook her to the core.

His lips tasted hers, teasing gently. *Kisses.*

It had been so long since she'd felt like this. Had she ever felt like this? Really wanted? Needed?

He deepened the kiss, ran his hand through her hair. This wanting, this needing, filled her to overflowing. She breathed him in. Tucker. The man who knew everything about her, the man who knew her every scar, inside and out. The man who loved her anyway.

Only he didn't know he loved her. Didn't know she was Sweetpea.

He was supposed to love Sweetpea.

Why was he kissing her? She felt betrayed. Then she felt silly because he was betraying her with *her*.

Even so, the feeling persisted. If he loved Sweetpea, how could he kiss Sabrina? She felt enraged on Sweetpea's behalf.

She pushed at his chest, breaking the kiss.

Her breaths came hard and short. She saw the confusion in his eyes before she turned. "Take me home."

"What's wrong?"

The answer to that question could fill a book. Did she have desperation written all over her? Is that why he'd kissed her? Wasn't he getting enough action from Arielle? The thought provoked her.

"I've had enough of the second show." She pulled the blanket more tightly around her, but the chill seeped right through.

He touched her hair. She flinched away. A lump the size of Texas lodged in her throat, and she feared she'd really make a fool of herself if he didn't put some distance between them. Why had she come out here with him? What was she hoping to prove?

Her thoughts from earlier washed over her, mocking her. *Pretend everything is different. Just for tonight. What could it hurt? Just to be with him and relax and let whatever happens happen.*

Stupid, stupid.

Now she knew what it could hurt. Her. The ache spread from her throat to her stomach and camped there.

"I'm sorry," Tucker said, still looking at her. "I didn't mean—"

Didn't mean what? Didn't mean to kiss her? Didn't mean he wanted her? Didn't mean to betray the woman he really loved?

She'd never know what he didn't mean, because after he said it, he went to start the boat, leaving her huddled against the cold.

Sweetpea: Kissing is highly underrated. Characters in movies go from first base to home plate in one giant leap. Doesn't anyone value the kiss anymore?

Harbormaster: I do. ;-)

Chapter Twenty-six

"So . . ." Arielle bombarded Sabrina the moment she stepped from her room the next morning. "Tell all. How was your date?"

Sabrina rubbed her temples and headed to the kitchen to start a pot of coffee. "I don't want to talk about it." It was bad enough that it kept her awake until all hours of the night. The quiet ride back on the boat. The tense ride home in the car. The awkward goodbye. Her mind had whirled like a hurricane all night.

Arielle followed her to the kitchen. "What do you mean you don't want to talk about it?"

"I mean I don't want to talk about it." Sabrina rinsed the pot and added water to the tank. "As far as I'm concerned, you're fit and healthy again. You go out with him tonight." Even as she said it, a stab of jealousy pierced her.

Thank goodness it was her day off. She didn't think she could face Tucker so soon after—

"I don't understand."

"You don't have to." It was Arielle he wanted to see. She'd only been a substitute last night. Maybe he'd been lonely and desperate or something. Maybe he wasn't the man she thought he was. The Tucker she knew would never have made out with one woman while in love with another.

Maybe he was like Jared after all. Maybe all men were.

She set the filter in the basket and plugged in the coffeemaker, shoving the bracelet up her arm when it got in her way. So much for the tangible reminder of heartbreak. She'd blocked everything sensible from her head the night before. Her head pounded now. She needed caffeine. She needed peace. She needed a new life.

"Did he say something?" Arielle asked.

Sabrina turned toward the living room.

Arielle took her arm. "He thinks I'm sick. This is your chance with him."

"I don't want a chance with him. He's all yours." Sabrina jerked away.

"Sabrina!"

"I'm taking a shower." Sabrina closed the conversation with the slam of the bathroom door, but not before she heard Arielle's growl of frustration.

Renny was potting a plant in the front yard when Sabrina was leaving for the post office. Her shadow fell over Renny's form like a dark cloak as she approached.

"Morning," Renny said. Her bare knees dug into the soil and her calloused heels were propped in the air.

The yard had become a profusion of color over the past several weeks. Sabrina wondered where Renny was going to fit the flowering plant once it was potted.

"*Gan Eden's* filling up fast," she said. "Are you stuck on your story? Do you want to brainstorm more?"

Renny scooped dirt from the bag into the terra-cotta pot. "No, I don't think so." She brushed her hair from her face with the back of her hand.

"I had some ideas the other day that might work."

Renny put down the scoop and sat back on her haunches. "Listen, I decided to give up writing."

Had the woman lost her marbles? "What?" Of all the zany ideas Renny had, this was the craziest of all.

"Don't worry, I want you to stay in the apartment, and I won't charge you rent. I love having you here; you're good company. More than that. You're like a daughter to me, really. But I'm done with writing. I'm going back to what I know. Gardening."

"You know how to write. You're extremely proficient."

"Not proficient enough."

"I've told you, it's just a matter of time!" The thought of all that talent wasted made Sabrina ill. "Someone is going to want *Danger*, just wait and see."

Renny retrieved the shovel and started scooping. "No, no, I don't think so. I'm tired of trying. I'll never be good enough."

"You're good enough *now*. You'll probably get the call any day."

"No, I won't."

How could the woman be so stubborn? "I guarantee it."

Renny laughed, not the pleasant kind. "I don't think so, *amita*."

There was something Renny wasn't telling her. "What's going on, Renny?" Something wasn't right. Why would Renny quit when she was still waiting to hear from several publishers? Unless she'd gotten the rejections . . .

"Did you—have you heard from the publishers?" Surely not. Sabrina couldn't imagine anyone saying no to *Danger*.

"No, I haven't." Renny patted the dirt with her bare hands, packing it tightly around the gnarled stem.

"Well, see then? There's still—"

"I didn't send them." Renny pulled her soiled hands back and grabbed another scoop of dirt.

"Are you still unsatisfied with the characterization? Do you want to work on it some more?"

Renny stood suddenly, rubbing the soil from her hands. She studied Sabrina as if trying to make a decision. Finally she said, "Come here."

She walked toward the porch, and Sabrina followed onto the brick stoop. They entered the foyer and walked past the airy living room into the dining room, which overlooked the ocean. Renny bent in front of the cherry hutch and pulled out a fat drawer. It settled in place with a squawk.

Renny stood upright. "There they are."

Sabrina looked into the drawer, filled to the brim with stacks of paper. "Your manuscripts?"

"All nine of them."

Renny's words from earlier soaked in. *"I didn't send them."*

That's not what she meant . . . that she hadn't sent them, any of them, to publishers. Was it?

"I never sent them." Renny crossed her arms over the toucan on her Hawaiian shirt. "I didn't mean to lie, but I couldn't do it."

"Why not?" All those years of writing, locked in a drawer? All the work Renny had done, all the work Sabrina had done, wasted? She didn't understand.

Renny went to the sink, turned on the faucet, and pumped some soap. "I was waiting until my writing was good enough. I was going to go back and fix the earlier ones." She shook her head.

Sabrina looked at the drawer of manuscripts. The earlier ones were weak in spots. Pacing problems, weak writing, stale characters. The last three, though . . . she'd wondered why some publisher hadn't snapped them up. Now she knew. Renny had never sent them.

"Why did you do it, then? Why spend all those hours—all those hours, Renny!—writing and brainstorming and researching? Why do all that work and just . . . stick it in a drawer?"

"I don't expect you to understand."

"You're right, I don't understand." Her words wobbled. All those hours she'd spent researching locations and killing methods and police procedure. All those hours reading and editing. She'd been paid for her work, but it felt empty. All for nothing. Where was the faith Renny clung to?

"What about God and his will that you talk about?" Sabrina asked. "How can he do his will when you won't do your part? Send them to your agent now. At least the last three."

Renny dried her hands. "I can't."

Sabrina reached into the drawer. "Then I will." It was a small matter to write a cover letter and stick them in the mail.

"Stop it!" Renny grabbed her arm. "Leave them be. It's not your place."

Sabrina straightened. Renny was right. It was her work. Her decision. She had to know one thing. "Did you ever intend to send them?"

Renny closed the drawer, and it creaked under its load. "I was going to send them when they were good enough."

Sabrina opened her mouth to say they already were, then shut it again. She'd already said it, many times over. One more time wouldn't make Renny believe it.

Harbormaster: Remember in sixth grade when we just had to ask a friend if so-and-so liked us? Life was much simpler then, huh?

Chapter Twenty-seven

Arielle was waiting for Tucker when he arrived at the Even Keel Cafe. He navigated the maze of tables and joined her in the corner against the rear wall. The scent of seafood and grilled steak tempted his taste buds, reminding him he'd skipped lunch.

Arielle had left a voice mail on his cell, asking to meet after work. She looked up as he approached, her wide smile absent.

"Hi." He slipped into the chair across from her.

"You got my message, obviously."

"I tried to call you back. Got the machine." He'd expected Sabrina would answer. Had half hoped she would. Maybe she had caller ID.

Before he could grab the menu, Arielle leaned forward, intent. "What did you do?"

"What? Nothing."

"You didn't tell her you knew?"

"No." He wondered why she thought that. Sabrina had been

so quiet all the way home, despite his efforts to initiate conversation. "What did she say?"

"She didn't say anything. And I mean nothing. She's been quiet as a mouse all day."

Was she angry he'd kissed her? He'd hoped Arielle might be able to enlighten him. He'd almost sent Sabrina a message that morning. But he could hardly mention the kiss when he wasn't supposed to know Sabrina was Sweetpea.

"What did you do?" Arielle was giving him the look she probably used on her preschoolers. Her arms were crossed now.

He shifted on the chair. He could say nothing. What was another secret between friends? Then again, what did it matter if he told her?

"I—uh. I might have kissed her."

Her eyes widened. "You *might* have kissed her?"

Was that such a bad thing? A man kissing the woman he loved? He had nothing to be ashamed of. Then why did he feel so rotten?

"Well, she kissed me back," he said in a small voice.

"But that's a good thing," Arielle said.

"You would think." It had sure felt good. It felt good every time he relived it too. Right up until the moment she pushed him away and demanded he take her home.

"Huh," Arielle said.

The server came and took their orders. The restaurant was noisy, the clatter of scraping utensils and the loud hum of too many conversations. It was giving Tucker a headache.

"So, what happened after the kiss, if you don't mind my asking."

"She pushed me away and asked me to take her home."

Arielle frowned. "That's it?"

He decided to skip the part about his heart beating madly. "That's it."

Arielle sipped her tea. "Huh," she said again when she set down her glass.

That's all he got? *Huh*? Weren't women supposed to have insight into each other's souls? They were cousins; she had to know something.

"She thinks you're cheating on her," Arielle said.

"What?"

Arielle took a white bottle from her cavernous bag, unscrewed the lid and dumped green powder into her water. It turned cloudy.

"You're supposed to be in love with Sweetpea, who you're supposed to think is me, and yet you went out with her and put the moves on her." She stirred the water and took a sip.

The stuff looked like algae water. Tucker grimaced. *And steak makes her ill?*

"She thinks you're cheating on her," Arielle said.

"You mean on Sweetpea?"

"Who is supposed to be me."

Tucker rubbed the back of his neck. For crying out loud.

"She feels betrayed."

"By her own self?"

"Think about it. You're not supposed to know she's Sweetpea, so what's she supposed to think when you're in love with Sweetpea, yet kiss her?"

So complicated. When had life gotten so complicated? What sense did Arielle's speculation make? How could he cheat on Sabrina with

Sabrina? Though, in a wacky sort of way, it made sense when you figured Sabrina didn't know he knew. He rubbed his eyes.

"I have a tincture for headaches if you want to try it."

He looked at the disgusting green water. "If it's anything like that, I'll stick to Tylenol, thank you."

She shrugged, capped the white bottle, and tossed it into the cavity of her bag.

"So what now?" he asked. "What am I supposed to do?" Arielle was her cousin. Surely she had some insight, some idea about how to make Sabrina crack.

"You connected online, and that's comfortable for Sabrina. That's your only real connection at this point. I suggest you go back to that."

"I want a real relationship with her."

Arielle gulped down the green stuff, gave a tiny shudder, then followed up with a sip of tea. "You just work on the relationship where she's comfortable." She smiled furtively. "And leave the rest to me."

Sweetpea: Have you ever told anyone about our letters?

Harbormaster: Just my sister.

Chapter Twenty-eight

Sabrina heard the ding of a message hitting her inbox and realized she'd forgotten to reduce the volume before turning in. She wasn't sleeping anyway. She crawled out from under the covers and crept into the living room. Arielle, a shadowed lump on the couch, breathed a soft snore.

Sabrina slid into the chair and moved the mouse, awakening the computer. It was Tucker.

Are you awake? he'd written.

Like she could sleep after fretting over Tucker and Arielle all night. Her cousin had returned with a mysterious grin that left Sabrina with an empty ache.

Yes.

Sabrina had wanted to ask Arielle how their date went. But each time the words had caught in her throat. What if she didn't want to know? A new message arrived with a ding. Sabrina muted the volume, then opened the message.

Wanna chat awhile?

Yes, she typed.

What was Tucker thinking about right now? Was he remembering his night with Arielle? Was he thinking about how beautiful she was in her gauzy white shirt and fitted jeans? Another message arrived.

Are you going to answer all my questions with a yes?

She smiled.

Yes.

It had been a while since they'd chatted on email. She missed it. She missed him. Her thoughts turned to the kiss they'd shared on the boat the night before. If she closed her eyes, she could still feel his lips on hers. *You have got to stop this! It's getting you nowhere.* She opened her eyes to a new message.

In that case, I'll have to come up with something more consequential to ask.

Her stomach fluttered. What would he want if he could ask anything, knowing her answer would be yes?

She placed her hands over the keyboard.

I'll ask the questions here. ☺ If you had one wish, anything you wanted, what would it be? Something for yourself—not world peace.

She sent the message and leaned back, ready for a wait. Instead, an email popped right back.

You first.

She smiled. No fair. She wrote the first thing that came to mind.

To be beautiful.

She sent the message, then wished she could reach into cyberspace and retrieve it. He would say she was beautiful because he thought she was Arielle. And Sabrina didn't want to hear him rave about Arielle's beauty.

She opened his reply with trepidation.

You have a lasting beauty, soul-deep. The kind that won't fade with age. Save your wish for something you need.

Sabrina reread his answer. Not what she'd expected. He hadn't raved about Arielle's beautiful smile or her gorgeous hair. His words warmed her.

She poised her fingers over the keys.

Your turn.

She speculated about what he'd say. More time to enjoy life? A family of his own? She realized she didn't know what Tucker wanted most, and that surprised her after all the hours, all the letters. How had they not discussed this before?

His message arrived, and she opened it eagerly.

I want to know you more.

What could he mean? They did know each other well. And he was now seeing her in person, or so he thought. She wanted to ask, but reconsidered.

Maybe you'd be disappointed.

She sent the message, then feared it had been a mistake. Before the anxiety peaked, she got his reply.

Never.

Sabrina closed her eyes. If only it were true. If only things were different.

This conversation was getting out of hand. It was getting scary. She needed to change the subject.

Tell me something about you that I don't know.

Maybe he'd tell her how he'd gotten the scar between the knuckles of his right hand. Or maybe he'd tell her about his first dance or his favorite place to think.

The email appeared in her inbox, and she clicked it open.

I love you.

Her lungs constricted, pinching off her air supply, making her next breath impossible. Her lungs were too big for her chest. Her skin too tight for her heart. The words, blurred on the screen.

The cursor's arrow pointed to the words, emphasizing them. He'd never said it before, when she was just Sweetpea. Why couldn't he have said it before Arielle had come? She wanted full claim on the words, wanted to snatch them up, draw them close like a favorite blanket.

But the words didn't belong to her. They were Arielle's.

Would Tucker have said them if he knew who she was? She didn't have to answer, didn't even want to. Had he told Arielle tonight? Is that what caused her mysterious smile?

Then she remembered the question that had preceded his words. She'd asked him to reveal something she didn't know. He couldn't have told Arielle. But what if he said it tomorrow night or the next? What if Arielle was falling for him too?

Another message appeared. Her pulse raced like a boat hitting the open sea.

I don't expect you to say anything. I just wanted you to know.

The truth was, and she couldn't deny it any longer, she loved him too. God help her, but she did.

You can't tell him. Yes, she knew that too. There was nothing she could say. Her breath came in quick puffs, drying her mouth. She had to put an end to this conversation before she found herself in deeper waters.

She took the mouse, her fingers trembling, and clicked on the X, closing the program before she did something really foolish— like telling Tucker the truth.

Sweetpea: My aunt and cousins keep trying to reach me. If I avoid them, will they go away? Sorry to be so snarky. I was never good at conflict resolution.

Chapter Twenty-nine

Only when Sabrina saw Tucker ambling toward his table did she realize she'd been hoping he wouldn't have the audacity to show. But there he was, seating himself at his usual table, looking too handsome, turning that crooked grin on Oliver.

Just the one peek of him with his cap pulled low over his curls sent her traitorous mind back to the boat where she'd been within arm's reach of heaven. *Deep breaths, Sabrina. Deep breaths.*

Resolutely, she grabbed the coffee and headed his way. *It's just another day at the café, another morning pouring coffee for Tucker, pretending I'm just his server.* Never mind his lips had been locked on hers two brief days ago.

Not helpful.

Mercifully, Oliver's mug needed to be topped. Two extra seconds' stalling time. "Thanks, Sabrina."

She drew a deep breath and turned. *Just another day . . .* "Good morning, Tucker." *Pour coffee. Do not make eye contact. Do not pass go. Do not collect two hundred kisses.*

Dollars.

"Sabrina." He nodded, or at least, she thought he did.

"I was wondering . . ." he began.

The kitchen bell dinged. Saved by the bell. "Excuse me." She rushed toward the window, but it was Char's order.

"I'll get it," Sabrina told the server, who was in the middle of making coffee.

"Thanks, hon."

No problem. She had to stay busy. Very, very busy. Her mind rewound Tucker's last words. What had he been fixing to say? *"I was wondering . . ."*

If we could talk?

If I could explain?

If we could go back to the break room and make out?

Bad, Sabrina.

She delivered the tray of food, and when three more tables filled in her station, she nearly shouted with glee. Thank God for summer people. They ran her for ketchup, extra napkins, and refills, and she was happy to oblige.

Her contact with Tucker the next half hour was limited to filling his mug twice, as she passed his table. Then finally, he was checking his watch. *Better go, Tucker. Can't be late for work.*

A few minutes later, the bell over the door jingled, signaling his departure, and Sabrina felt the weight of an oil barge lift off her shoulders.

The day was exhausting. The café hopped, but the tips were worth the hard work. By the time she pulled into her drive, however, she was ready for a brisk jog. Arielle had borrowed her bike to ride the Surfside bike path to the other side of the island so she'd be gone awhile. It was the perfect time to slip away and—

Someone was sitting on the steps to her loft. At the sound of her tires on the gravel, Tucker straightened from his slump.

Her heart found a new gear and, unfortunately, it wasn't Reverse. What was he doing here? He must be waiting for Arielle, but her cousin wouldn't be home until this evening. Why wasn't he at work?

She turned off the engine and exited the car, steeling herself against his boyish charm. Her eyes flickered over his broad shoulders and the thick forearms that rested on his jean-clad knees. Nothing boyish there.

A-hem.

"Sabrina." He pulled his cap off and stood.

"Tucker. Arielle's out for a bike ride, and I don't imagine she'll be back for a while." She moved toward the steps, but a body was in her way.

He put a hand on the railing, further blocking her path.

Sabrina hitched her purse strap higher, impatient to pass. Impatient to hide in her apartment.

"I came to see you," he said. Those eyes said things that held hers captive.

She cleared her throat and tore her gaze away. "You saw me this morning."

"I wanted to talk about the other night."

Oh, boy. She didn't want to go there. "I—uh—I was going to—"
Go for a jog. Wash my hair. Organize my sock drawer.

"It'll just take a minute." He shuffled his cap in his hands, turning it in clockwise circles. He was nervous?

Well, he should be. He was the one who—

"Sit down a minute? Please?"

At one glimpse of his baby blues, her mouth went dry. So not fair. Her trembling legs gave way, and she settled beside him. His shoulder bumped hers as he sat, and she edged sideways, which put her knees against his thigh. She shifted again.

Get through this. Hear him out. It'll be over in a few minutes, and you'll be pounding the pavement in no time.

"I know this is . . . awkward . . ."

You think?

"But I'd rather address it and move forward than pretend there's no white elephant in the room."

Sabrina clutched her bag in her lap and watched an ant traverse the step below them. White elephants were underrated.

"The other night I—" He raked his hand through his hair like he might find the rest of the words in there somewhere. "I know you must be confused by what happened."

The kiss flashed in her mind, along with all the feelings it had evoked: desire, tenderness, joy. She had to stop this.

"I'm not sorry," he said in that deep voice that made her miss all those other things email lacked.

He was looking at her, but she was not going to look back. She wasn't. She'd be lost if she did. The other night, darkness had veiled her emotions, but now it was daylight, and she didn't know if she could conceal her thoughts. She was weak, fresh from the memory of that kiss.

"Unfortunately," he continued, "I can't explain why I kissed you. But I don't regret it."

The words brought a mixture of relief and fear and confusion. He couldn't explain? It made no sense. If he were in love with Sweetpea/Arielle, shouldn't he be sorry? Wouldn't his actions make him a first-rate jerk? Yet, she knew Tucker, and that description didn't fit. Not by a long shot.

"I'm sorry for the confusion I've caused. I want to be friends, and my only regret is that I've made things awkward between us."

Friends? Is that what they were? And what would happen when Arielle went home? Or would Tucker ask her cousin to stay? What reason could Arielle give for refusing to see him again, and where would that leave their online relationship? Why did this have to be so confusing?

"Sabrina?"

She had to focus. "Yes?" The black ant was hauling a chunk of something half the size of its body. Probably taking it home to feed its family of five.

Tucker bumped her shoulder, playfully.

She looked at him and fell smack into his shadowed blue eyes. As if the sight of him awakened her other senses, she became aware of his musky cologne, of his hip grazing hers. Have mercy. She could almost taste the kiss they'd shared, feel the tenderness of his lips as they brushed hers.

Now, she watched as those lips parted, as if he were fixing to speak. Her gaze flitted back to his eyes. Yes, he was about to say something. Something important.

She felt herself being pulled in, and she went willingly, all her fight draining away.

And then a memory. The smell of cigarette smoke, the taste of alcohol, the sound of a sheet ripping clear of a mattress.

She cleared her throat and broke eye contact. "Everything's fine, Tucker. Thanks for stopping by." She stood and clutched her bag to her stomach like a leather shield. "I'll have Arielle call when she returns."

She brushed past him, her feet taking the steps quickly as if she were late for an appointment. She heard Tucker's quiet goodbye in the beat between steps and wished her own life crisis could be tweaked and reworked like the plot of one of Renny's stories.

Sweetpea: Why is it so hard to get back on track once something has derailed? Your faith journey, your relationships, your career . . . sometimes it seems like the impossible task.

Chapter Thirty

Sabrina toweled off, then slipped into her favorite capris and a button-down blouse. She cleared the fog from the mirror and ran a comb through her wet hair. Arielle had been gone when she'd returned from work, probably out buying something else for the loft. The air smelled of paint, and the kitchen walls were still damp.

Sabrina surveyed the pale yellow she'd approved several days ago. It was drying to a nice buttery color. Arielle had worked hard to get it painted over the weekend.

The furniture had been rearranged again too. Sabrina frowned as she surveyed the room. Maybe she would get used to it.

She shook the thought and checked the time. Sabrina thought she and Arielle might go to 'Sconset to see the village and take a stroll along the Bluff Walk. Arielle would love the doll-sized houses in 'Sconset and the tiny picturesque gardens. It was Sabrina's favorite part of the island.

They could make sandwiches and take a picnic up to Sankaty Head Lighthouse. It was the least she could do after all the work her cousin had done. Arielle hadn't seen much of the island and, although she hadn't complained, it seemed a waste. Maybe on her next day off they could go out to Altar Rock for a view of the moors, cranberry bogs, and harbor. It was Sabrina's favorite view from the island.

Sabrina worked her hair quickly into a ponytail. It would be nice to spend time with her cousin. And with Jaylee's wedding looming only a few weeks out, she needed the wedding details so she could mentally prepare.

Between the frustration of Renny's disclosure and her confusion at Tucker's declaration of love, the idea of escaping the house, getting away from work, and hanging with her cousin appealed.

In the kitchen, she fished the deli roast beef from the fridge and made a quick sandwich for herself. She filled a pita with the deviled tofu Arielle made the day before, wrinkling her nose at the tangy smell and chunky texture. A wedge of cheese and a bag of chips rounded out the meal. She bagged it and set it in the fridge; then, as she closed the door, she heard Arielle enter the loft.

Her cousin rounded the corner, her ponytail swinging and her cheeks flushed.

She set a bag on the counter. "It is so gorgeous out there! I found a couple cute baskets at a shop in town," Arielle said.

"Thanks." Sabrina pulled the two Nantucket baskets from the bag, one a tightly woven cane with cherrywood rims, the other a door hanger basket in a pleasant honey color. "I like them." She set the baskets to the side, then poured two glasses of iced tea.

"Thanks." Arielle gulped half the glass at once. "Say, is Renny all right? I saw her on my way in, and she was raking the same patch of mulch over and over. She didn't even respond when I said hello."

Sabrina told Arielle about her confrontation with Renny over the manuscripts.

"She's been stuffing her stories in a drawer all this time? But isn't she paying you?"

"Indirectly. She lets me stay here in return for my help."

"What does that mean for you? Aren't you two pretty close?"

"I'm not worried about the apartment. Renny wants me to stay."

Sabrina rinsed her glass and set it in the sink. "What exasperates me is that she doesn't recognize her own talent. You know I don't dish out undeserved compliments, but that woman can write." Sabrina slapped the counter with her palm. "It's so frustrating. But at least now I know the problem isn't with a bunch of incompetent editors."

"No, it's a crazy writer who doesn't believe in herself."

"Apparently."

"Can't you send the stories?"

"I was going to. Renny went postal on me." She'd thought Renny was going to rip her arm off when she reached for those manuscripts. "And she's right. It's not my place. I can't make her want to risk rejection."

A thoughtful silence settled between them. Maybe with time Renny would find the courage to send her manuscripts. Sabrina had done all she could, and she'd have to let it go.

Enough brooding. They had the whole afternoon ahead of them.

"I have a surprise. I packed a picnic and thought I'd take you up to Sankaty Head and 'Sconset. It's my favorite place on the island. You have to see—what's wrong?"

"I didn't know you were planning something. Tucker asked if I could go for a boat ride to the other side of the island. I just have enough time for a bath and—hey, I have an idea."

"Why am I thinking I'm not going to like this?"

"Why don't you come along?" Arielle said with the enthusiasm of someone who'd just invented fried tomatoes.

"Like I want to be the third wheel of your bicycle built for two. No, thanks."

"Come on. We can bring your picnic. It'll be fun."

"Fun."

Arielle frowned. "It's not like you have anything better to do. You'll only sit here with your nose in a book."

"I like having my nose in a book." But even as she protested, her mind went there. She missed Tucker. She wanted to be with him. Heaven knew she'd relived those moments on the boat a thousand times. But this wouldn't be like that night. Instead she'd be subjected to watching Tucker fuss over Arielle, watching him touch Arielle, watching him gaze at Arielle as if she hung the moon. Same boat, different day.

"Again, no, thanks. The whole idea was for you to put your time in with him, remember? We had a deal."

Arielle stared her down, her jaw jutting out.

Stubborn. Sabrina crossed her arms. Let her stare. It wasn't going to work.

Her cousin finally surrendered. "Fine, be that way. It's not like he's a pill to go out with." Arielle stood, and, with a flip of her pony-tail, exited the room. "I'm taking a bath."

⁂

"This isn't working," Arielle called over the wind.

Tucker watched Arielle's hair settle on her shoulders as he slowed the boat and shut off the motor. Water lapped the hull as the boat drew to a stop and seagulls called from the beach. In the distance, the red and white of Sankaty Head Lighthouse was barely visible.

"What's not working?" he asked.

"This whole Sabrina thing. We have to kick it up a notch."

The words opened a hole in his gut. He hated this. He was starting to wish Arielle would go back to wherever she came from so he could pick up the pieces of his relationship with Sabrina.

"Are you mentioning our dates in your emails?" she asked. "Details and stuff that'll make her jealous?"

"Not really. I don't want to hurt Sabrina. I hate thinking about how she feels, knowing I'm with another woman. If it were me, it would be driving me crazy enough without the details." It had bugged him just to watch Cody ogling her, asking her over for dinner. He couldn't imagine how he'd feel if she were right next door with another man.

The sun was sinking in the sky, glowing pink behind a thin layer of clouds. Maybe it was time to call it quits. It was getting him nowhere. He wanted Sabrina to tell him who she was, but if she were going to, she would've done it by now. At this point, he just wanted the intimacy he'd had with her on email. Her letters were different since Arielle arrived, guarded. And how could he blame her?

He shifted toward Arielle. "Maybe it's time for a change of plans."

"What'd you have in mind?" A dainty brow arched.

"Have you considered going home early?"

"Tonight?"

"No, I mean leaving the island."

Her mouth parted, then slowly a look of hurt dimmed the light in her eyes. He didn't know what to make of that. It wasn't like they were buddies or something. She was there to help him achieve his goal, to help Sabrina lower that wall.

"This has been harder than I thought," Tucker said. "And we're not making headway with Sabrina."

"We need to give it more time." The hurt look was gone, shadowed by some other expression he couldn't interpret. "What if she sees us together more?"

"You already tried to convince her to come tonight. She's not going to agree to that. Can you blame her?"

"What if I invite you over when she's not expecting it?"

He sighed. "Arielle . . . I don't want to hurt her any more." God knew that was the truth. He had to do something soon before his relationship with Sabrina was damaged beyond repair.

"I love her," he said. He needed Arielle to understand how difficult this charade had become.

That look again. What was up with that?

"Maybe we can arrange for you and Sabrina to be together again, alone," she said finally.

"I don't think she's going to buy another illness." Still, the idea of being alone with her was tempting. If only they could make it work.

"I get migraines sometimes. Sabrina won't think anything is amiss if I have to bail out on a date at the last minute."

Maybe that would work. Still . . . "Last time we were alone, it didn't go so well. Actually it went too well." He grinned, feeling sheepish at his admission. "I seem to be short on self-control where your cousin is concerned."

Arielle looked away, admiring the sunset, he supposed.

"Maybe if we keep it fun," he wondered aloud. "No moonlit boat rides or romantic strolls on the beach."

"Maybe you could do something Sabrina enjoys."

"Yeah, something like that." Hope pried its way in, wedging open the door again. The boat rocked gently in the waves as he racked his brain for an idea. He mentally went through Sabrina's letters, searching for some activity she wouldn't turn down. What was she obsessed with? What activity would she do anything to participate in, even if it meant being stuck with him?

He felt a grin work its way onto his face. "I have an idea," he said.

Chapter Thirty-one

The front door slammed and, moments later, Arielle appeared in the kitchen. "Couldn't you have a more interesting hobby?"

Sabrina had tried to read all night. Too bad she hadn't gotten her mind off Tucker and Arielle long enough to finish a chapter. Finally, she'd given up and started a batch of cupcakes. Sometimes a girl needed chocolate.

"You have something against cupcakes?" Sabrina pulled the pan from the oven, and the sweet aroma filled the kitchen.

"Not *that* hobby. The book thing."

What was Arielle carrying on about? Whatever it was, she didn't seem pleased. "What are you talking about?"

"He's taking me to some dead writer's house in Boston. He cleared his schedule for a day, already bought tickets, and now I have to fake interest in some ancient property and probably a zillion artifacts. Booooorrrinnng."

A stitch caught in Sabrina's stomach. A writer's house in Boston? There were many of them, but only one she'd mentioned online. "Who? Which writer?"

251

Arielle pinched off a piece of hot cupcake and slid it in her mouth. "Henry Fellow Longsworth or whatever it is."

Sabrina's insides felt weighted with lead. "Henry Wadsworth Longfellow?"

"Yeah, that's it. Ugh! Within blocks of all those wonderful boutiques and I'll be stuck in some moldy old house."

It wasn't fair. Sabrina would give her right arm to go there. "Charles Dickens visited that moldy old house, and so did Nathaniel Hawthorne." Sabrina loosened the cupcakes from the pan and set them to cool on a wire rack.

Arielle sighed. "Unless they're interested in having me redecorate it, I couldn't care less about some dumb old house."

Her cousin's acting skills were going to be tested. "Well, you'll have to feign interest. He knows how badly I want to go there."

"No kidding. Hey, these are pretty good."

Sabrina watched Arielle take a hot cupcake and bite into it. Steam rose from the center, carrying the sweet scent, but suddenly she didn't feel like chocolate. She didn't have an appetite at all.

"I think I'll turn in." She didn't have to be up early for work or she would've turned in long ago. Besides, she was too busy fretting over Tucker and Arielle to sleep.

"I'll wrap these when they've cooled." Her cousin took another bite of the cupcake.

"Thanks." Sabrina retreated to her room and slid under the covers, feeling the familiar stab of jealousy.

A pounding at the door roused Sabrina from a deep sleep. She checked the clock. It was early. Too early for Renny.

The trip to Boston. Were Arielle and Tucker leaving this early? She hadn't heard Arielle moving around, hadn't heard the water running in the bathroom.

Sabrina peered through her bedroom window. Tucker stood on the landing, his hands tucked in his pockets, bouncing on the balls of his feet like he couldn't wait for the day to start.

"Arielle?" she called, swinging open her bedroom door. The living room was dark, and her cousin was a shadowed lump on the couch.

"Arielle, Tucker's here." She shook her cousin.

"What?"

"Tucker's here. You're going to Boston today, you overslept."

Arielle moaned. "I have a migraine."

Another tap sounded at the door. "Come on, Arielle, he's waiting."

Arielle pressed her fingertips to her temples. "I can't go."

"You're not just trying to get out of this, are you?"

She moaned again.

"Maybe it'll go away if you take something."

"I already did, hours ago."

The cupcakes. Chocolate gave Arielle migraines. She wondered how many her cousin had.

Tap, tap, tap. The knock was louder. She had to answer the door before he woke Renny.

"Tell him I can't go. Apologize for me, okay?" Arielle rolled away as if it were a closed matter.

Great. Not only was Tucker going to be disappointed, but Sabrina had to deliver the news.

She sighed and went to the door, wishing her hair wasn't matted and straggly, wishing she wasn't wearing her pajamas. She gave her hair a futile fluff and pulled open the door.

Tucker's smile was disarming. "Good morning."

"Uh—hi, Tucker." She cast a glare at the lump on the couch. "Um, I'm afraid I have bad news. Arielle has a migraine this morning."

His eyes registered surprise, but the smile hung around. "Oh. Is she going to be okay?"

"She gets them occasionally—I mean, she said she does. She said she doesn't feel up to going today. She asked me to apologize for her."

His smile faltered. "Oh." He looked toward the yard.

Sabrina followed his eyes toward the yard, down the tree limb to where the robin's nest still clung for dear life. She could hear the hum of Tucker's car from the front of the house. She felt bad that he'd cleared his schedule for the trip, and now it was canceled. He looked vaguely disappointed, and she was so tired of disappointing him.

Then he turned his full attention on her. "Hey, I have an idea. You want to go with me? Arielle said you were a fan of Longfellow too."

Her traitorous heart jumped the curb, and she clearly saw a sign marked "Danger Ahead." "Oh, I don't know—"

"Come on, it'll be fun. I already reserved tickets, and I cleared my calendar for the day. I was looking forward to it." He gave her the puppy dog look. So not fair.

Reasons. She needed reasons to say no. She couldn't think of a single legitimate one.

"It's your day off, right?" he asked.

She clenched her jaw. He knew way too much about her. "I

have to go to the grocery. And read. I was going to read today." *Lame, lame, lame.*

"You can do that any day. Come on, you're already up. Doesn't a trip to Boston sound fun? It's a beautiful day for a boat ride. The Longfellow House . . . Please?"

Tempting, it was so tempting. And it was a beautiful day. Already the sky was clear blue, and the temperature promised a mildly warm day. Still . . .

"I'm not ready. I just got up, haven't even showered yet." *Is that the best you can do?*

"We have time. I'll wait in the car, just come down when you're ready."

"But—" She had no more words, but it didn't matter, because Tucker was already traipsing down the steps like a kid just dismissed from school.

Sweetpea: I think courage resides deep inside of everyone. But sometimes it's impossible to reach because of all the stuff piled on top.

Chapter Thirty-two

Sabrina strolled through the gardens beside Tucker. Every now and then his arm brushed hers, especially when they toured the crowded house. The artifacts had been fascinating, and though she knew most of what the guide recited, just seeing the rooms and desk where Longfellow had written had been a dream come true.

The garden showed off its summer wardrobe, a riot of colors and textures. Blue delphinium, pink hollyhock, vibrant purple Japanese iris, and dozens of other varieties crept and climbed the surfaces of the garden. Renny would be in heaven.

"What's that?" Tucker pointed.

Sabrina caught sight of the bronze object nearby. "That must be the sundial. Longfellow's daughter placed it here. She put her father's favorite motto on it."

"How do you know so much about this place? I think you could've led the tour."

She shrugged. She'd never mentioned it in email, so it was

safe to do so now. "I wrote a fifty-page essay on Longfellow in college."

Tucker leaned over the inscription on the sundial. "I can't read it."

"You don't speak fluent Italian?" she teased, then caught herself when he turned his crooked smile on her. "It means something like 'Think that this day will never dawn again.'"

Tucker straightened, and she felt his eyes on hers. She'd felt him watching her throughout the day. On the long boat ride to Boston, over their quick lunch once they'd docked, through the house tour. Did they mean anything, those looks? She was confused.

"Think that this day will never dawn again." She thought it was meant to be inspirational, but today the thought depressed her. She wished this day could dawn over and over for all eternity.

She ran her fingers over the sundial, wondering what Tucker was thinking. A bird twittered, serenading them. Tucker was probably thinking about Arielle, wishing she were here instead. Though he had been a lighthearted and entertaining host. He'd made her laugh repeatedly, and Sabrina realized she hadn't had so much fun in—well, she didn't remember the last time.

Now, though, an awkward silence had fallen. Even the bird stopped his song, as if waiting expectantly.

She had to break the silence before whatever Tucker expected, whatever she hoped for, happened. "It's too bad Arielle couldn't come." The name of her cousin had an instant dampening effect, at least on her.

"I'm having a great time. You're a fun and knowledgeable date." He cocked a grin at her before starting along the path again.

She fell in step beside him. The sun was sinking in the sky, had fallen behind the trees. A mild breeze cooled her skin.

"How about we find an air-conditioned café for a quick supper before we head back?" he said.

"Only if you let me pay my half." He'd insisted on buying her lunch.

"Have it your way, stubborn."

She bumped her shoulder into his arm, delighting too much in the sturdy feel of him.

Tucker pulled his car onto Sabrina's street. Tired though he was from the long day, he dreaded its end. He'd enjoyed Sabrina. Seeing her in her element, talking about her passion. It made him fall more deeply in love with her. It made him want to end the secrecy between them.

Just tell her you know.

No, I can't risk losing her.

All the way back on the boat, he'd waffled back and forth.

Back and forth, back and forth. He was about to drive himself crazy with indecision. It wasn't like him. But the cold, hard facts were that he'd spent another day with Sabrina, and she was no closer to telling him the truth. Whatever it was, whatever was holding her back, it had her by the heart and wasn't letting go.

Now, he pulled his car into her drive, feeling reasonably settled about the decision he'd reached. He flipped off the ignition and unbuckled his seatbelt.

"You don't have to walk me up. Arielle's in bed already," she said quickly. Sabrina had called twice to check on her cousin.

"I'll see you to the door." He exited the car before she could argue. They weren't done yet; she just didn't know it.

He followed her up the steps, admiring her form from behind, wishing he could set his hand at the small of her back. *You have no right to be looking, much less touching. What would she think if she knew the direction of your thoughts?*

Sabrina fished her key from her bag and aimed it at the knob.

Tucker took her fist in his. "Wait. I wondered if we could talk a minute." They'd had all day. Why didn't he do this earlier?

Because you were hoping she'd do it herself.

"I—I should probably check on Arielle."

"You called an hour ago, and she was in bed."

She looked at the door as if hoping it might open up and swallow her. "I haven't thanked you for today. I enjoyed seeing the mansion and—and everything." She was looking everywhere but at him as she pulled her hand from his grasp.

He leaned against the door frame, conveniently blocking the knob. He saw right through her parting words, an attempt to end the evening quickly. "I'm glad you could go." If she only knew how glad. If she only knew how badly he wanted to prolong the night.

But it was late, and they both had work tomorrow. Still, there was the matter of that one last piece of business. He took a breath, digging deep for courage.

"Sabrina, I feel like we've gotten to know each other pretty well recently." He waited for a response, but got none, save a long swallow.

"I want you to know, if there's anything you need, anything you ever want to talk about, I consider you a close friend."

She tucked in the corners of her lips, a cross between a smile and a grimace. "Thank you."

Her eyes darted over his shoulder, then to the ground between them, then to her hand that held the key. He was pretty sure the words *I've got to get out of here* were tumbling around that pretty little head.

He wanted her to be still long enough to hear him. He wanted her full attention. He nudged her chin up with his finger until she met his gaze.

She was a frightened doe. Those big brown eyes overflowed with panic. Worry lines creased her forehead, and her shoulders were plywood stiff. He regretted his words if only because they'd changed Sabrina back into the Ice Princess.

His hope withered slowly under a scorching light of realization. He didn't know why—why she wouldn't tell him, why she hid behind email, why she'd gone to such great lengths to protect herself.

But if she needed to hide, for whatever secret reasons, didn't he love her enough to wait? In the space where hope had resided, a seed of mercy sprouted. *Ah, honey. I'm sorry I pushed you. You're worth the wait.*

He tried for a smile he didn't feel. "You're tired. Get to bed." He pressed a kiss to her forehead and felt the softness of her hair under his lips, smelled the sweet scent of ocean and lilac in her hair.

He'd scarcely pulled away before her key found the lock, and then she was gone.

Sweetpea: Everyone yearns to be loved for who they are. Not for what they look like or what they do or what they've accomplished. I wonder how many people actually find that.

Chapter Thirty-three

A cab waited in front of the house when Sabrina returned from work. Maybe Arielle was going somewhere.

For three days Sabrina had been lost in thought, remembering every moment of her date with Tucker. The morning after, Arielle had quizzed her about the day, and she'd told her cousin everything. Except the kiss. But it wasn't a real kiss, just a brotherly kiss on the forehead.

Only it hadn't felt brotherly at all.

She entered the loft and kicked off her work shoes. Arielle was hunched over her floral suitcase, pushing on the swollen bag, struggling with the zipper.

A glance around revealed a lack of all things Arielle. The sandy spot by the door where she usually kicked off her sandals was bare, the end table where she piled her clothes was empty. Dread welled inside Sabrina. "Where are you going?"

Arielle gave the zipper one last tug. "Home."

She watched her cousin haul the suitcase off the sofa and set it at her feet. "What do you mean?"

"I've had enough of this charade, cuz. It's time for me to go. I'm catching the ferry, and I booked a flight from Cape Cod."

Had something happened between her and Tucker? This was totally out of the blue and utterly unfair. "What happened?"

"Nothing happened. I have to get back. I just—I can't do this anymore." A flicker of something—fear?—flared in her eyes before her eyelids shuttered them.

Now that Sabrina looked closer, Arielle's face looked strained, her lips tipped uncharacteristically down at the corners, her brows pulled together. What was going on?

"It's only a few more days, Arielle. We had a deal."

"Deal's off. I don't expect you to come to the wedding, so you're off the hook."

What in the world? Arielle had begged her to attend Jaylee's wedding. It was the only reason she'd come. "What reason did you give Tucker?"

A nonchalant shrug. "I didn't tell him. I'm sure you'll come up with something."

"You didn't tell him?" What explanation could Sabrina give? *Sorry, Tucker. The love of your life disappeared as quickly as she'd appeared.* Why was Arielle doing this?

Her cousin was wheeling her suitcase past her, toward the door. Sabrina grabbed her arm, panic building. "Why are you doing this? What are you so afraid of?"

Arielle whirled on her heels. "Don't question *me* about fear.

You're hiding behind some email name because you're afraid to have a real relationship. You're worse than Renny, hiding her manuscripts in a drawer."

Arielle's anger, her words, stopped Sabrina cold. Her hand fell from her cousin's arm.

"Go back to your safe little emails, Sabrina. Never mind that you're missing out on a real relationship with a wonderful man . . ." Arielle's words wobbled as the sentence trailed off.

When the door closed behind her cousin five seconds later, Sabrina knew with sudden clarity why Arielle was leaving the island, why fear laced her eyes, why angry words were spilling from her tongue.

Arielle had fallen head over heels for Tucker.

Sweetpea: I haven't been to church since the Jared/ Jaylee episode. I just haven't been able to bring myself to go.

Chapter Thirty-four

Sabrina paced the length of the loft as the taxi pulled away. So, Arielle had fallen for Tucker. Was it any surprise? He was a wonderful man, just as she'd said. It was a miracle some woman hadn't snatched him up already. But did it have to be her cousin? Was Sabrina destined to lose every man she loved to one of her beautiful cousins?

Sabrina kicked the chair Arielle had placed against the wall, and it toppled over, hitting the floor with a *thwack*. It was so unfair. What right did Arielle have stealing the only man she cared about? It had been stupid to encourage those dates. Stupid! Sabrina couldn't have done a better job sabotaging herself if she'd tried.

She reached the windows and turned. Arielle's feelings aside, the relevant question was, where did Tucker stand? He was caught in a triangle and didn't know it. Was he in love with Sabrina or Arielle or some bizarre combination of them both? Sabrina ran her hands over her face. What had she done?

And how was she going to tell him Arielle was gone? What

reason could she give? A family emergency? But what excuse could she give for keeping the relationship online now?

Was it time to admit defeat? To send him a final letter ending the relationship?

She imagined coming home to an empty inbox, facing Tucker at the café every morning with no hope of having that intimate communication again . . .

How her heart ached at the thought!

She couldn't do it, she just couldn't. It was all she had of him. All she could ever have, and it would have to be enough.

And yet, was it fair to tie him down to a relationship that could never go deeper than email? *But he loves you.*

Why, God? Why, of all people, did it have to be Tucker? Why, of all men that night, did it have to be his brother-in-law?

But it was what it was. Begging and praying would change nothing. She had to focus on the problem. She had to decide what to tell Tucker and how to say it. Arielle had left a fine mess, leaving in a snit as she had.

Sabrina stopped pacing, her feet stopping on the braided rug Arielle had bought. Arielle had left Sabrina in a bind, but the fact that she'd left, despite her growing feelings for Tucker . . .

It was so obvious she'd almost missed it. Arielle was leaving for Sabrina. Despite her cousin's testy words, she was removing herself from the picture out of love for her. Leaving so that Sabrina wouldn't get hurt again.

And Sabrina hadn't been nice about it.

She cringed. She'd let her confusion and anger blind her, but everything was clearer now.

A knot of anxiety tightened inside. She couldn't stand that they'd parted on bad terms. Especially now that she realized Arielle was willing to sacrifice a possible relationship with Tucker for Sabrina's sake. She snatched her bag, slipped into sandals, and ran down the steps.

⌁

Traffic in town was heavy, and pedestrians littered the sidewalks, waiting to cross the street. Sabrina had to stop pedaling at every crossing, further delaying her mission. As she neared the wharf, the congestion thickened with passengers arriving from Hyannis, exiting the ferry with their fat suitcases and dog-weary grins. Taxis lined the street, waiting to drive tourists to their hotels and rentals.

After parking, she hurried up the concrete dock, dodging pedestrians, feeling like a trout swimming upstream. She hoped Arielle hadn't boarded. She scanned the ferry's rails for a glimpse of her cousin. Someone on the middle deck had long, blonde hair and looked—

Thwack! She slammed into another body and staggered backward. "I'm so sorry." She reached out to steady the woman, eager to move on.

But her eyes caught on the woman's face. On those icy blue eyes she could never forget. They'd haunted her ever since that day. That morning in the house in Madaket.

Maybe the woman wouldn't recognize her. Sabrina averted her eyes quickly, turning her head. She had to get away quickly. "I'm sorry." Giving up her mission to fight the crowd, she turned toward town for a quick escape.

"It's you." The woman's voice rose over the din of voices and footsteps.

Sabrina broke into a run, trying to disappear in the throng. She prayed Tracey wouldn't follow. If she could just make it to her bike . . .

Tucker hadn't said his sister was coming. But why would he mention it to Sabrina? He'd probably told Arielle, and her cousin had no knowledge of that fateful night. Tracey had probably come to meet Arielle. And now Arielle was gone and—

Tucker.

He was probably here to pick up Tracey. Here somewhere in this mass of humanity. He would be parked in the same area as her bike.

Changing direction, she turned up Water Street. She'd go back for her bike later, long after Tucker and his sister left. She hustled up the sidewalk, making a left when she reached India Street. The crowd had dispersed, making her more visible. It was irrational to think Tracey had followed her, especially when she'd been encumbered with luggage. But what if Tracey told Tucker she'd seen her? What if they were both looking for her?

Where could she hide? In the distance, the steeple of First Congregational Church, Renny's church, poked into the sky like a pointy finger. Quickening her pace, she headed toward the building. She would hide there until the sun sank. Then she'd sneak to her bike under the cloak of darkness.

When she reached the church, she darted up the steps, out of breath. An elderly man stood just inside the door. "I'm sorry, the tower is closed for the day."

"Oh." Did this mean she couldn't enter? "I wasn't coming to

climb the tower. I was—" She looked over his frail shoulder into the sanctuary.

Sanctuary. The word had a nice ring. "I wanted to—to pray." It might have been a lie, but Sabrina suddenly realized it was true.

"By all means," the man said, ushering her forward.

She couldn't take her eyes from the altar. It drew her like a magnet. She did want to pray. Like Renny. Like Tucker. Like *her*, before her life fell apart. She *needed* to pray.

Maybe she'd find answers or, at least, solace. She'd missed that and only now realized how much.

She needed to pray because the web she'd become ensnared in was too big, too sticky to escape on her own—it didn't take a genius to see that.

And yet, after seeing Tucker's sister, after the reminder of what she'd done that night, of all she'd done since . . . she felt unworthy.

She stopped at the sanctuary's entrance. It was so . . . white in there. White walls, white pews, white altar and pillars. Did her presence sully the place? Did she have the right to be in a holy sanctuary? In the presence of a holy God? Would the usher have thrown her out if he knew what she'd done?

Would God strike her dead for having the nerve to enter his house? Because she realized with sudden clarity that he did know. Knew everything she'd done, from that first week on the island through her lies and charade. She'd blocked it from her mind all these months, pretending he didn't see or didn't care enough to notice.

Yet, what hope did she have on her own? Would he mind her return if she was seeking his help?

A movement at the altar caught her eye. A woman was hunched

over the bottom step of the pulpit in prayer. There were others dotting the pews. Their presence gave her the boldness to take one step and then another.

Her courage grew as she neared the altar, but her heart took a dozen beats for each step down the long aisle. She didn't recognize the woman at the altar until she was nearly upon her.

"Renny." Sabrina didn't mean to say it aloud, to disturb her friend from prayer.

Renny raised her head. Her eyes were red rimmed. "Sabrina . . ."

She'd never seen Renny cry. Not even when her beloved pet bird died suddenly. She knelt by her friend, forgetting her own troubles. "What's wrong? Did something happen?"

Renny wiped her nose with a tissue that was wadded in her fist. "I'm fine. I'm here about my stories."

"Your stories?"

Renny nodded, wiping her eyes.

Sabrina waited for her to continue.

Renny laid her hand on her heart. "I've really been fighting *El Shaddai*—God—on this one."

"What do you mean?"

"I was afraid. So afraid, it paralyzed me. I couldn't send them, I just couldn't."

Sabrina settled down lower beside Renny. "Oh, Renny."

"Can you believe fear can be so paralyzing? I've been afraid my whole life, hiding away in my big house with nothing but a view of the ocean. My fear has been a wall that's separated me from freedom. It kept me from pursuing my dreams and living a full life. I'd write a story, intending to send it. Then I'd hit that wall of fear and decide it was too hard to get to the other side. Too thick, too high. Too scary. Rather than face the anxiety, I'd hide on the safe side of the wall, where it's not so scary."

"But you can change that."

Renny dabbed her eyes. "With God's help, I'm going to do it. I'm going to send my babies out there, all nine of them. If they all come back, I'll find a way to deal with it. He'll help me through it."

"I'm so glad to hear that." Sabrina patted her shoulder, wishing, not for the first time, that she was a hugger. She was sure Renny could use one. Spontaneously, she reached over and put her arms around the woman.

Renny gave her a tight squeeze, then released her a few moments later. "Well, enough of my blubbering. What brings you here, *amita?*"

Sabrina breathed a laugh. "I've been doing a little hiding of my own. I'm so confused." She rubbed her temple.

"I left my scalp massager at home . . . that always clears my confusion." Sabrina smiled, but Renny wasn't joking. "Well, never mind that. Want to talk about it?"

Before she could lose her nerve, Sabrina spilled the whole story. Renny already knew about Jaylee and Jared, but Sabrina had never told her friend about the night of her transgression or the charade with Arielle. She finished the story with the moment on the pier that now seemed like hours ago.

Renny listened, offering nods of encouragement and sighs of sympathy. When Sabrina was finished, Renny pulled a clean tissue from her pocket and handed it to her.

They'd shifted and now they sat on the altar steps, their backs to the pulpit. The others who'd come to pray or think had left.

"I'm tired of doing this alone," Sabrina said.

"Doing what alone?"

"I turned on God after Jaylee and Jared betrayed me. And then I committed adultery with another woman's husband and felt too ashamed to return."

"Ahhh . . . The same sin that separated you and God, separated you and Tucker."

"I never thought of it that way, but you're right. I have a wall just like you, and it's right between me and God. I don't want it there anymore."

"Oh, honey, it doesn't have to be. He's received many a prodigal child, myself included. Just come back to him. It's called *teshuvah*. Returning, a repentance of sin."

Was it that simple? Would he receive her after she'd rejected him? After she'd committed that despicable act?

She'd royally messed up. She'd done to another woman what Jaylee had done to her. She felt ashamed and unworthy. Unworthy of freedom and happiness. Unworthy of God's mercy. Her wall *was* too thick. Too high.

"What I did was so—I still feel dirty. I knew better, and yet I . . ."

"God is standing at the top of the wall with a rope. You only have to take hold of it. You can trust him, Sabrina."

Can I, God? "But, I've got this huge mess . . ."

"He knows that. And he's not going to wave a magic wand and make it disappear, but he'll help you do what's right. Help you overcome your fears—just like he did mine."

Sabrina thought of Renny's years of hard labor. "You've been fighting that one a long time."

Renny grinned. "Okay, so it took me a while. You're a faster learner than I am."

Sabrina was tired of hiding on this side of the wall. Tired of the limitations when the other side offered so much freedom.

All right, God, I'm grabbing the rope. Are you okay with that?

"He loves you, Sabrina. So much, *amita.*"

Sabrina stared into the darkened sanctuary, feeling calm for the first time in months. The wall was still thick. It was still high. But Jesus held the rope, and he'd help her over it. Somehow, some way, he'd get her safely to the other side.

Sweetpea: I hate being the bearer of bad news. Once, Jaylee double-booked herself for prom. I had to tell the guy who came second that she'd already left with someone else. I'll never forget the look on his face.

Chapter Thirty-five

Dear Tucker,

Sabrina typed the words, then stared at the blinking cursor until it mesmerized her. She'd emailed Arielle as soon as she'd returned from the church. She'd apologized for her harsh words and said she understood why Arielle had left. She'd even managed to thank her cousin. Arielle would get the message when she returned to Macon, and they'd undoubtedly settle things over a phone call.

But her letter to Tucker . . . What could she say? She tapped her fingers on the keyboard. He would expect her to give some reason for leaving the island. And she had to let him know she couldn't see him again.

She wanted to tell him that she and God were back on speaking terms. Maybe she could include that too. He'd be thrilled for her.

But first, how could she explain Arielle's departure without telling another lie? She was adamant about avoiding more lies. All that deception had gotten her nowhere.

Tucker's words from the week before popped into her mind. *"Unfortunately, I can't explain why I kissed you. But I don't regret it."*

That's what she would do. Offer no explanation and ask him to trust her.

The phone rang, and she was grateful for the disruption. Probably Renny calling to set up a brainstorming session now that the creative neurons were firing again.

"Hello?" Sabrina tucked the phone into her shoulder and swiped away cookie crumbs Arielle had left behind.

"Sabrina?"

Tucker. She dropped the crumbs in the trash and rubbed her hands together. Was it too late to hang up?

"Yeah." She could hit herself for not writing Tucker as soon as she'd returned.

"Hey, how's it going?"

"Fine." *Except everything is fixing to fall apart.* She covered her face.

"I was wondering if I could drop by tonight. My sister's visiting for the weekend, and I wanted her to meet you. I mean, you and Arielle."

This cannot be happening. "Uh . . . Arielle's not here." Sabrina paced across the room.

"Will she be back soon?"

Here goes. Sabrina swallowed the dry lump in her throat. "I—I have something I need to tell you."

"What's wrong? Are you okay?" The concern in his voice about broke her.

"Arielle left. I mean, she left the island." She gentled her voice, stealing herself against the pain she was causing. "I—I don't think she's coming back." Her heart hurt for him. She wanted to coat the words with chocolate or something to make them go down easier, but there was no way to sweeten them.

"She left?"

Sabrina heard the surprise in his voice. "I'm sorry, I—I don't know what to say." An understatement. A huge understatement. *Please don't press for details.*

"Did she say why?"

A question she could answer honestly. *Thanks, God.* "Not really. She was packing when I got home from work, had a cab waiting. I'm sorry she left without an explanation. I'm sure she'll be in contact soon." *She's in the middle of writing you as we speak.*

A silence ensued. A long one that made her wonder if Tucker was still on the line. Then finally, he spoke. "It's okay, Sabrina. I think I understand."

He did? Had something happened between Tucker and Arielle after all? Had he kissed her? Told her he loved her?

Please, no. She couldn't bear the thought of him whispering those words into her cousin's ear, of seeing Arielle wrapped in his arms the way Jaylee had been in Jared's. She scrubbed the image from her mind.

"Sabrina?"

He didn't sound hurt or depressed. She was confused. "I'm here. Just be watching for that email."

"I will."

"Yeah, so I'll—uh—see you bright and early, then."

"See you tomorrow."

She turned off the phone and set it in the cradle, their final words ringing in her ears. She couldn't go to work the next day. Or even Sunday. What if Tucker brought Tracey? She could ruin everything with just one word.

Sweetpea: My dad whistled when he was happy. That was before my mom died, so I was little, but I still remember the tune, the way his lips puckered, and the way it made the whole house cheery.

Chapter Thirty-six

The next morning there was no email response from Tucker. Sabrina puttered around the house, cleaning and reading all day, hoping the time would pass quickly, eager to hear from him. She'd taken two personal days and asked Char to fill her spot so Gordon would have no cause to complain.

When evening arrived, she opened her email again. In her message, Sabrina had said as little as possible about her departure from the island. Arielle's departure, she corrected herself. She'd spent most of the email expressing her joy at finding peace with God. She knew Tucker would rejoice with her.

While writing the letter, Sabrina also had come to grips with her anger toward Jared and Jaylee. How could she hold a grudge against her cousin after God had forgiven her? It was time to let it go. She'd told Tucker that too.

Now, she opened her email program and smiled when she found Tucker's reply in her inbox. Finally.

I'm so happy for you. I sense a new freedom in the tone of your message, and I couldn't be more pleased. Isn't it amazing how God accepts us right where we are, regardless of where we've been or what we've done? It's such a foreign concept in this world that it's hard to fathom.

I'm also glad you've found it in your heart to forgive your cousin and ex-fiancé. I can't believe you're going to the wedding—I'm so proud of you. I'd love to go with you, if you'll have me. I admit that it relieves my mind to know you're able to put Jared behind you completely. Does that make me a selfish jerk?

I want to talk with you more about all this, but my sister, Tracey, is visiting for the weekend so my spare time will be limited for a couple days. Know that I'm thinking about you and missing you.

Sabrina couldn't keep the smile from forming. She reread his letter and noticed he hadn't said anything about her leaving except that he missed her. Obviously he couldn't go to the wedding, still a few weeks away—but, oh, how she wished he could be there with her.

She sighed. He'd probably be out of touch until Sunday night when his sister left, and until then, she had only one goal.

Stay out of Tracey's sight.

Sabrina felt like singing when she awoke early on Monday. She'd survived the weekend without running into Tracey, and her relief was tangible.

When she exited the bathroom, her eyes caught on her own image in the oval mirror Arielle had hung there. She stopped in front of it. Well, her cousin was gone now. Sabrina grasped the maple frame in her palms, ready to pull it from its spot, but something stopped her.

She uncurled her fingers, releasing the frame, and stepped back from the mirror. The honey color of the wood contrasted nicely with the sage color Arielle had painted the hall. The mirror had a beveled edge that was simple and elegant, and the face staring back from the middle of it really wasn't so bad.

Sabrina watched herself grin. Maybe she could live with the mirror after all. Happy with her decision, she turned toward the kitchen, but when she rounded the corner, she bumped her leg on the end table. Straightening, she surveyed the room with fresh eyes. She really didn't care for the way Arielle had arranged the furniture. She preferred to face the window looking over the ocean, not the TV.

Before she knew it, Sabrina was scooting the table, sofa, and recliners into new positions. As she gave the sofa one last shove, her bracelet caught on the fabric. She worked the heart charm loose from the material and straightened.

Why was she wearing this stupid bracelet? That part of her life was over. Sabrina unfastened the clasp, walked to the wastebasket, and dropped it inside. It landed at the bottom with one last jingle.

Turning, she surveyed the living room critically. It was good. She didn't know why she hadn't thought of the arrangement before. She liked it much better. Not only did it open up the room, but it seemed brighter and cheerier somehow. Giving a satisfied nod, Sabrina used the extra few minutes before leaving for work to peruse *The Inquirer and Mirror*.

When she reached the back section, a help-wanted ad drew her eye. It was for an editorial position at Mill Hill Press, right here on the island. Maybe it was time she did something with that literature degree.

But if she weren't working at the café, she wouldn't see Tucker every day. The thought put an ache in her stomach.

But she'd still have the email relationship. Was it worth the trade-off? Maybe it would be easier not seeing him all the time. Anyway, she might not even get the job. She'd put in her application and see where it led.

The thought put an extra bounce in her steps as she exited her loft. Dark clouds obscured the sun, but not even a gloomy day could dispel her good mood. The lyrics from "It's a Beautiful Morning" hung in her head like harbor fog on a warm spring morning.

Once she was at her station, Sabrina tied her apron and tucked an order pad in her pocket.

"What's with the mysterious smile?" Char asked as Sabrina made fresh coffee.

Sabrina shrugged. "Just in a good mood."

All was well. She and God were hanging out again. Arielle was gone. The charade was over. And she'd survived the weekend without running into Tucker's sister. Oh, yeah, life was good.

"Oliver's trying to get your attention," Char said. "Probably wants to stump you with another word, poor man. He'll never give up."

The kitchen bell rang, and Sabrina trayed an order, collected a couple refills of milk and juice, and headed to the corner table.

"Promise you won't say anything," Tucker said. He loaded the last of his sister's luggage and closed the trunk.

Tracey limped to the car as the first drops of rain fell; then Tucker slid behind the steering wheel and turned the key. "Tracey . . ."

"What?" She flashed wide baby blues at him.

"We're not going unless you promise."

"Let's get this straight. This is the woman you love, the woman who's stolen your heart"—she covered her heart—"who gives breath to your very—"

"I'm waiting."

Tracey sighed, still in drama mode. "Oh, all right. Party pooper. I came here for nothing."

"Who asked you?"

"You did."

"Yeah, well, I didn't know you were going to be such a pain in the patootie."

"Are you going to get this thing in gear? We'll have to skip the café if you don't hurry. I'm not missing my ferry."

"Maybe that's not such a bad idea."

"I promised to be a good girl. Now, let's go. I have to see this shining example of womanhood."

Now that Tracey's divorce was final, her life was settling down. She'd lost the emaciated look she'd had since she and Sebastian split, and she was starting a new life in a new city. Her new job as a hospital dietician was giving her a purpose and allowing her to meet new people. He was starting to see her trademark steel will reappear.

"I still don't understand why you don't just tell her who you are."

"I told you, she's been hurt. Did I ask for your advice?"

"I'm your sister, honey. You don't have to ask." She patted his shoulder. "I'm always here for you."

"Your generosity overwhelms me." Tucker backed from the drive and put the car in forward gear. The weekend had passed quickly. He'd assigned some of his trips to Nate to make time for Tracey, but his sister didn't seem to mind hanging around his house while he worked.

"All joking aside, bro, I had a great time this weekend. After the lousy start, that is."

Tracey had been upset after running into the woman she'd caught Sebastian with, but she'd been determined to stay. And when Tracey was determined, nothing stood in her way. Tucker's goal had been to keep her so busy she didn't have time to dwell on it. Besides, the island wasn't that small, and presently it was crowded with summer people. Chances of running into the woman again were slim.

As Tucker pulled to the curb and parked diagonally, a butterfly or two fluttered in his stomach. "Not one word."

"I promise! Sheesh."

"Or look."

"I'm here to see her, Tuck."

"You know what I mean."

Tracey rolled her eyes and reached for the door.

Tucker hit the lock button, and all the locks snapped downward.

Tracey glared.

He couldn't believe he was so nervous. It wasn't like Tracey was a blabbermouth. She could be a brat when she wanted to but she'd never hurt him.

"She means a lot to me, Trace." *Everything, actually.*

Tracey's face softened, and she laid her hand on his. "I get that. Relax. I won't do anything to draw undue attention, okay?"

Tucker gave a sheepish grin and hit the button, unlocking the doors.

They ducked through the drizzle, slowed by Tracey's uneven gait; then he opened the door for Tracey and ushered her to his table. Oliver was already at the neighboring table with his steaming mug of coffee.

He introduced the man to his sister, and they made small talk as they settled in. He handed Tracey a menu.

"How am I supposed to see her when I'm facing the street?" she whispered.

"Stop whining. She'll be around soon with coffee." Sabrina was loading a tray at the kitchen window. Her uniform was still spotless as far as he could tell, and her ponytail was caught in her collar, but he knew one flip of her head would set it free.

"Bacon and eggs are good, and so are the pancakes if you're in the mood for them."

"I'm starving," Tracey said.

It was good to see her appetite back. She'd lost too much weight the last year. "Get the Hungry Captain then. It has a bit of everything."

Sabrina delivered food to a table at the back, then retrieved the coffeepot as Oliver drained the last drop in his cup.

"Okay, here she comes," Tucker whispered to Tracey, feeling his heart pounding into his throat. "Act natural." He turned his mug over and settled back in his chair, striking a casual pose.

Chapter Thirty-seven

Sabrina's mind was so occupied, she was at Oliver's table before she felt Tucker's presence behind her. Was it that late already?

She filled Oliver's mug and removed the empty creamers from his table. He had a word coming, she could smell it.

He didn't disappoint her. "Did you hear about the *opprobrious* behavior of the students here on summer break?" Oliver asked.

Someone squeezed between the tables, and Sabrina leaned forward to let them by.

"Hey, Sabrina," Tucker said after they passed.

She turned with a bland smile, steeled against Tucker's charm.

She met his gaze and was extending the coffeepot when she became aware of the other person at the table.

Her eyes collided with the blue gaze of Tucker's sister.

She was supposed to be gone. She'd come for the weekend, and it was Monday. She should be far, far away by now. Sabrina's nerves rattled like a stack of dirty dishes on a rickety table.

The woman's friendly smile turned down, and the twinkle in her eyes turned as dull as old ice.

The pot shook in Sabrina's hand. Mechanically, she poured the coffee. The stream of liquid shimmied dangerously close to the rim.

Please, God.

"*Opprobrious* behavior, I'm telling you." Oliver's voice was a dull buzz somewhere in the distance.

Sabrina finished filling the mug.

"Sabrina, this is my sister, Tracey," Tucker was saying. "She came all the way from Atlanta to—What's wrong?"

Sabrina couldn't move. Couldn't tear her eyes from Tracey's rigid face. A rush of dizziness hit her like a rogue wave, sudden and debilitating. "I—I have to—"

Leave.

Now.

Before Tracey tells you.

She couldn't be here when he found out. And he would find out. The look on Tracey's face confirmed it.

Sabrina wavered under the dizziness, then took a step toward the kitchen. Char blocked the path with a large tray of food.

"Sabrina." It was Tucker's voice.

Could she dash out the front? A family of five clustered around the entry, waiting to be seated. She was trapped.

"*Tucker.*" His sister's whisper was like the slicing wind of a hurricane, harsh and angry.

She had to leave. Sabrina spun, sloshing coffee over her wrist. The burning pain was a welcome distraction. She bumped Char on her way by.

"Sabrina . . ." Char scolded, but Sabrina kept going. She heard Tucker calling her name and prayed he wouldn't follow. But no, his sister was no doubt informing him who she was, telling Tucker she was the one responsible for breaking up her marriage.

She dropped the pot at the station and darted to the back. Grabbing her bag, she exited through the rear door. She should've told Char or Gordon she was leaving. She'd never walked off a job, but she couldn't go back now, couldn't go back and see the look on Tucker's face when he learned the truth.

Tucker watched Sabrina skirt the tables and exit the room; then his gaze swung to his sister. Between Sabrina's panic and Tracey's— what? anger? hurt?—he didn't know what to think.

"Was it something I said?" Oliver's befuddled voice barely registered.

Tracey's nostrils flared twice. She wrung the napkin until it split in two.

Dread clogged Tucker's throat, but he squeezed the words out. "What is going on?"

Her gaze bounced off his. "Not here."

Oliver watched them with interest and, across the room, Char cast a curious glance their way.

"Come on." He stood, taking Tracey's arm. He ushered her outside, through the drizzle and into his waiting car.

Tracey's breaths came heavily, fogging up the windows. "It's *her.*" She peered through the passenger window. "I can't believe it's her, of all people."

The dread spread downward, a thick ball of trepidation. "Tell me, Trace," he said, but suddenly wasn't sure he wanted to know. He watched a raindrop trickle down the windshield, collecting others in its path, growing larger.

"The woman I found Sebastian with is your Sabrina, your *Sweetpea*." She drilled him with a look.

No, it couldn't be. She was mistaken. He shook his head, a firm denial.

"Did you know?" she asked, pricking him with darts of accusation.

"No, I didn't know. I can't believe you said that."

"Well, I'm a little freaked right now!"

Freaked didn't come close to what he felt. Tracey was wrong. She had to be. Sabrina wasn't the kind of person who would—

"Look," Tucker began, "calm down and let's think this through. It was probably dark that morning you found Sebastian. And it was over a year ago . . ."

"It was *her*. You think I can forget the face of the woman I found my husband in bed with? And she ran off, didn't she? Clearly she recognized me."

He needed a little healthy denial right now. He ran his hand over his face. This couldn't be happening.

He thought he'd known Sabrina . . . Sweetpea. She'd never said anything that indicated she was capable of something like this. She'd mentioned mistakes in the past. But this—this went beyond anything he'd imagined.

Suddenly his words from a letter resurfaced. He'd told Sweetpea about Tracey finding Sebastian with another woman and eventually about the divorce. Tracey had been in anguish at the discovery of his affairs, and he'd felt so helpless. He'd vented with

Sweetpea. He'd said harsh things, knowing she wouldn't judge him for it.

The realization kicked in.

"That's why." His whispered words barely penetrated the patter of rain on the rooftop.

He'd been ruthless in his summation of the events, his feelings toward Sebastian and the woman Tracey had found her husband with—had he called her a whore?

Oh, God. That's why she wouldn't meet me, isn't it? Why she wouldn't admit who she was. She knew what she'd done to my sister and pronounced herself unforgivable.

It was making sense. The refusal to meet, the photo she'd sent, the charade with Arielle. It all made sense when viewed in light of this new piece of information.

"I need to get out of here." Tracey laid her head back, closing her eyes as if she wanted to forget the whole mess.

And he was right in the middle of it. "Maybe you should stay awhile. We could talk. We can get you on a later ferry."

"I think I've had enough of Nantucket. No offense."

Tucker squeezed her hand, then started the car and pulled onto the street heading toward the wharf. Why did this have to happen now, when Tracey had just recovered from Sebastian's betrayal?

Betrayals, he noted the plural. The discovery of Sabrina and Sebastian was just the eye-opener that revealed his other affairs. But his sister didn't need that reminder. He wasn't pouring salt in the wound.

"I'm sorry, Trace." *And what are you going to do now? How can you choose between your sister and the woman you love?*

He thought of Sabrina, no doubt panicked and devastated, and he felt torn.

But Sabrina knew. She knew what she'd done, who his sister was, and she'd let him fall for her, opened up to him and let him in.

When he reached the parking lot, his sister waved him off. "No, just drop me at the wharf. You need to get to work."

"I can wait with you."

"I need to be alone, Tucker." She crossed her arms over her chest, avoiding his eyes, and he knew she felt he'd betrayed her somehow.

A defense rose on his lips, but he held his tongue. She knew he was innocent, but feelings could be deceiving sometimes. Time would sort it out. He only wished he could be there for her while she did the sorting.

When he pulled the car close to the terminal, he helped Tracey with her luggage. He didn't want to leave, felt like he was dumping her at the curb. "Are you sure you don't want company? I can call Dorothy and—"

"I'm sure." Her eyes were bloodshot, but her shoulders were back, her head up.

He felt like a heel. Helpless, he put his arms around her and drew her into a hug. "I'm sorry, honey."

She stood stiffly for a few seconds, then embraced him, her face turned into his T-shirt. "It's not your fault. I know that. I just need some time to work through this."

Forgiving Sabrina seemed impossible, but he knew Tracey was capable of the impossible. If she could prove the doctors wrong and learn to walk again, she could forgive Sabrina someday.

He kissed the top of her head. "You got it." He hated the timing, hated that she was returning to a big city where she hadn't yet established close friends.

"Go on, now. I'll be all right." She straightened and grabbed her luggage.

It was only as he was pulling away from the terminal that he realized his relationship with Sabrina, everything he'd fought for, everything he desired, was now in jeopardy.

Sweetpea: Some mistakes can't be undone.

Chapter Thirty-eight

Sabrina had to get out of there, off the island. She had to leave. What other choice did she have? She grabbed a suitcase from the closet and began jamming it with clothes, then realized she needed to call a cab.

Before she took two steps, she stopped. It was pouring rain. Every tourist in town would be calling for a cab, and she didn't have an hour to wait for one. She'd have to ride her bike. Realizing the suitcase was too big to transport, she pulled a smaller one from the closet and dumped the contents into it. Her hands shook. Her body trembled.

Pajamas, socks, toothbrush . . . What else? She pulled the rubber band and ran her hand through her hair. She couldn't think.

Tucker. *Oh, God, the look on his face.* The confusion, the concern. And his sister. She didn't even want to think about the accusation in those eyes. And Sabrina deserved all of it.

Toothpaste. Yes, she needed that and her vitamins. She was getting a pounding headache, the kind that required one of Arielle's nasty tinctures.

A knock rattled the front door.

She sucked in a breath and stared at the white door like it might bust off the hinges and assault her.

But reality was worse, because Tucker could be on the other side of that door. Would he do that? Would he confront her with his sister's accusations?

A sudden thought brought another wave of panic. What if his sister was with him? What if—

Another knock sounded, harder this time. She wouldn't answer. The blinds were drawn; maybe they'd think no one was home. But her bike was out front.

Look through the peephole, Sabrina. Just check.

She made her feet move by force of will. She approached the door and leaned in, careful not to touch it. Maybe it wasn't Tucker at all. It might be—

Renny. The sight of the woman's face, distorted in the glass, brought an exhale that fogged the peephole. She caught her breath, then opened the door.

"I did it!" Renny spun in a circle, a one-woman party, her fluorescent orange Hawaiian shirt blooming at the waistline. "Wahooo!" She waved her hands, oblivious to the rain trickling down her face.

"Did what?"

Renny singsonged her answer and accompanied it with a little jig. "I sent off my manuscripts, my manuscripts, my manuscripts . . ."

Sabrina allowed a tiny smile at her friend's exuberance. "That's wonderful, Renny."

"I saw you ride up the drive and just had to come tell you. Can I come in? I have to celebrate, I feel so . . . free!" She spun her way past Sabrina. "Why's it so dark in here?" she asked when she finally stopped.

Sabrina had forgotten to turn on the lights. She flipped the switch and shut the door.

"Why are you home so early?" Renny asked. "And what's this? I didn't know you were going somewhere. Did you change your mind about your cousin's wedding?"

Her suitcase sat open and full on the same sofa where Arielle's had sat only three days before. So much had happened since then. Some of it good, and some of it bad. It was the bad part that was eating her lunch.

"Sabrina?"

"I'm fine. I'm just . . . taking a trip." And she was still shaking. With fear? Anxiety? Desperation? It was impossible to separate the emotions spiraling through her.

"What's wrong, amita?" Renny had finally curbed her excitement enough to notice something was amiss. She laid her hand on Sabrina's arm.

Sabrina didn't have time for explanations. She had to leave before Tucker actually did come knocking on her door, possibly bringing his sister just for fun.

She grabbed her light sweater off the hook by the door and folded it hastily into a lump. "Nothing's wrong. I decided to take a vacation." A permanent one.

"Where to?"

She hadn't gotten that far. Hadn't thought beyond the ferry that would take her off the island. She could go home to Macon, but the thought of seeing her family . . .

She rejected the idea with unwavering certainty. She needed time to digest her feelings before she went home for the wedding.

"Something's wrong, I can see it on your face."

Sabrina shoved the sweater in the suitcase.

"You're shaking, Sabrina. Sit down and talk to me."

Sabrina didn't argue as Renny led her to the chairs in the corner. Rain drizzled down the window behind Renny and pattered on the roof.

"Now, what is going on?"

"I have to leave for a while. Something happened this morning. That's why I'm home early."

"What happened?"

At the question, the scene at the café played in slow, horrifying motion. The memory was like a punch to the stomach. "It's Tucker. He brought his sister to the café this morning to introduce her to me."

Renny sucked in a breath. "The twin sister? The sister that—"

"Yes." If only there were another.

"Maybe she didn't recognize you."

Sabrina gave a wry laugh. "Oh, she recognized me all right."

"What did she say? Did she tell Tucker?"

"I didn't stick around long enough for that special brother/sister moment." Her sarcasm was alive and well. Good to know.

Why was she sitting here when every moment heightened the possibility of a confrontation with Tucker?

"I have to finish packing." She jumped from the sofa and pulled her sandals from the floor.

"Wait, child. Where are you going? Let's think this through."

"There's nothing to think about, Renny. I can't stay here now that he knows. He'll hate me."

"Well, he might hate Sabrina, but he won't hate Sweetpea."

Sabrina set her shoes in the suitcase. That was true. It was something, at least. But she couldn't face him every day at the café, knowing what she'd done and what he thought of her.

"You still have your email relationship."

Thank God for that. It was salvaged at least. Maybe she should write him now. But no, that would slow her down. And she was supposed to be at work and he'd wonder why she was—

Another realization dawned. He was going to write tonight and tell her about his discovery. He would tell her exactly what he thought of Sabrina. She was going to hear every vicious thought running through his head—not that she didn't deserve it.

But she couldn't bear to know what he thought of her now.

"Or maybe . . ." Renny was massaging her scalp with all ten fingers. "Maybe you should tell him everything."

Renny had missed the point. "He already knows everything."

"Not *everything*." Renny's eyes were wide as she nodded her head slowly.

Sabrina sighed. "The only thing he doesn't know is—no. No, I can't tell him I'm Sweetpea."

"Why not, *amita*? What've you got to lose?"

"Tucker." Well, not Tucker, but Harbormaster. Sabrina shook her head. Such a mess. She grabbed a novel from the end table and stuffed it in the suitcase. Like she'd be able to read.

She had to make a plan. She could take her bike on the ferry, but she'd have to rent a car in Hyannis. Thank God money wasn't an issue. She didn't make great money at the café, but she spent little of it since she didn't pay rent.

Renny laid a hand on her arm. She hadn't even noticed the woman approach. Renny's sympathetic expression contrasted with the wildness of her hair after her "massage."

"All you have is a correspondence with the man. If you love him, tell him the truth. Maybe there's *tikva*."

"English, Renny."

"Hope. Maybe there's hope."

Sabrina was already shaking her head. "You didn't see his sister's face. She was livid. I wanted to die on the spot."

"That's her. Not Tucker."

"You don't know how close they are. You don't know the things he said when he was telling me—telling Sweetpea—what happened with his sister and her husband. He used a word to describe that other woman—me, Renny!—that I don't even want to repeat, much less think of being!"

She had to go, had to finish packing. Renny was only holding her up.

"What about honesty? What about doing the right thing and trusting God to work things as he wills? You're strong enough to do the right thing. You've already come through so much." She shrugged. "I'm just trying to be the voice of reason here."

Ha! There was nothing reasonable about that plan. She had to think. She needed to take her address book, her cell phone and charger, what else? She saw the paper on the counter, opened to the editorial ad. So much for that new job.

"Sabrina, stop for a moment and think."

"I can't think with you hounding me, Renny." She regretted the snap of her voice as soon as the words were out. "I'm sorry. I'm just—feeling a little scattered." She walked toward the door. "Thanks for telling me about your manuscripts. I'm happy for you, really. I know there are wonderful things in store for you. But I need to finish packing now."

She wondered for a minute if Renny was going to take the hint. Renny finally lumbered toward the door, but she wasn't quite finished.

"One more thing and then I'll leave."

Sabrina sighed heavily.

"Last spring I was eager for gardening season, and I started some seeds indoors. A few varieties, but among them were sweet peas."

Sabrina barely kept from rolling her eyes. "I feel a metaphor coming on."

Renny ignored her comment. "The seeds have a hard coat that can cause the plant to sprout slowly or unevenly. Before you plant them, it's recommended that you chip away a piece of the shell. Once they go through that, they sprout quite nicely and will even survive a hardy frost."

Sabrina checked her watch. The meaning wasn't lost on her, but she didn't have time to psychoanalyze herself.

"Okay then. I'll let you get back to your packing." Renny turned on the landing, her eyes wet. "I'll be praying for you. Call me when you find a place tonight and let me know you're all right."

Hearing her gentle words, Sabrina really regretted the tone she'd taken. She nodded. The woman loved her, was only trying to help. "I will."

Renny patted her shoulder and left. Sabrina started to close the door but stopped when her eyes settled on the branch outside her door. She followed the length of it once. Twice. Finally settling in the empty crook where two branches met.

It was gone. The nest had finally given way to the wind and fallen. When had it happened? The emptiness that filled her defied all logic.

She closed the door and returned to the task at hand. After changing out of her uniform, she went to the bathroom and gathered the shampoo and a few rubber bands. She chucked the things in her suitcase, then went to the kitchen for her vitamins, checking her watch again.

A pink patch blotched her wrist from the spilled coffee. It still burned, but there was no time for such trivialities. She was going to be too late for the early ferry, but she could catch the next one. Hopefully there was space. She should call and reserve a spot.

The light was flashing on her machine. Char, no doubt, calling to say Gordon was in an uproar about her MIA status. Ignoring the pulsing light, she looked up the number for the fast ferry and dialed.

As she punched in the last numbers, a knock sounded. Renny must've massaged out another metaphor and was back to give her another reason to stay. The line rang while she went to the door.

She was going to tell Renny she didn't have time for this. She'd call her from the ferry or something. They could talk it out then.

On the other end of the phone, a woman picked up. "Hy-Line Cruises, how may I help you?"

Sabrina swung open the door, signaling just a minute with her finger. But her hand froze in the air. Her fingers tightened on the phone.

"Hello?" the voice on the other end of the phone said. "May I help you?"

Sabrina needed more help than the woman on the phone could offer, because the face she was staring into wasn't the pudgy face of her eccentric friend, but the strained, rain-dampened face of the man she loved.

Sweetpea: Happy endings are for fairy tales, right?

Chapter Thirty-nine

"Hello?" the woman on the phone repeated.

Sabrina stared at Tucker, watched as rivulets of rain ran down his face. His hair hung in wet strands, matted to his head.

The other end of the phone went dead, but Sabrina didn't know what to do. Invite Tucker in? Slam the door and lock it?

He made the decision for her, squeezing past, out of the weather. When a recording came on the line, Sabrina turned off the phone.

Tucker took a few steps into the room. The lighting suddenly seemed as bright as a spotlighted stage, and the bulging suitcase, square on the sofa, was the star of the show.

The doorway, still open, beckoned. If only she could dart through the door. How could she face him now?

But she needed her suitcase. She needed her purse, lying on the table across the room.

Tucker turned, looking her in the eye.

What was he thinking? She couldn't tell, couldn't read the features that were normally so easily discerned. Unable to meet his gaze any longer, she turned and closed the door.

You deserve everything you get. Just face it like a woman. Straightening her shoulders, she turned, though she couldn't bring herself to meet his eyes.

"Tell me everything." His words were barely discernible over the pattering of rain.

"I think you pretty much know everything now."

He took one step closer, then stopped as if his sandals were glued to the floor.

She wanted to melt into a puddle and pour through the floorboards. To think he knew what she'd done. That she'd behaved so loosely, that she'd slept with a married man—his sister's husband, no less. It was what Jaylee had done to her. Worse, even.

"I want to hear it from you."

"Do you doubt your sister?" Was he giving her the benefit of the doubt? Surely not. And yet, why would he care about her side? She'd done it, she was guilty.

"I don't doubt Tracey. I want to understand."

Sabrina laughed bitterly. "I have no excuse, Tucker. Everything you're thinking about me is true."

"How do you know what I'm thinking?"

"Because anyone would be thinking it!" She crossed her arms over her heart as if she could protect it from the coming pain.

"I'm not just anyone. And neither are you."

"I'm the woman who slept with your brother-in-law. The whore who broke up your sister's marriage." The phrase slipped out, and she recognized her blunder.

He winced, looking away. She watched the straight line of his back as he walked toward the patio door and looked out.

Did he remember his own words sent to Sweetpea all those months ago? But he knew she'd read the emails right there in his office. He just didn't know she'd originally read them as Sweetpea.

His broad shoulders hunched as he crossed his arms. She couldn't believe he was so calm. Why didn't he just have his say and leave?

Because he was Tucker. That's not who he was.

But his words from that long-ago email pricked her. He'd been angry when Tracey had told him about that morning, about Sebastian's infidelity. He'd been ready to hunt the man down and beat him to a bloody pulp. He'd made no secret what he thought of the woman his brother-in-law had been with. What he thought of *her*.

"Tell me what happened." He was facing her again.

Her mind went back to that night. Back to the depressive state she'd been in when she'd come on her solo honeymoon. He wanted to know everything, and what could it hurt? It didn't excuse what she'd done, but Tucker deserved to know the whole story.

But she had to be careful. Tucker knew Sweetpea's story. She had to be vague.

"I was going through a—a dark time when I came here. I was alone and depressed. Barely made it out of my hotel room for days. I—" She could hardly find words to describe her desperation, to describe how the pain of betrayal had swallowed her whole.

"Go on." His gentle tone spurred her on.

She picked at the cuff of her blouse where it had frayed. "After a while I found an effective, if not necessarily brilliant, way to escape my sorrows. I went to a bar and got drunk." Shame flooded her face as she recalled the way the night culminated. But she was going to be woman enough to admit in broad daylight what she'd done under the cover of night.

"There was a man across the room. He was nicely dressed, and he was looking at me. I—I couldn't believe someone who looked like that could find me interesting, but he bought me a drink." Her eyes sought out his, testing the waters. But Tucker was silhouetted by the light from the patio door.

"I went home with him. I don't remember everything. I never even noticed his ring . . ." Such a feeble excuse.

"I didn't realize until the next morning when his wife—when Tracey—came in." Mortification cloaked her. Her hand went to her throat. She was so dirty. And admitting her transgression to the man she loved was beyond humiliating.

And yet, it didn't compare to what Tracey had suffered.

Nothing she said would rectify or justify it. Jaylee's words, spoken the night she'd discovered her with Jared, haunted Sabrina now. *"We didn't mean for it to happen—didn't mean for you to find out like this."* They were empty words that changed nothing.

Sabrina had still been betrayed, just as Tracey had been. Sorry didn't change a thing. Tracey's marriage was still over.

The air felt heavy, unbreathable. Sabrina needed to get out of there, she wanted to run as far away from this place, away from Tucker and his steady gaze, as she could. She could send for her things later. There was no returning, she knew that now.

She rushed to her suitcase and closed it, pulling the zipper.

"What are you doing?"

She hauled the case off the couch and set it on the floor. Her purse was beyond Tucker. She went for it.

He took her arm. "Sabrina."

She shrugged out of his grasp and grabbed her things. "I've got to go."

"Where?"

Sabrina pulled her suitcase across the floor. It snagged on the rug's edge, and she jerked it loose.

Tucker grabbed the handle.

"Let go!"

"Tell me where you're going."

"Out of here, away, what does it matter?" She tugged the suit-case from his grasp and pulled open the door.

He followed her down the steps. Rain poured down her face and soaked her clothes within seconds. The suitcase was heavy and awkward.

"You're running," he said. "Where are you going to hide? You can't hide from what you did."

The accusation stung. She blocked out his words, pretended the rain washed them away. There was nothing he could say to make her feel worse, was there? And yet, his presence convicted her, made her ever more cognizant of her offense.

She reached the bottom of the steps. Tucker caught her arm. The suitcase slipped from her wet palm and tipped, landing on the gravel with a thud. Her purse fell to the ground afterward.

Before she could stop him, Tucker snatched it.

He had her purse, and where could she go without money? She felt trapped, and it wasn't a feeling she liked. "Give it back." She glared.

"Not until we talk."

"We have talked."

"No. You've talked and I've listened. Now it's my turn."

Her eyes burned. She wanted to cover her ears with both hands. She didn't want to hear what he had to say. It would hurt too much, and she was tired of hurting. Maybe it was selfish, but she wanted to go away and forget everything that had happened. She wanted to start over fresh someplace where she hadn't done so many wrong things, hurt so many people.

"Give me the bag." She reached for it, but he held it away. Thunder cracked.

"Five minutes," he said. "Let's get out of the rain." He took her arm.

She jerked it away. How dare he hold her hostage. "I want my purse!" A stare-off ensued. Tucker's eyes looked dark under the storm's shadows. Dark and stubborn.

"Fine. We'll do it right here then." He tightened his fist around the strap of her bag.

She crossed her arms, a futile act of defiance. He could have his say. She didn't have to listen, didn't have to respond. He wanted to settle the score. Let him say all the awful things he could, call her all the names she deserved.

At the thought, a whimper rose in her throat, but she strangled it before it escaped.

He was quiet so long she wondered if he'd changed his mind. But no, he was only waiting for her to look at him. Rain trickled down his face like tears. His spiked lashes framed eyes that were full of something that contradicted her expectations.

"I know you're not the woman who did that dishonorable thing."

She searched his eyes, confused. "What? Yes, I am—"

He put his fingers over her mouth. "Shush, it's my turn." When she quieted, he spoke again. "I know you did it, but it doesn't define who you are. It was one night, one mistake."

He was letting her off the hook? It didn't make sense. Somehow it angered her. Where was the justice in that? The justice for Tracey.

"Don't make excuses for me. Of all people, you shouldn't be defending what I did. You should detest me on your sister's behalf. What I did destroyed her marriage."

Tucker gave a sad smile. "You were one in a long line for Sebastian. Tracey discovered the truth after that morning. She would've been able to forgive him the one indiscretion, but he has a problem that goes beyond that one night with you."

There'd been others? The divorce hadn't been her fault alone? The news removed a bit of weight from her shoulders. Still, how could Tucker be so . . . so . . . ?

"I don't hate you, Sabrina. I—"

She wished she could pull the words from his tongue. But they seemed stuck there. His gaze roamed over her face, making her conscious of her own state of dishevelment.

Sabrina wiped the rain from her cheeks.

"I forgive you." His words washed away every other thought. "You don't need to leave. Nothing needs to change. Don't go."

It was so tempting, everything he said. But could she continue with the way things were when he didn't know the truth? Forgiving Sabrina the café waitress for her perfidy was one thing, but could he forgive Sweetpea for the same crime? Could his sister ever forgive her?

Of course not. It was more complicated than Tucker dreamed.

And she was weary of the pretense. Weary of loving a man who thought she was someone else. The relationship that meant everything to her was nothing but a lie because Tucker was in love with an illusion.

"Sabrina?"

She looked at the man she loved and knew with sudden clarity that he deserved more than she'd given him. More than she could ever give him.

It was over. All of it. She would tell him the truth and let the chips fall where they may. Then Tucker would hate her. Then Tucker would gladly return her purse and let her leave the island.

The thought carved away a section of her heart, the part where courage resided. She didn't have the guts. Didn't have the strength to face him when he learned who she was, and found her profoundly lacking in integrity and basic morality. She wasn't at all who he thought she was.

Renny's words played back. *"What about honesty? What about doing the right thing and trusting God to work things as he wills?"*

But what if . . . what if she couldn't handle it? What if it cut her to the core?

Do you trust me? The small, familiar voice came from somewhere deep inside.

"Sabrina, talk to me."

She took one last look at him as he was now, savoring the compassion in his eyes for a moment longer. He was a good man. He deserved better than she could offer. He deserved someone who wasn't dragging her past around on a heavy chain. Someone like Arielle. The thought appeared out of nowhere.

Of course.

Sabrina had been nothing but selfish through the entire relationship. She could do this one selfless thing. It would hurt, but it was time to let Tucker go, set him free. It was time to tell him everything.

She whispered a quick prayer for courage. "Okay, you've had your say. Now I need to have mine." She suddenly felt shy, remembering all the words she'd said, all the letters she'd written. He knew more about her than anyone. To tell him the truth was to expose herself, to be vulnerable. All the things she'd thought she was done with.

"Go on."

"I—" *Dear Lord, how can I say it? Give me the words.* He looked so innocent, and she was going to hurt him. She hated that more than anything.

He wiped a trickle of rain from her cheek with the back of his fingers. "Go on," he said again.

She closed her eyes against the touch, then forced them open. "I—I have something to tell you that may come as a shock. I've done something—I'm afraid it's going to hurt you and—" Tears burned at her eyes, clogged her throat with a lump the size of a boulder.

"Just say it." His tender look was about her undoing.

He was going to hate her afterward.

Do you trust me?

"I'm not who you think I am, Tucker. I—" *Just say it.* "I'm Sweetpea." Once the boulder came loose, she couldn't stop the flow of words. "I've been her all along, since the beginning and—"

"Sabrina."

"—when you sent the photo, I was afraid because—because I had feelings for you, and I didn't think you could possibly love someone like me, and then later I realized what I'd done, that Sebastian was your brother-in-law—and then you asked me to find her—to find *me*, and I didn't know what to do, so I pretended to look for her—"

"Sabrina."

"—but I felt so guilty taking your money, so I donated it to Nantucket Soundkeeper, and then Arielle showed up—she's my cousin—and then you saw her and—"

"*Sabrina!*" He dropped her bag and took her face in his hands. "Would you just shut up?"

Her thoughts spun slowly to a halt, like a vacated merry-go-round.

And then her mind began spinning slowly again, this time with questions. Why was he touching her so gently? Why was he looking at her like that—with such tenderness?

"I *know*." He looked at her as if to drive each word home. "I know who you are," he repeated in a whisper.

He knew she was Sweetpea? But how, and when? And why did he hire her?

"Aw, honey, I've waited so long for you." His thumb grazed her cheek, sending a shiver down her arms.

"But how—when?"

"From the beginning. I sought you out."

"But why?"

"I wanted to know you."

"But you hired me . . ."

"To spend time with you. I wanted to be with you. I wanted you to tell me who you are."

His words filled the empty places in her heart. "But Arielle . . ."

"I wanted to knock you silly when you stuck me with that woman. But then Arielle told me she wasn't Sweetpea, and I told her I already knew who—"

"You knew all along?" Sabrina felt dazed. He wasn't in love with Arielle? She remembered his letter that night. *"I love you,"* he'd written. And she'd thought the words were for her cousin. But the words had been for her alone.

She remembered their date, the boat ride. "The kiss . . ." she said.

One side of his mouth tilted in a grin. "The kiss."

He'd let his feelings run away that night. He'd wanted to be with her, not Arielle. He'd wanted to kiss her, not Arielle. Could it be true? Even now, she was afraid to believe.

That morning suddenly rushed to the front of her mind. It seemed so long ago, though it had been an hour at most. She'd seen the look on his face, the look on his sister's face. He hadn't known that part. She stepped back now, needing distance. His hands fell away from her face.

"What's wrong?"

How could anything come of their relationship when they had that between them? Even if Sebastian had made a hobby of sleeping around, could Tracey ever forgive what Sabrina had done?

Her lip wobbled, and she bit it still. "Tracey."

For the first time since her admission, his face sobered. A rivulet of rain traced a path down his temple, his jaw.

"How could she ever forgive me?"

"Same way I did."

"But I don't deserve it."

Tucker pulled her against him. She curled into his wet torso and hid her face in the wall of his chest.

"None of us do, Sabrina. You think I haven't made mistakes?" His words rumbled in her ear. He lifted her hand and kissed the tender flesh of her wrist where the coffee had spilled. "You think Tracey hasn't made mistakes? She's a strong and compassionate woman. She'll come around in time because she knows how much I—"

The sentence hung in the misty air, but Sabrina was enjoying the heavy thud of his heart too much to leave the comfort of his embrace.

But she felt Tucker's hands on her arms, felt him pushing her away. Felt him looking at her with eyes that spoke all the words she needed to hear. "She knows how much I love you." He squeezed her arms firmly and gave her a little shake. "*You*, Sabrina. No one else."

She soaked it up, all his eyes had to say, all his words meant. If she heard it a million more times it wouldn't be too much. The words turned her legs to noodles and warmed a path clear to her heart, seeping into all the dark crevices. The journey had been long and hard, but the destination was worth the trouble. More than worth it.

Tucker.

He lowered his head, and his mouth tested hers. She was sure he could feel her heart banging against his stomach, but soon, she forgot about her heart. All she could think of was the way his lips felt on hers, soft as a feather's touch. When he pulled away, she wanted to protest.

"Our first kiss." He brushed her wet hair from her cheek.

"Second," she corrected.

He grinned. "That one didn't count. You thought I was a two-timing creep."

Her thoughts returned to the uncertainty, the confusion of that night. "No, I didn't."

He gave her a look.

"Maybe a little."

"I couldn't help myself. You were so beautiful sitting there on the water, with the moonlight on your hair. You must've been so confused." He dried her face, the rain and tears, with the back of his hand. "Don't be confused about this, though, Sabrina. I love you with all my heart, and nothing's going to change that."

Were lovelier words ever spoken? She wanted Tucker to feel the way she did now. She wanted to tell him the rest of it, the part that mattered most.

"I love you, too, Tucker. So much." Emotion closed her throat.

"I've waited a long time for those words," he whispered, then dropped a quick kiss on her lips. After a pause, he was back for more. Sabrina wrapped her arms around his neck, ran her fingers through the curls at his nape. She couldn't get enough of him. He smelled like Tucker and tasted of heaven.

His lips were strong and gentle all at once. His touch sent a shiver of pleasure down her spine into the farthest reaches of her heart. When he ended the kiss, it was only to gather her closely in his arms.

"I meant what I said about going to the wedding with you. If you'll have me."

She smiled. "I'd love that." Peace enveloped her, and she remembered Renny's words from weeks ago. *"God will give you peace on this. I know it."* Now Sabrina knew it too.

She was all wrapped in Tucker's embrace, a chick under his wings. She could get used to this, she decided. The rain pummeled them, but they were already drenched and she wasn't going anywhere.

"Not in a hurry to get out of the rain after all?" she asked.

"What rain?" he whispered. And with one last grin, his lips closed over hers again.

Dear Friend,

I hope you enjoyed your brief journey to Nantucket through the characters of Sabrina and Tucker. My goal in this Nantucket series has always been to show the love of Christ through the relationship of the hero and heroine. Writing it has made me think long and hard about Christ's love for us and the human response to it.

You may have noticed that Tucker loved Sabrina in a God-the-Father kind of way, that he sought out the relationship, pursuing her until she was ready to come to him fully. Conversely, Sabrina was intent on hiding, shamed by the sin she committed "against" him. She's not so very different from us!

I'm so thankful to have a God who seeks me out, one who persistently pursues me—despite my efforts to hide and build walls—and lavishes love on me like I'm his only child. I hope you've discovered that same kind of love on your own faith journey and that *Seaside Letters* has somehow given you a fresh view of Christ.

Blessings!
Denise

Reading Group Guide

1. Sabrina hid behind the facade of the Ice Princess because of past suffering. What are some of the events that caused her to withdraw from relationships?

2. Sabrina was unattractive as a child, and though she grew out of it, she still viewed herself as homely. What baggage (words, attitudes, or actions) from your childhood do you hang on to even though it's not necessarily true?

3. What were some of Tucker's characteristics and actions that reflect Christ?

4. Tucker knew Sabrina was Sweetpea from the beginning. How did his activities at the beginning of their relationship reflect God's actions toward us?

5. Things began to spin out of control for Sabrina after she told her first lie—sending the photo of Arielle to Tucker. Have you

ever found yourself getting deeper and deeper in your own pit of deceit? How did you extricate yourself?

6. When Sabrina asked Tucker what he wanted most, his reply was that he wanted to know her more. Do you think God feels this way about you? Why or why not?

7. Why did Sabrina use email to keep Tucker at a distance? What do you use to keep the ones you love at a distance? What is preventing you from true intimacy? Do you keep God at a distance? How does our sin create a wall between us and God?

8. Isaiah 43:25 says, "I, even I, am he who blots out your transgressions, for my own sake, and remembers your sins no more." What does this mean, and how did Tucker's actions reflect God's reaction to our sin?

9. Renny didn't mail her manuscripts for fear of rejection. What are you most of afraid of? How has fear affected your actions? What steps can you take, with God's help, to overcome it?

10. Renny couldn't quite believe she was a talented writer, despite Sabrina's encouragement and compliments. Do you have a God-given talent you aren't using? What's stopping you?

Acknowledgments

Every author knows it takes many people working together to make a book happen. I'd like to give a shout-out to all those who put up with me, helped me with research, double-checked me, and encouraged me along the way.

I have to start with the Thomas Nelson fiction team. I'm so honored to work with this creative, hardworking, and dedicated team of publishing professionals: publisher Allen Arnold, Amanda Bostic, Jocelyn Bailey, Kathy Carabajal, Jennifer Deshler, Natalie Hanemann, Chris Long, Ami McConnell, Heather McCulloch, Becky Monds, Ashley Schneider, Katie Schroder, and Micah Walker.

I have to give an individual shout-out to Ami McConnell, who amazes me with her insight. Her editorial advice makes me look so much better than I am. I also owe a debt of gratitude to Jessica Alvarez, my second editor on this work—see, it takes two of them to keep me in line.

My agent, Karen Solem, intercedes, encourages, and does all that annoying contract stuff. Melissa Hankinson graciously offered to read the manuscript with an eye toward getting the Nantucket details right. Thanks to Joy Geiger for her help on research—we'll keep the specifics to ourselves.

My best buds from Girls Write Out (www.GirlsWriteOut.blog spot.com), Kristin Billerbeck, Colleen Coble, and Diann Hunt: God knew what he was doing when he put us together.

My family is a constant source of joy, encouragement, and research material! Thanks, Justin, Chad, and Trevor—you impact my writing in more ways than you know. And Kevin, my partner in crime. I can't believe it's been twenty years!

Lastly, thank you, friend, for joining me on this journey to Nantucket. It's a real treat to share my stories with others, and I'd love to hear from you. Send me an email at Denise@DeniseHunterBooks .com or visit my Web site at www.DeniseHunterBooks.com.

On the beautiful island of Nantucket,
salt and roses scent the air,
and a storm-tossed soul seeks safe harbor.

A NANTUCKET LOVE STORY

THOMAS NELSON
Since 1798

She wrote the book—literally—
on finding the right mate. But does she really
understand what love's about?

A NANTUCKET LOVE STORY

THOMAS NELSON
Since 1798

Driftwood Lane

For the latest on the
Nantucket Love Story series,
please visit www.denisehunterbooks.com

Coming Summer 2010

A NANTUCKET LOVE STORY

THOMAS NELSON
Since 1798

She wished she could go back and change things
but life doesn't give do-overs . . . or does it?

A Woman of Faith Novel

THOMAS NELSON
Since 1798

An Excerpt from *Sweetwater Gap*

one

*J*osephine Mitchell was up to her wrists in dirt when she heard the whistle. She looked past the ornamental iron railing down to street level where Cody Something shut the door of his '79 Mustang.

He approached her veranda, shading his eyes from the sun with his hand. "Hey, Apartment 2B, my friend came through." Cody tugged two tickets from the back pocket of his khaki shorts. "Louisville versus UK."

Josie pulled her hands from under the wisteria's roots and patted the dirt down. "Answer's still no." She smiled to soften the rejection, then poured more of the sandy loam around the vine's woody roots.

"Forty-yard line. Biggest game of the year . . ." A shadow puddled in his dimple.

"Sorry."

He sighed. "When are you going to break down and say yes?"

Josie's cell phone pealed and vibrated simultaneously in her pocket. "Saved by the bell." She wiped her hands on her jeans and checked the screen.

1

A frown pulled her brows. Her sister hadn't called since she'd gotten the big news four months ago. Josie hoped she was okay.

"Sorry, gotta take this," she told Cody, then flipped open the phone. "Hey, Laurel."

There was a pause at the other end. "Josie? It's Nate. Your brother-in-law." As if Josie didn't know his name or voice. He'd only dated her sister four years before finally proposing.

But Nate had never called Josie, and the fact that he was now only reinforced her previous suspicion. "Is everything okay? Laurel and the baby?"

"They're fine."

Thank God. Laurel and Nate had wanted a baby for so long. They'd been ready to start trying, but then Laurel and Josie's dad had the stroke, and the newlyweds had to move in with him and take care of him and the family orchard. Laurel hadn't had the time or energy for a baby.

Josie sat back on her haunches and wiped her hair from her eyes with a semiclean finger.

"I'm calling about the orchard." Nate's tone was short and clipped. "I think it's high time you hauled your city-slicker fanny back here to help your sister."

She almost thought he was joking—Nate was as easygoing as they came, and she'd never heard him sound so adamant or abrupt. But there was no laughter on the other end of the line.

Words stuck in Josie's throat. She swallowed hard. "I don't understand."

"No, you don't. *Responsibility* is a foreign word to you. I get that. But there comes a time when a person has to step up to the plate and—"

"Wait a minute."

"—help when they're needed. And Laurel needs your help. We can't afford to hire anyone else, you know."

This didn't sound like Nate. True, she hadn't talked to him in ages, but he'd always been the picture of Southern hospitality.

Below the veranda, Cody caught her eye and waved the tickets temptingly. When she shook her head no, his lips turned down in an exaggerated pout, his chin fell dramatically to his chest, and he sulked toward the apartment's main door. But not before he turned and flashed his dimple one more time, just to let her know he wasn't too heartbroken. They both knew he was already mentally sorting through the other candidates in his little black book.

Nate's angry voice pulled her back to the conversation, which, she realized belatedly, had been silent on her end for too long.

"I don't know why I thought you'd care," he muttered. She could barely hear his words over the roar of a passing motorcycle. "You didn't bother coming after the stroke, or for the funeral, why would you care about this?"

"What *this*? Would you please tell me what's going on?"

His breaths were harsh, as if he expected a fight.

"Laurel is having twins. She just found out yesterday at the ultrasound."

Twins. The word brought back a cluster of memories, none of them good.

But Laurel was undoubtedly thrilled. Josie was surprised she hadn't called, but then again, they hadn't spoken much since the funeral almost a year ago. "Well, that's great news."

"The doctor wants her to take it easy. And you know Laurel."

With harvest just around the bend, there wasn't much that was easy about working an apple orchard this time of year. The phone call was making sense now. All except Nate's antagonism. But then he'd always been protective of Laurel.

"When I came home from work today, I found her painting the nursery, and yesterday she spent the afternoon packing apples in cold storage for a new vendor she got. Every time I turn around, she's sneaking off to work somewhere, usually the orchard because she's so worried about it."

Josie stood, stretching her legs, then leaned her elbows on the railing. "She's never been one to be idle."

"She really wants these babies, Josephine. We both do. And after what happened with your mom . . ." His voice wobbled as the sentence trailed off, pinching something inside her.

"Of course, I completely get that." It was all sinking in now. She knew why he'd called. And she knew she wouldn't say no, because, despite the distance between them, she loved her sister.

"She needs help, that's the bottom line. I don't need to tell you how much work is involved this time of year, and she can't do it. We can hardly afford to hire more help."

"No, she can't work the harvest," Josie agreed. His words from a moment ago replayed in her head like a delayed tape. "You said you can't hire someone." Laurel hadn't mentioned financial troubles. She talked about their manager, Grady, as if he were God's gift to apples.

"Not after last year's failure."

"Failure?" Her sister hadn't said anything of the kind. True, they didn't speak often, but when the topic of the orchard did come up, Laurel said everything was fine. At least, Josie thought she had.

"Laurel didn't tell you? There was an Easter frost. We lost the apples."

"Frost?" An orchard could lose a whole crop to frost, though this was the first time it had happened at Blue Ridge. Why hadn't Laurel said something?

Nate sighed. "I'm sorry. I thought she told you."

What else had her sister omitted? Laurel was always trying to protect her. Josie should've inquired more directly. "How bad is it?" The fragrance from her lavender plant wafted by on a breeze, and Josie closed her eyes, inhaled the calming scent, letting it fill her up, soothe her frayed nerves.

"The place is a money pit. We don't have anything else to put into it."

This changes everything, Josie. Do you realize that?

The selfish thought materialized before she could stop it. Her plans . . . How could she follow through now? When Laurel was overburdened with a failing orchard and pregnant with twins?

Nate was speaking again. "Grady insists he can turn the place around, but I'm wondering if we shouldn't sell it."

She and Laurel were the third generation to own the orchard, and as far as Josie knew, not one of the Mitchells had thought those words, much less said them. And she'd thought Laurel would be the last one to do so.

"Laurel's considering that?" Their father's death had left Josie with shares that tied her to the place. Even three hundred and fifty miles away, it dragged behind her wherever she went, weighing her down like an anchor. But if Laurel was considering a sale . . .

Now that she'd slipped the thought on for size, it was starting to feel more comfortable, like her favorite pair of Levi's.

"I haven't exactly broached the topic," Nate said.

That was precisely what needed to happen. It was something

her father should've done long ago, before he'd saddled Laurel with his own care and the care of the orchard.

"How does this year's crop look?"

"Promising. She was hoping this year would put us in the black. But a strong crop means extra work and plenty of hands on deck. And I can't afford time off."

Nate ran Shelbyville's one and only insurance agency. Good thing they'd had his income to fall back on.

"So can you come back and help us through the harvest?" he asked.

Josie's eyes flitted over the lacy white alyssum, past the potted strawberry plant toward the haven of her darkened apartment. She closed her eyes and was, in an instant, back at Blue Ridge Orchard. She could almost smell the apples ripening on the trees. Hear the snap of the branch as an apple twisted free. See the ripples of Sweetwater Creek running alongside the property.

And with that thought, the other memories came. The ones that had chased her from Shelbyville six years ago. The ones that still chased her every day. The ones that, at the mention of going home, caused a dread, deep and thick in her belly.

"Josie, you there?"

She opened her eyes, swallowing hard. "I'm here."

"I know you've got your photography job and your plans and your life."

She breathed a wry laugh. Ironically, none of that mattered. The one plan that did matter could still play out. Same tune, different venue.

What mattered most now was seeing that Laurel's life was settled. And Laurel's life wouldn't be settled until she was out from under the orchard. Josie saw that clearly now. And it wouldn't happen, she knew, without a lot of coaxing. She only hoped there was enough time.

"I wouldn't have called if we weren't desperate."

Josie took one last deep breath of the lavender, shoved down the dread, and forced the words.

"I'll come."